to Lynne

Penguin Books
The Doctor is Sick

Anthony Burgess was born in Manchester in 1917 and is a graduate of the University there. After six years in the Army he worked as an instructor for the Central Advisory Council for Forces Education, as a college lecturer in Speech and Drama and as a grammar-school master. From 1954–60 he was an education officer in the Colonial Service, stationed in Malaya and Borneo.

He became a full-time writer in 1960, though he had already by then published three novels and a history of English literature. A late starter in the art of fiction, he has previously spent much creative energy on music, and has composed many full-scale works for orchestra and other media. His Third Symphony was performed in the U.S.A. in 1975.

Anthony Burgess believes that in the fusion of musical and literary form lies a possible future for the novel. His *Napoleon Symphony* attempts to impose the shape of Beethoven's *Eroica* on the career of the Corsican conqueror. His other books include *The Long Day Wanes: A Malayan Trilogy*; the Enderby novels (including *The Clockwork Testament*); *Tremor of Intent*; a biography of Shakespeare intended to act as a foil to his Shakespeare novel, *Nothing Like the Sun*; *Honey for the Bears*; *The Wanting Seed*; *MF*; *Urgent Copy*; *Beard's Roman Women*; *ABBA ABBA*; *A Clockwork Orange*, made into a film classic by Stanley Kubrick; *Ernest Hemingway and His World*; *1985*; *Man of Nazareth*; the basis of his successful TV script, *Jesus of Nazareth*; *Earthly Powers*, voted in France, 1981, the best foreign novel of the year; *The End of the World News*; and a collection of his journalism, *Homage to Qwertyuiop*.

Anthony Burgess

The Doctor is Sick

Penguin Books

Penguin Books Ltd, Harmondsworth, Middlesex, England
Viking Penguin Inc., 40 West 23rd Street, New York, New York 10010, U.S.A.
Penguin Books Australia Ltd, Ringwood, Victoria, Australia
Penguin Books Canada Limited, 2801 John Street, Markham, Ontario, Canada L3R 1B4
Penguin Books (N.Z.) Ltd, 182–190 Wairau Road, Auckland 10, New Zealand

First published by William Heinemann 1960
Published in Penguin Books 1972
Reprinted 1979, 1983, 1986

Made and printed in Great Britain by
Richard Clay (The Chaucer Press) Ltd, Bungay, Suffolk
Set in Linotype Baskerville

Chapter One

'And what is *this* smell?' asked Dr Railton. He thrust a
sort of ink-well under Edwin's nose.

'I may be wrong, but I should say peppermint.' He
awaited the quiz-master's gong. Beyond the screens that
had been wheeled round his bed the rest of the ward
could be heard eating.

'You *are* wrong, I'm afraid,' said Dr Railton. 'Laven-
der.' Gong. But he was still in the round. 'And this?'

'Probably something citrous.'

'Wrong again. *Terribly* wrong. Cloves.' There was a
tone of moral indictment in the gentle voice. Gently Dr
Railton sat on the edge of the bed. Gently, with womanish brown eyes, long-lashed, he looked down at Edwin.
'Not so good, is it? Not at all good.' The knives and forks
percussed and scraped weakly, an invalids' orchestra.

'I have a cold,' said Edwin. 'The sudden change of
climate.' The dying English year rattled at the ward
windows, as if begging for a bed. 'It was well up in the
nineties when we left Moulmein.'

'Your wife came with you?'

'Yes. Officially as my nurse. But she was air-sick most of
the time.'

'I see.' Dr Railton nodded and nodded, as though this
was really very serious. 'Well, there are various other tests
we shall have to try. Not now, of course. We'll get down
to work properly on Monday.' Edwin relaxed. Dr Railton, seeing this, pounced with a tuning-fork. He brought
it, sizzling like a poker, up to Edwin's right cheek. 'Can
you feel that?'

'Middle C.'

'No, no, can you *feel* it?'

'Oh yes.' Dr Railton looked grim, allowing Edwin no triumph. He got in quickly with:

'How would you define "spiral"?'

'Spiral? Oh, you know, like a spiral staircase. Like a screw.' Both of Edwin's hands began to spiral in the air. 'Going up and up, turning all the time, but each turn getting progressively smaller and smaller till the whole thing just vanishes. You know what I mean.' Edwin begged with his eyes that this definition be accepted.

'Exactly,' said Dr Railton with his new grimness. '*Exactly.*' But evidently he did not refer to the definition. 'Now,' he said. He got up from the edge of the bed and brutally pushed the bed-screens away. They freewheeled squeakily a yard or so, and a wardful of ice-cream-eaters was disclosed with appalling suddenness. 'Get up out of that bed,' said newly brutal Dr Railton with a no-more-of-this-malingering gesture. Edwin's pyjama trousers had lost their cord somewhere between Moulmein and London, and he blushed as he drew up the stripy folds from around his ankles. The ice-cream-eaters looked on placidly, as at a television commercial. 'Now,' said Dr Railton, 'walk in an absolutely straight line from here to that man over there.' He pointed to a tense-looking patient who nodded, as showing willingness to participate in any helpful experiment, a patient imprisoned in cages and snakes of rubber tubing. Edwin walked like a drunk. 'All right,' said the tense patient encouragingly. 'You're doin' all right, truly you are.'

'Now walk back,' said Dr Railton. ('See you later,' said the tense patient.) Edwin walked back, drunker than before. 'Now get back into bed,' said Dr Railton. Then, as if none of this really had to be taken *too* seriously, as if he were only paid to be like that and over a couple of pints you couldn't meet a nicer man, Dr Railton boyishly laughed and play-punched Edwin on the chest, tousled his hair and tried to break off a piece of his shoulder.

'Monday,' he promised laughing at the door, 'we really start.'

Edwin looked round at his ward mates who now lay back replete and tooth-sucking. The tense patient said:

'Know who he was?'

'Dr Railton, isn't it?'

'Nah, we know that. What he was before is what I mean. Mean to say you don't know? That's Eddie Railton.'

'Really?'

'Used to be on the telly when he was learnin' to be a doctor. Played the trumpet lovely, he did. Just goes to show you, dunnit?'

A Negro ward orderly came to Edwin's bedside. He caressed the bed-clothes lingeringly, looking liquidly through thick intellectual spectacles. 'Now,' he said, 'you eat.'

'No, really, I don't think I want to.'

'Yes, yes, you eat. Must eat. Everybody must eat.' The deep tones of a Negro sermon. He marched gravely towards the door. The tense patient called from his nest of tubes:

'Here, fetch us an evenin' paper. There'll be a bloke sellin' 'em in the 'all just about now.'

'I have no time,' said the Negro orderly, 'to fetch evening papers.' He marched out.

'There you are,' said the tense patient in disgust. 'Just goes to show you, dunnit? There's a right good bleedin' specimen of a good Samaritan for you, ennit? I mean, it shows you, dunnit? Fair drives you up the bleedin' wall, dunnit? Straight up it does.'

Edwin toyed with steamed fish and a scoop of mashed potato, depressed as he looked round the ward. Everyone was in bed except his immediate neighbour. Most wore white turbans like Mecca pilgrims, though signs not of

9

grace but of shaven heads. A ward full of sick hajis. Edwin's neighbour sat on his bed in a dressing-gown, gloomily smoking, looking out to the London evening in the still square. His face wore a clinical sneer, part of a complex syndrome. That afternoon, shortly after Edwin's arrival, two visitors from another ward had come, also with sneers, to compare sneers. A sort of sneerers' club. They had sneered good-bye to Edwin's sneerer neighbour and then sneered off. Very depressing.

A staff nurse, depressingly healthy, jaunted in, and the tense man of the cage and tubes said, 'Evenin', staff.' The staff nurse jaunted on to the end of the ward, not replying. 'There,' said the tense man, 'shows you, dunnit? What the bleedin' 'ell I done wrong now? Says good evenin' to her and she don't say good evenin', kiss my arse nor nuffin. Drives you up the wall, dunnit?'

'No,' said Edwin, 'I don't want ice-cream. No, thank you very much, no ice-cream. No, please, no. No ice-cream.'

'Relax,' came the Negro preacher's tones. 'You relax, my little friend. That's what you here for, to relax. Nobody's going to make you eat ice-cream if you don't want ice-cream. So I just leave the ice-cream here by your bedside just in case you change your mind and want to eat ice-cream some time later on.'

'No,' said Edwin, 'no. I don't like ice-cream. Please take it away.'

'You relax now. Maybe you want to eat it some time later on.' The Negro orderly gravely walked off. In a jumpy temper Edwin got out of bed, picked up the chill melting saucerful, ready to throw it. Then he thought: 'Careful now, careful, take it easy, they'd love you to do something like that.'

'If you don't want that,' said the tense man of tubes, 'give it to me. I'll give it to my youngster when he comes in tonight. Loves anythin' like that, he does. Anythin' cold. Fair laps it up, he does.'

Edwin put on his dressing-gown, a Chinese silk one crawling with dragons, and padded over to this man's bed. At its foot there was a glory of many charts – water intake and output, rate of saline flow, protein content of cerebrospinal fluid, as well as temperature and pulse graphs showing peaks, deep valleys. The name on all these was proud and simple – R. Dickie. 'Like me to show you round the gas-works?' said R. Dickie. 'This here tube with that bottle upside down up there is like pouring sort of medicine into me, and this tube here is attached to my old whatnot, and that one goes into my back, and I'm not quite sure where that one goes to. And that sort of crane is so as how I can lift myself up, and that kind of cage is to stop things touching my legs. Marvellous what they can think up, ennit? Mind you don't kick that bottle on the floor over because that tube fixed to it at one end is fixed to my old whatsit at the other. Keeps drippin' in all day it does. Later on they measure it. Marvellous, ennit? Straight up.' He had a red fifty-year-old face and hair much disordered, as if his hospital stay had really been a strenuous cruise in a trawler.

'What happened to you?' asked Edwin.

'Fell off a bleedin' ladder at work. Me, I'm a builder.'

A simple and dramatic accident, a proud hazardous trade. Edwin thought of his own trade, his own accident. A lecturer on linguistics in a college in Burma who had one day, quite without warning, fallen on the lecture-room floor while lecturing on linguistics. He had been talking about folk etymology (*penthouse, primrose, Jerusalem artichoke*) and then, quite suddenly, he had passed out. He came to to find concerned, flat, delicate-brown Burmese faces looking down on him, himself saying: 'It's really a question of assimilating the unknown to the known, you see, refusing to admit that a foreign word is really foreign.' While he lay on the cool floor he could see quite clearly, on the fringe of the group that surrounded him, one or two students taking down his words in their

11

notebooks. He said: 'While we honour none but the horizontal one.' That, too, was taken down.

The doctors had taken a serious view of the matter, giving him a very dull series of medical examinations. A lumbar puncture had shown a great excess of protein in the cerebrospinal fluid. Dr Wall had said: 'That shows there's something there that shouldn't be there. We'd better send you back to England to see a neurologist.' Here he was, talking to a builder who had fallen off a ladder.

'In Germany it was,' said R. Dickie. 'Perhaps if it had happened here it might have worked out different. Here they come now, you see. They're lettin' them in.'

They were letting them in. The flowers were being wheeled out on trolleys, the water-bottles filled for the night, and they were letting the visitors in. To R. Dickie's bed came various grey women and a small thumb-sucking boy who began to eat Edwin's ice-cream. To the supine Mecca pilgrims came cheerful grape-laden families, including hearty men in pullovers with copies of *The Autocar*. To Edwin Spindrift came Sheila Spindrift. With Sheila Spindrift was a man, unknown to Edwin.

'Darling,' said Sheila. 'Look, this is Charlie. It *is* Charlie, isn't it? That's right. I met Charlie in the pub and he was sweet enough to bring me round here. I wasn't too sure of the way in the dark.' Sheila had a slight unfocused look about her; her black hair was untidy; powder had caked on her face. Edwin could gauge, almost to the nearest cubic millimetre, how much she had been drinking. He didn't blame her, but he wished she hadn't picked up this Charlie.

Charlie took Edwin's right hand in both his large warm horny paws. 'So you're Edward,' he said warmly in a furred Cockney baritone. 'Your wife's been telling the whole lot of us in the public bar about you being ill. It's a real pleasure to me,' he said, 'this is.' He was darkly coarsely handsome in a working-class best blue suit.

'And he brought me all the way here,' said Sheila, 'because I wasn't too sure of the way in the dark. And he's been so sweet. See what he bought for you. He would insist on stopping at the tube station bookstall to buy these. He said you'd want something to read.'

'It's a real pleasure,' said Charlie, and he pulled from his side-pockets bunches of gaudy magazines – *Girls, Form Divine, Laugh It Off, Vibrant Health, Nude, Naked Truth, Grin, Brute Beauty*. 'Because,' he said, 'your wife here tells me you're a reading man, same as I am myself, and nothing passes the time better when you're ill than a good read.' He fanned one periodical open, as in demonstration, and male and female nudes grinned wanly, postlapsarianly, under the ward ceiling lights. 'Let's sit down, shall we?' said Charlie, and Edwin, feeling he was being a bad host, led his visitors over to his bed. 'Now,' said Charlie, 'what is it your wife here says that you do?'

'Linguistics.'

'Aha.' The three of them sat, leg-swinging, on the bed. '*I've* never heard of it,' said Charlie, 'and that's a fact. Mind you, I'm not saying there's no such thing, but no mention of it has ever come my way before.'

'Oh,' said Edwin, 'it does exist.'

'That's as may be, but, if it does exist, it'll be above the heads of people like me and her.' He jerked his head towards Sheila. 'Me, I clean windows. Anybody can understand what that is, and you don't get put into places like this one if you do a job like that. Mind you, you can get put into a hospital if you're a window-cleaner, but not in a hospital like this one, because window-cleaning doesn't affect the brain. Not, that is, if you're made as you can do the job. Some can't do it, and I should think it's more than likely that you yourself couldn't. I'm not trying to be insulting, but every man to his trade. If you got up there on a ladder you'd as like as not get froze. I've seen these young ones just starting –

"tumblers" we call them – get froze stuck up there on a ladder, and nothing that anybody can do can get them down if they're not ready to come down. What I mean is, they can only get unfroze of their own accord. I remember hacking away at the hands of one of these tumblers, twenty storeys up, who'd got himself froze. It was a very high wind, and there I was on the window-sill hacking away at him with the side of my hand, but nothing I could do could get him unfroze.'

Edwin was an acrophobe. His head began to spin, and he gently lowered his feet to the floor.

'And what are they going to do, darling?' asked Sheila.

'They're going to do tests,' said Edwin. 'I suppose they're going to try and look inside the brain.'

'You keep them off that,' said Charlie. 'If you're not crackers already they'll make you crackers. Then they shut you away and you can't get out and you can't convince anybody that it's all been their fault, not yours. Your brain's your own property and you don't want them fiddling about with it. Catch them trying to see inside my brain,' he said with scorn. 'Very delicate piece of machinery the brain is, not unlike a watch or a clock.'

An Indian sister with a moustache and sideboards came up from behind and said: 'Meesees Speendreeft? Doctor would like a word with you in the office.'

'If they're trying to get your permission,' said Charlie, 'to do things to his brain what they otherwise wouldn't dare to do, you just tell them no. Just that, no. The shortest word in the language and one of the most telling.' But Sheila had already gone to the large glass tank of an office at the end of the ward.

'On a point of information,' said Edwin, 'that isn't the shortest word in the language.' He felt that, shorn as he was of everything but pyjamas, a bed and a water-bottle, he had to confront this dark horny window-cleaner with a show of the only authority he had. 'The indefinite article,' said Edwin, 'in its weak form, of course, is the shortest. It's a single phoneme. I refer, of course, to the form of the indefinite article used before a word beginning with a consonant.' He felt better after saying that. But Charlie said:

'A fine girl, your wife is. I say "girl" without intending any offence, meaning more a woman or perhaps a young woman, according to opinion. I'd say she was about the same age as you, and I'd give you thirty-eight, although you've still got a good head of hair. She came into the public bar at the Anchor today and beat Fred Titcombe at darts. She's drunk pint for pint with me. You've got to hand it to her.'

Edwin felt rising another of these unwonted fits of irritation which showed him that he was sick. 'You don't see my point,' he said, 'about the indefinite article. And you don't even ask me what a phoneme is. And I'm quite sure you don't know.'

'Well,' said calm Charlie, 'that's neither here nor there, is it? It's not to the purpose, so to speak. There's lots of things I don't know, and it's too late to start learning them now.'

'It isn't, it isn't.' Edwin held back a gush of tears. 'You know perfectly well it's never too late.' Some of the nearer visitors, longing for the bell to ring them out, having said all, and more, that they had to say, looked towards Edwin hopefully. But, in check, he sat down quietly on the bed again, blinking back the water.

'You'll be all right,' said Charlie. 'You mark my words. You'll get over it and be as right as rain.' Sheila came back at that moment, too bright, too cheerful. She said:

'Well, it seems that everything's going to be all right, there's nothing to worry about at all.'

'Is that all,' asked Edwin, 'that he wanted to tell you?'

'Well, yes, pretty well. He says that you're going to be perfectly all right. That's what he said.'

'Just what I've been telling him,' said Charlie. 'And I'm no doctor.'

15

A Nigerian nurse, her head an exquisite ebony carving, came in with the bell. 'All visitors out,' she said, 'if you don't mind.' Relief stirred down the ward. Sadly Edwin saw that his wife was only too ready with her kiss, her promise to come the next day, her quick swirl of lipstick for the healthy world outside. Charlie said:

'You read those books I brought you. Keep you cheerful. Stop you brooding about things.'

With the departure of the visitors a sigh of quiet satisfaction seemed to be exhaled through the ward: the bell had rung out what were, after all, aliens. They were, with their bright voices and natty clothes, the frivolous world. Now everyone could go back to the serious business of disease, disease being ultimately the true human state. Grapes and magazines from the alien world lay untouched for a time, time for them to become acclimatized, assimilated. The near neighbour of Edwin, who had had no visitor, who had sat unmoving on his bed, smoking thoughtfully, now spoke to Edwin for the first time. Through a twisted immobile mouth: 'Your wife's a real smasher,' he sneered. 'I like them like that. Brunette, too.' Then he sneered in silence.

Chapter Two

Edwin drew the thermometer from the warm pit where it had lain, read it, and handed it to the nurse. 'Ninety-eight point four,' he said.

'You are not supposed to know your temperature,' scolded the nurse. She was a grim sallow Slav, large-footed. 'You are not even supposed to know how to read the thermometer.' She frowned over his pulse, threw his wrist away, and recorded the evening data. 'Have you your bowels open?' she asked.

'Yes,' lied Edwin. Otherwise, what purgative horrors might she not devise? 'Very much so.'

'It is not necessary to say that. To say yes is enough.'

'Sorry,' said Edwin. And then he added, as she moved away: '*Spasebo, tovarishch.*'

'You need not thank me. It is my duty. Besides, I am not Russian.'

Edwin lay back, his bedlamp flooding warm on his face. He leafed through one of Charlie's gifts, page after page of nudes. Nude; naked. These were nude, not naked. It worried him that he could grow more excited over the connotatory differences between the two words than he could over the nude, or naked, flesh itself, in reality or in representation. Dr Mustafa, plump dark interrogator in the Tropical Diseases Clinic – whither Edwin had first been sent – had worried about that too. 'Can you feel no desire for your own wife? For anybody else's wife? For any woman at all? For nobody?' Then he had leaned forward in quiet excitement. 'Not for boys? Not for goats?' There was a true scientific approach. 'And how about fetishes?' Dr Mustafa had asked. 'Shoes? Underwear? Spectacles?' Dr Mustafa had sighed deep, deep, deep commiseration. 'Something has gone wrong with your libido. It is very sad.'

Indeed very sad. Vicariously sad, though. The man who had overcome tobacco addiction was universally congratulated. Was this other, though involuntary, loss of an appetite of a very different order? Yes, because, despite Barrie's whimsy, nicotine was not a lady. A lady was not nicotine. One's wife was not a packet of Senior Service. It was, therefore, vicariously sad.

Edwin stared, though now unseeing, at a nude named (why the quotation marks? he had wondered) 'Felicity'. He thought not of felicity but of fidelity. He and Sheila had long ago agreed that sexual infidelity was not really infidelity at all. You could accept a drink or a cigarette from somebody, why not also an hour or two in bed? It was the same sort of thing. Even when she had not been able, for some obscure reason of fancy, to reciprocate a friend's or stranger's desire for her body, she had always been willing to lie still, be the passive food for that appetite. '*Ça vous donne tant de plaisir et moi si peu de peine.*' A favourite slogan of hers. The real infidelity, according to her, should draw to itself total and ultimate condemnation, unforgivable, the sin against the Holy Ghost. To prefer just to *be* with somebody else, to engage of one's own free will in spiritual intimacy with another, that was true adultery.

It had been easy enough to accept this view of morality with one's brain, thought Edwin. It was when promiscuity changed from a concept to a percept that trouble began. Curious how women, so irrational, could exalt reason, could be genuinely puzzled that even a doctor of philosophy should want to bring out a knife when he actually *saw*, actually *heard*. Edwin had actually seen, actually heard, only once, and that had been fairly recently, in a hotel in Moulmein. Sheila had sweetly forgiven his rage; after all, the failure of his libido had already taken place; he was not quite normal.

What Edwin now feared was that his marriage would fail completely because choice had been taken away from her, her right to choose between his bed and all the others in the world. She needed a base from which to conduct her forays; she might now, without deliberately searching for it, find a new one. Edwin did not believe that anyone in any hospital, neurologist or psychiatrist, could put anything fundamental right. The libido had failed for good; the latest phase of one's personality must always be the final phase; he wanted to ensure that he never fell down unexpectedly again while lecturing on folk etymology, but if he smelt cloves as peppermint who was to say that he was wrong? And though he worried vicariously about the end of his sex-life, the test of the durability of his marriage must surely be taken on this very issue. Some day, all marriages had to become sexless, but then they usually had more than fifteen years to look back on. Thirty-eight was (Charlie had been right in his estimate) much too young to pack all those instruments away.

The sneerer next to Edwin was already asleep, toiling hard in it. At intervals he would announce a football result, the scores fantastic.

He really preferred, Edwin decided, being worried over the loss of sexual desire to being cured of this loss by people like Dr Railton. He knew this was unreasonable and ungrateful, but he felt that, in feeling that, his right to choose was being vindicated. Then he remembered that it was this very right to choose that was being denied Sheila. He was very confused. Then, into the darkened ward with its few burning bedlamps, tiptoed Dr Railton, as if to come and resolve the confusion. Dr Railton smiled. He said:

'I'm glad you're not asleep yet, Mr Spindrift. There are just one or two little things –'

'We'd better get this business straight,' said Edwin. 'This business of honorifics. I'm *Doctor* Spindrift.'

'Doctor?' Dr Railton looked wary: delusions of grandeur setting in?

'Yes. I was awarded the degree of Doctor of Philosophy by the University of Pasadena. For a thesis on the semantic implications of the consonant-group "shm" in colloquial American speech.'

'Semantics,' said Dr Railton. 'You didn't do very well with that "spiral", did you?'

'I wasn't intended to do very well,' said Edwin.

'Now,' said Dr Railton, sitting on the bed and speaking softly, 'I'm going to tell you a little story. Then I want you to re-tell the story in your own words. Right?'

'Right.'

'Once upon a time,' said Dr Railton, 'in the city of Nottingham, a policeman came to the door of the house of a gentleman called Mr Hardcastle, on Rook Street. Everybody along the street said: "Ah, they've come to arrest him at last, I knew he'd get found out sooner or later." But actually the policeman had only come to sell Mr Hardcastle a ticket for the annual police ball. Mr Hardcastle went to the police ball, got rather drunk, drove his car into a lamp-post and was, in fact, arrested, so that the neighbours were, in a prophetic sort of way right. Now tell that in your own words.'

'Why?' asked Edwin. 'What are you getting at? What are you trying to prove?'

'I know what I'm doing,' said Dr Railton. 'Tell that in your own words.'

'Nottingham has a castle, so that gives the gentleman his name,' said Edwin. 'A castle is a rook, so that explains the name of the street.'

'Now the story,' said Dr Railton, 'please.'

'I've forgotten the story. It's a silly story anyway.'

Dr Railton made rapid notes. 'All right,' he said. 'What's the difference between "gay" and "melancholy"?'

'There are various kinds of difference,' said Edwin. 'One is monosyllabic, the other tetrasyllabic. One is of French, the other of Greek, derivation. Both can be used as qualifiers, but one can also be used as a noun.'

'You've got this obsession, haven't you?' said Dr Railton. 'With words, I mean.'

'It's not an obsession, it's a preoccupation. It's my job.'

'Let's try numbers,' said Dr Railton, sadly, patiently. 'Take 7 away from 100, then keep on taking 7 away from the remainder.'

'93,' said Edwin confidently, then, less confidently, '86 ... 79 ... 72 ...' A voice came from a darkened bed, saying:

'It's all right if you play darts, ennit? That's all takin' away, ennit?' And he machine-gunned: '65, 58, 51, 44, 37, 30, 23, 16, 9, 2. Easy, ennit, if you play darts?'

'Thank you, Mr Dickie,' said sarcastic Dr Railton. 'That will do very nicely.'

'Have to, wunnit? That's the end of the numbers, ennit?' Then the sleeping sneerer next to Edwin began to intone fresh results:

> 'Blackburn 10, Manchester United 5.
> Nottingham Forest 27, Chelsea 2.
> Fulham 19, West Ham 3.'

'I suppose,' said Dr Railton, sighing, 'we've really done enough for one day.'

'Pools on his mind, ennit?' said R. Dickie. 'Got them on his mind, that's what it is. Pools.'

'Do you want a sleeping tablet?' asked Dr Railton. 'To make you sleep,' he explained. Edwin shook his head. 'Very well, then. Good night, *Doctor* Spindrift.' And he went out.

'Proper sarky, enny?' said R. Dickie. 'Proper takin' the mickey. As if you'd be here if you was *really* a doctor.'

Edwin put out his bedlamp, the last. The ward was

now dark except for a dim pilot-light overhead and a lamp as dim on the night-sister's desk, a desk hidden cosily in an improvised hut of bed-screens. The night-sister was having supper somewhere.

'Tellin' stories about Nottingham,' said R. Dickie. 'I bet he was never in Nottingham in his life. I had a sister got married there. Used to go and see her sometimes, I did. Nice little place, Nottingham. Marvellous the way they talk about what they don't know nuffin about, ennit?'

Chapter Three

Edwin sat on the edge of his bed, his heart thudding, dragging on his cigarette hard, wondering why she hadn't come. Sunday morning had pealed and tolled itself away, rustling with the *News of the World*, a day without doctors or inflicted pain yawning ahead to be broken by two periods for visitors, an extra helping, a Sunday treat. But not, it would seem, for Edwin. Two struck in the tower across the square, half of the visiting time already gone, and she did not appear. R. Dickie was saying: 'That's right, yes, that's right, true enough,' to a voluble woman about eighty years old, probably his mother; the sneerer had a crafty-looking small clergyman with him, the one whining, the other sneering, about the love of Jesus; farther down the ward a young man, chinned and humped like Punch, sat up in bed wearing a kind of ski-cap, discussing car engines with a lip-chewing nodding male relative. The two slices of Sunday roast beef had put new life into the patients. Agitated, Edwin found that his bowels wanted to move. It would serve her right, he snivelled, if she came and found him not there, perhaps thinking him wheeled away dead, it would serve her right.

He sat in the lavatory, trying to remember which hotel she had now moved to, some place near this hospital. He could ring her up, perhaps, in this pub she seemed now to frequent, this pub where she picked up window-cleaners. But it was after two now, and two was closing-time. Then, as his bowels eased, a bolder thought struck him. He would dress, leave the hospital, look for her. The

Anchor, that was the name of the pub, somewhere round there. A restaurant, probably.

It was easy enough. The lockers were opposite the washplaces. To the music of the lavatory's flush he opened his own and, trembling, took out his crumpled trousers, his sports jacket, his tie and a shirt. It was no good, of course, seeking permission. But nobody would know. He entered one of the two bathrooms and began to dress. In the mirror he saw a face sane enough looking, young enough, healthy enough, a mass of brown hair only a little grey. He put on further health and sanity with his clothes, combed his hair sleek, lit a cigarette. But he still felt insufficiently armed. Money, of course, the lack of money. He had given the whole of his two months' salary, paid in advance in Moulmein, converted now to five-pound notes, to his wife. His wallet was thin and his pockets, save for a few shillings, empty.

Nobody commented, nobody seemed to notice as he passed the glass case of the ward office. The nurses in there were giggling about something which belonged to their world without uniform, world of frocks and dances. Out of the tail of the eye they saw, perhaps, the clothes of a visitor. Edwin shut the heavy outer ward doors behind him and began to run downstairs. In the corridor that led to the vestibule were busts of bearded medical giants, set high in niches, a plaque of commemoration he had no inclination to read. Nor time, for, behind him, he heard a singing Negro voice, that of the grave giver of ice-cream.

Bells for the departure of visitors rang. It was incredibly easy. He passed the porter's desk jauntily, swinging his left arm. Outside, the main doors behind him, he was hit full in the chest by autumn. The doggy wind leapt about him and nipped; leaves skirred along the pavement, the scrape of the ferrules of sticks; melancholy, that tetrasyllable, sat on a plinth in the middle of the square. English autumn, and the whistling tiny souls of the dead round the war memorial. Edwin shivered, walked across the square and down an alleyway – flats on one side, a cut-price chiromancer on the other. He crossed a street of Sunday autumn strollers, turned a corner and came straight to the heartening façade of a tube station. Tubes meant both normality and escape. He looked down at his feet and saw that he was still wearing bedroom slippers. He wondered whether to whimper to himself, but then saw, across the street on a corner, the pub called the Anchor. He crossed, uncertain. Next to the pub was a narrow alley which a truck tried vainly to enter. The truck roared, thrust and backed, chipping two walls, clanging a mudguard on a street-post. Edwin skirted the truck, found beyond the alley a mean restaurant. From it came that percussion of knives and forks he had heard beyond the bed-screens last night, but this was robuster. The eaters could be seen through the two smeared shop-windows. One of them was Charlie, eating spaghetti un-handily, rolling sauced bales on to his fork and patiently watching them collapse back to his plate. By him was a wall-eyed man in a beret, lunching off beans. Charlie, his mouth open for a new attempt, turned towards the win-dow and saw Edwin. He kept his mouth open but now ignored the load on his fork. 'In,' he mouthed through the window, jerking head and free thumb inwards. Edwin, with gestures of regret, pointed downwards at his bedroom slippers. 'Hardly right. People might think eccentric.' Charlie pressed his brow to the window, mouth still open, trying to look down. He saw no dog. He hesi-tated between eating the forkful and coming out to Edwin. His jaws pounced. Nodding triumph to the wall-eyed man and to Edwin, he chewed and swallowed; stray spaghetti-ends were drawn in, as if fascinated. Chewing, he came out to Edwin.

'You shouldn't be here. You should be back there. Who said you could come out?' he bullied. 'You're ill.'

'It's my wife. Sheila. She didn't come.'

'You have it out with her,' said Charlie. 'I wash my hands of the whole business. If you collapse now on the street I'm not taking any responsibility.'

'Where is she?' asked Edwin.

'Where is she? How should I know where she is? I'm in there having a bite to eat with my mate. Spaghetti, as you can see. I'm not responsible. Now you get back to that hospital in double-quick time.'

'I must see her first.' His feet were cold in their bedroom slippers. He had a perverse longing for the sick warmth he had just left.

'You might try just down there,' said Charlie, pointing to the end of the grey street. 'A lot of them go there at throwing-out time. A club, you might call it. They have no members, only customers. It won't be long before the law gets on to them. If you go there, don't stay too long. Look good, won't it, you a sick man picked up by the law for illegal boozing. And in carpet slippers.'

'I'll try there.'

'All right, but watch out. Now I'm going back to this spaghetti. Very hard to eat. Italian stuff it is.' He returned to the restaurant with a cross look. Edwin walked down the street, passing dim Indian restaurants that, he knew, should smell of turmeric but seemed instead to smell of size. He came to a corner, a shop of no name, its single shop-window opaque with blue paint, its door, the same blue with khaki panels, ajar. The passage floor, he saw as he gingerly entered, was littered with bits of old racing editions, fag-packets, a doll's torso, a flabby ball, dirt. Two doors on the left wall were padlocked. Another led to buried noise and music. Uneasy Edwin went towards this and opened it. In a blast of heat the noise rose up the cellar stair-well, warming the cold damp cellar-smell which, to Edwin, was curiously flowery. Unsafe precipitous stairs led to the ultimate door. Should he knock? No, said the door, opening violently. A wet-mouthed corner-boy in a turquoise sweater with the name, in stitched yellow on the chest, of JUD, was ejected with noise and protest. Edwin pressed to the wall.

'Try vat once more,' said a youngish Semite in an old suit, 'and you won't just be frown aht. You'll ave certain fings done to you first. Fings vat will ensure you won't try vat sort of fing no more. Not only 'ere,' he promised, 'but everywhere.' He was growing untidily bald; his chocolate-brown double-breasted suit, sagging at the bosom, bagged at the knees. He began to push the corner-boy by the rump up the stairs. The boy snarled street words. The Semite, sad-eyed, raised chin and arm for a back-hander.

'Bleedin' plice,' said the boy. 'Lot of old bags.' No whit daunted, he whistled his way up, each step resounding like a thumped herring-box. The Semite said to Edwin:

'Vat's what you get. I've ruined vis place lettin' yobbos like vat one in. It's me who's ruined vis place and nobody else.' Sadly, and with a remnant of ancestral Levantine courtliness, he ushered Edwin in. A vast man in striped sweatshirt and snake-clasp belt stood facing them, beer in hand, very still, like a turn of human statuary Edwin had come to see. 'I'd have done that,' he said, 'if you'd asked, but you never asked.' He had small not unhandsome moustached features set, as print in some expensive edition, in a face with wide margins. Edwin looked for her over the heads of, in the gaps between, far uglier men and dishevelled women: though one trim drunken middle-aged woman in a smart hat twirled sedately to the music, her partner a glass of Guinness. The Semite shook his head in sorrow, his brown eyes full of sadness. 'Ve fings we get in 'ere,' he said. 'I *ate* vis place,' he said, with bitter Mosaic passion, 'I 'ate it like I've never 'ated anyfin' else.'

Edwin got to the bar, pushing, excusing himself, and there was Sheila, smart in her green costume. She opened her shocked eyes wide as, into him, relief pumped rapidly. 'Darling,' she cried, holding out wide a cigarette

27

and a gin-glass. 'You've escaped,' she said. 'They've taken your shoes,' she said, missing nothing.

'You didn't come,' said Edwin. 'I was worried.'

'But it's tonight I come, surely.'

'Sundays are different. You can come twice on Sunday. On Sunday there's an extra session.'

'Oh,' she said, 'I'm so sorry. I should have known. It was stupid of me.' What Edwin could not understand was that the Semite was in two places at once, moaning in tie and suit at the plywood counter, serving cheerfully in shirt-sleeves behind it. Out of this Dr Railton could make a nice quiz question. 'How did you know I'd be here?' she asked. 'Yes,' she said, 'I see your trouble. They're twins, you see, Leo and Harry Stone. That's Leo, behind the counter. They run this place, if you can call it running. A Greek tailor's just asked me how much for the afternoon, that dark man there pinched my bottom, and there's a sort of Englishman who dances in the most peculiar way.'

'Could you perhaps,' asked Edwin, 'buy me a small whisky or something?'

'Not whisky,' said Sheila. 'You've been told to lay off drink for two years. A light ale.'

Edwin was served with a golden water tasting of soap and onions. 'Not so good, is it?' said Leo Stone. His baldness, Edwin noticed, was more advanced than that of his twin. His accent had a patrician overlay, as if he had sometime been a superior salesman. From the juke-box in the far corner two light American voices, of the new generation of castrati, sang of teenage love amid recorded teenage screams. Clumsy dancing began. A tattered dog arose from sleep and barked. 'All right,' said Harry Stone. 'Vey won't touch you, I can promise you vat. If one of vem was to lay a bleedin' 'and on you I'd 'ave 'im.' The dog yawned, comforted. Behind the counter an electric kettle suddenly sang. 'Vere,' said Harry Stone, 'your dinner's nearly ready. Just give it time to cool dahn. A lovely bullock's 'art,' he said to the vast moustached man.

'Could bleedin' near eat it myself.' The vast man belched on a draught of beer and converted the belch into Siegfried's horn call. He followed this with a cry of *'Nothung! Nothung!'* and ended with a bar or two of the burning down of Valhalla. 'Take no notice,' said Harry Stone to Edwin. 'Works at Covent Garden, 'e does.' And he shook his head, his eyes frantic with pain, at the world's folly, looking at Edwin as though they two were in a conspiracy of sanity. The bullock's heart was pincered out of the kettle with two crown-cork bottle-openers; it steamed on the wet counter. 'You wait, Nigger,' said Harry Stone. 'Or, 'ere, Leo, just 'old it under ve tap.'

A Medusa, her long coat as shabby and dusty-black as the dog's, came up to Edwin and asked him to dance. 'I shouldn't really,' said Edwin. 'I should be in hospital really.' But he was borne off, too much the gentleman, into the jigging crowd. He looked for Sheila, but he had become separated from her by two new drink-buyers – thin young Guardsmen, blind behind their peaks. Frantic shoving dancing went on before the golden calf of the juke-box – a man who had taken his teeth out for fun; a woman whose breasts bounced lazily up and down, out of time with the music; a Mediterranean man shaven to a matt blue; a coach-driver in his cap; a genteel woman in a raincoat, tremulous with gin; two flat-chested girls who danced woodenly together, talking German; a middle-aged blonde with a bull-dog's face – all seemed somehow mixed in one moving mush, like pease pudding. Edwin and his partner were added to the boil, and the partner, her snake-hairs waving, was vigorous. Edwin soon found that one of his bedroom slippers had been kicked off. He danced as though guying a bent-backed old man, looking under feet, under the juke-box, into corners. It was not to be seen. He lost the other one and then, still dancing, felt spilt beer soaking his socks. When the music ended everybody helped.

'What's he lost?'

'It sounded like slippers, but I don't see how it can be that.'

The genteel woman in the raincoat said carefully to Edwin: 'I can see that you're artistic, just the same as I am. I modelled for the best painters, the very best. John, Sickert, that other man. There's one of me in the Tate, you must have seen it.'

'It's my slippers,' said Edwin, kneeling down, looking between the legs of the seated. 'There's one there,' he said, crawling on his knees towards the two German girls, one of whom was in the other's lap.

'Edwin,' said Sheila, 'whatever are you doing?'

'It's my slippers.'

'You shouldn't have come out, you know you shouldn't. I'm going to call a cab and take you straight back there.'

The loss of his slippers, the fact that he had been dancing in his socks had suddenly, for some reason, endeared Edwin to the man who had taken out his dentures. 'Drink this, major,' he said gummily. 'Take it in your right hand and repeat after me.' He wore a good suit but no collar or tie. Edwin, flustered, found himself holding a glass of Scotch. 'You're a man as likes a lark, same as it might be myself. I could see that soon as you come in.' The club customers seemed quick at finding affinities.

'I'm going to take you back,' said Sheila, 'as soon as I've finished this drink. Dancing in your stocking-feet indeed. You want your head seeing to.' The shocking aptness of this struck her. 'Oh,' she said, 'I didn't mean in that way, you know I didn't,' and she hooked her hand on to his arm.

'Tomorrow morning,' said Edwin, 'they start.'

'Yes, darling, and tonight I think you'd better get as much sleep as you can. I shan't come to see you. After all, we've seen each other this afternoon, haven't we?'

'Oh,' said Edwin. 'Well, that's up to you, I suppose.'

'I'll come tomorrow evening, naturally.'

'I can see you lookin' at vem shelves,' said Harry Stone to Edwin. 'Not much vere, is vere?' There was a half-bottle of gin and a plastic nude statuette. 'Can't get no credit, can't carry much in ve way of stock. Ashamed I am when I fink of ve way I've ruined vis place. But vat's perhaps because I 'ate it so much.' The dog Nigger chewed away at the remaining ventricle. 'We buy retail from ve public bar of ve Anchor at closin' time and stick a bit on. It's no way of doin' business, really.'

The German girls brought a slipper each. *'Danke sehr,'* said Edwin. Then he heard the big man who worked in, or at, Covent Garden talking on philology. 'Italian's a lovely language,' he was saying. 'I've heard some of the finest Italian singers of all time. It's the best language to sing in, they reckon. Stands to reason,' he said illogically, 'because it's the oldest. Italian's only a kind of Latin, and Latin's the oldest language.'

'Oh, there are older languages,' said Edwin. 'Sanskrit, for instance.'

'Well, that's a matter of opinion, isn't it?' The big man spoke a kind of northern English which, slowly, over long years, had been modulating towards Cockney.

'Oh no,' said Edwin, 'it's no matter of opinion, it's a matter of fact.' He settled himself to a lecture. Sheila said:

'Come on, we're going back.' She tightened her hold on his arm.

'In a minute, dear. I just wanted to show our friend here –'

'My name's Les.'

'How do you do? To show Les here –'

'Come on.' She began to lead him out. Edwin had the impression – but he might have been wrong – that she made a quick face to the Stone brothers, a face indicating that her husband was not quite normal, that he mustn't be encouraged to start talking. He was sure that she did not point her finger to her temple, however. Fairly sure.

Chapter Four

They walked back to the hospital, Sheila's hand firm on his arm. It was not even tea-time yet: his outing had been brief. Only on the steps before the main entrance did Edwin ask her what he'd wanted, yet feared, to ask. Sheila said:

'I think I'm sure of the way now. Even in the dark. I'll be able to come on my own.' A cold breeze suddenly blew, crinkled leaves scuttled along the pavement. Edwin said:

'What did Railton want to see you about?'

'Railton?'

'You know, the doctor. Look,' said Edwin, 'it's cold. Come into the vestibule for a bit.'

'I'd rather not. Really I wouldn't. I'll be so glad when you're out. I hate hospitals.'

'What did he say?'

'I told you, didn't I? That everything's going to be all right and that nobody's to worry.'

'Come off it. He didn't have you in just to say that. What did he really say?'

'There was a bit more, but it was me who did the talking, really. He wanted certain things confirmed, things in the original report.'

'Such as?'

'Oh, you know as well as I do. About you collapsing and so on. How much you drank. Our married life. Whether we were happy and so forth.'

'Well, were we, are we?'

'Of course we are.' She didn't sound too convinced. She

put her hands in the tiny pockets of her costume jacket. 'It's cold. Thank God I brought my fur coat back.'

'And about sex, of course?'

'About sex. Look, it *is* getting really cold, isn't it? I don't think it's good for you to stand out in the cold.'

'What do they suspect is wrong with me?' asked Edwin.

Sheila hesitated. 'They don't know what they suspect. They say that there's obviously something wrong but they hope soon to find out what. They don't think it's too serious.'

'How can they think that when they don't know what to suspect?'

'I don't know. I'm not a doctor. Look, I'm cold. That's all that was said, honestly.'

'Right,' said Edwin. And then: 'I'm sorry about the sex life.'

'Oh, everything will be all right. I'm sure of that.' She stamped daintily, dancing up and down in the cold. 'It was silly of you to come out in your bedroom slippers.'

'Yes. What are you going to do this evening?'

'Oh hell,' said Sheila, 'what can I do? It's not much fun for me, either, you know, stuck here in a cheap hotel, knowing nobody.'

'You know a window-cleaner and a couple of Jewish twins.'

'Oh, don't be silly. You know perfectly well what I mean. They're *half*-Jewish, anyway. Leo knows Burma, or says he does. He was in the Navy.'

'I suppose I'd better go in.' He wanted the cosy ward, tea brought round by the Italian ward-maids, a read of the article on morphology in the latest *Language*.

'It's no fun.' She seemed ready to resume at length. 'What do you want me to do with my evenings?'

'There's the cinema, ballet –' He couldn't think of anything else. 'The theatre,' he remembered. 'Opera.' They all sounded dull.

'I can't go on my own, you know.'

'Some women do.'

'This woman doesn't. There's a man with a beard who comes into the Anchor. He said he'd take me to a club he belongs to. He's a writer or painter or something. That might make a change.'

'Do be careful. There are some pretty queer types in London.'

'I'm not a child exactly. He said he was sorry to hear that my husband was in hospital. He said that I must be very lonely.' Sheila giggled, then shivered. 'It's *so* cold,' she said. 'I *must* go.'

'And you won't come this evening?'

'You've had your ration of me.' She smiled. 'Try and get to sleep early. I'll be in tomorrow.'

'All right. Oh, this hotel.'

'Yes?'

'This hotel where you are now. Where is it, what's it called?'

'I don't want you out of bed ringing me up, catching cold and whatnot. Anyway, I'm not quite sure of its name. Oh yes, the Farnworth. They've got it at the hospital, anyway. Address of next of kin.'

The leaves scurried. 'I'm sorry about all this,' said Edwin. 'But it's a change for you, isn't it, a bit of a change? A sort of holiday? A nice change from Moulmein?'

'My dear sweet Edwin, why should you be sorry – in that way, I mean? It's not your fault. And it *is* a change from Moulmein, yes. Colder, a little more squalid. But yes, yes, I do like London, I was only joking. I'll make out somehow. Now go in and have your tea or whatever it is.'

'*You* must eat. I'm sure you're not eating enough.'

'I'll eat all right. Now you go in to your nice nurses.' She danced up and down again; the leaves, like kittens, danced around her. 'I *must* go now,' she said, 'and warm up a bit. Oh,' she added, 'I nearly forgot.' She gave him a cold kiss; cold, he assumed, because her lips were cold, because she wanted to get away to warmth. 'It is warmth,' he thought, 'that we are finally faithful to.' She went off quickly like a schoolgirl. Edwin entered the hospital: the crankhouse, he thought, those two German girls would call it. The porter called to him from his desk:

'Too late for visitors, sir. You can come again this evening.'

'Do I look as fit as that?' said Edwin.

'Patients going out,' said the porter severely, 'are to leave their names at the desk. I've got no name written down here.'

'Dr Spindrift.'

'Oh, sorry, sir. I didn't know, sir. I *do* beg your pardon.'

Edwin did not use the lift; he hated lifts. He walked up the stairs slowly to his ward. There was nobody around to rebuke him. He went softly to the locker and took out his pyjamas and dressing-gown, changed quietly in a bathroom. He examined his face again in the mirror: it seemed a normal enough face. Then he remembered that he had forgotten to put a final frank question to Sheila. Did she think he had changed? But she would have been evasive. In pyjamas and dressing-gown he entered the long warm sick place which was now home. Tea was coming round. R. Dickie said:

'Where've you been? Everybody's been askin' for you.'

'What did they want me for?'

'Nuffin, really. They just wanted to know where you was.'

'I've been to the—' Though a philologist, he was ashamed of using certain words in public. He sought a euphemism and, automatically, it was one of R. Dickie's that came out. 'The old whatsit,' he said.

'You was a long time.'

'It was rather a slow and frustrating business,' said Edwin.

'They'll be givin' you a black draught if you tell 'em that. Straight up they will. Frustratin', eh? That's a good un.'

Chapter Five

Next morning Edwin was introduced to a subterranean world of female technicians – crisply permed, white-coated young women who were jauntily self-assured. Their status seemed equivocal. Despite their lack of clinical knowledge, their mere narrow mastery of certain machines, they deferred to no one. They seemed to have access to a special laundry which blanched their coats to a blinding snow, making the medical staff's array look almost grubby. Their high heels were quick on the corridors, their heads erect. Edwin shambled after one of these pert creatures to the X-ray department.

He pressed his cold chest to a plate on the wall and heard its picture clicked off. He was strapped to a bed and had, from many angles, his grinning skull recorded. 'Webster, too,' he said, 'saw the skull beneath the skin.'

'Who was Webster?'

'A poet.'

'Oh, a poet.' She thrust in a new plate fussily. 'Don't move,' she said. 'Keep absolutely still.' There was another click. 'I don't go in much for poetry,' she said. 'It was all right at school, I suppose.'

'You think it's better to be a radiographer than a poet?'

'Oh yes.' She spoke with vocational fervour. 'After all, we save lives, don't we?'

'What for?'

'What do you mean, what for?'

'What's the purpose of saving lives? What do you want people to live for?'

'That,' she said primly, 'is no concern of mine. That didn't come into my course. Now, if you'll just wait here, I'll get these developed.'

Edwin was left a long time on his own. He looked out of the window on to a squad of dustbins. Two fat cats slept in the grey autumn morning, too fat to feel cold. What did they get fat on? Discarded cerebral tissue, perhaps. The shining machine seemed to be staring at his back. He turned on it to stare it out. There must be a flaw somewhere to mar this squat elegance. He had cured his young man's diffidence in the presence of the smart and beautiful by looking for the microscopic but qualifying mark of negligence – spots of dandruff on black serge, a wisp of pastry at the mouth-corner. He walked over now to the heavy polished apparatus and found, to his pleasure, a fleck of rust. Moreover, in a cardboard box on the windowsill there was, among metal terminals and fuses, a solitary white button. He felt exhilarated. The radiographer returned to find him doing a stately dance across the floor.

'They're all right,' she said, staring at him fearfully. 'They're quite clear. Can you find your own way back to the ward?'

Edwin could. He entered it to find a ward-round in progress – a great man proceeding from bed to bed with his satellites, one of them Dr Railton. This, he knew, was Mr Begbie, eminent neurologist, famed discoverer of Begbie's syndrome. The Negro orderly, awed and hushed as at a pontifical high mass, motioned Edwin to his bed, made him, with poultry-shooing movements, enter it. Both waited, perfectly still, as for the eucharist to come.

Mr Begbie had a tic under his left eye. So dentists sometimes had visible caries, so the cobbler's child was the worst shod. 'And you,' said Mr Begbie, 'must be Mr Spindrift.' The satellites in white gave encouraging smiles; Dr Railton seemed anxious as a lance-sergeant at a general inspection.

'*Doctor* Spindrift.' That had to be made clear. 'Doctor of Philosophy,' he expanded. All smiled more broadly.

'Yes. 'And you were sent here by —'

'I was sent by the Tropical Diseases Clinic. I went straight there from Moulmein.'

'Yes. And who actually employs you?'

'The I.C.U.D. The International Council for University Development.'

'Very well,' conceded Mr Begbie. He wrinkled his nose as though this organization were suspect. He looked through the file he held with greater concentration. 'Yes, yes,' he said. 'What's all this about a battleship?'

'A battleship?'

'You seem to be obsessed with battleships, according to this.'

'Oh, that.' Edwin laughed. 'I see what's happened. I get migraine sometimes. The pain seems to be accompanied by a vision of a battleship sailing straight into my frontal lobes.' There were smirks at the extravagance of the image; the ward sister looked outraged at Edwin's pretence to anatomical knowledge.

'That', said Mr Begbie, 'doesn't sound like migraine at all. Well, we shall see, we shall see what can be done.' He sighed, with the weariness of one who has helped so many, received so little gratitude. The procession proceeded to the sneerer. He was patted on the back by Mr Begbie. 'We'll straighten that face out,' he promised. 'Never fear.' The face, to Mr Begbie, was just another limb. The white birds swooped on to R. Dickie. His voice came through, muffled, with compulsive question-tags: ennit? wunnit? It was, agreed Mr Begbie, it would.

Just before luncheon another of the legion of the cool, the neat-haired, in a white smock with bare pink arms, came to conduct a sort of pummelling therapy on the Punch-chinned, Punch-humped young man in the winter-sports cap. She punched him vigorously, and he responded by coughing profoundly and spitting into a sputum-cup. A brisk trade was done in bedpans. Bottles were called for; sly micturition was achieved under the bedclothes. And then Edwin's afternoon treat was announced.

'A lumbar puncture,' said the sister. She was a pinch-nosed Scot who trilled the r's with relish. 'They're going to take some of the fluid from your spinal cord. Then they'll take it to the laboratory. Then they'll see what's wrong with it.'

'I've had that done already,' said Edwin, 'twice.'

'And,' said the sister, 'ye'll have it done again.' Mistress of repartee, she returned to her office.

Some humorist in the catering department had decided on stewed brains for luncheon. Softer-hearted, some other cook had provided potatoes cooked in four different ways, a tiny potato anthology. The black man came with the ice-cream, gleaming sardonically at Edwin. Edwin read his philological magazine – a humourless American word-count of *The Owl and the Nightingale*. Stewed brains, indeed.

In the pleasant time of afternoon torpor, haunted still by the taste of after-luncheon tea, the bed-screens were wheeled round Edwin. 'Good-bye, mate,' said R. Dickie. 'See you in the next world.' A doctor in glasses, mild of face and younger than Dr Railton, came to Edwin, announcing himself as Dr Wildbloode. 'My colleague,' he said, 'is at a rehearsal. He plays the trumpet, you know.' The sister hovered behind. Edwin was made to lie on his side, his buttocks and lower back exposed. 'Nice clean skin,' said Dr Wildbloode. 'This won't hurt much.' He shot in a local anaesthetic. 'There,' he said. 'Lovely.' There was a fumbling and clatter of tiny glass and metal. 'Now,' he said, 'I'm going to draw off a few c.c.'s. Just lie quite still.' Edwin was aware, as though several miles away, of a deep prick, and then his vertebrae seemed, dully, to collapse. 'Lovely,' said Dr Wildbloode, 'coming

39

away nicely.' Edwin felt unmanned, the core of his being slowly being extracted. He said, as though it were an important discovery:

'It isn't pain that's the real trouble ever, you know. It's the feeling of disintegration, however subjective.'

'Never mind,' said Dr Wildbloode, 'never mind. It's coming away nicely. Nearly finished now.' The sister, Edwin saw from the tail of his eye, had a test-tube ready. 'Right,' said Dr Wildbloode, 'I think that's it.' Edwin heard a faint squirting out. He said:

'Can I see that?' The sister coyly granted a quick peep of the tubeful. 'Like gin, isn't it?' said Edwin.

'Burnett's White Satin,' said the sister, surprisingly. 'That's a lovely one taken neat.'

'Now,' said Dr Wildbloode, 'you just lie quite still till tomorrow morning. Lie on your back, quite still.' He went away, nodding mildly. The bed-screens were squeaked away, and Edwin lay exposed to the ward, a new recruit to the brigade of the prone.

'Marvellous what they can do these days, ennit?' said R. Dickie.

It was, in a way, refreshing to be prescribed complete passivity, to be ordered to become a mere thing. It was satisfying, too, to know that one was contributing to the uniformity of the ward. There was now not one who was not rooted, like a flower, in bed. Even the sneerer lay staring at the ceiling, beguiled by hopes of a mended set of nerves. But the becalmed order could not last. Wellmade men in caps and uniforms arrived to take away a patient in a far corner. He, drooling and evidently incurable, responded to valedictions with 'Urr', propped in a wheel-chair.

'Good-bye, Mr Leathers.'

'Ta ta, mate.'

'Keep smiling till we meet again.'

The vacuum was speedily filled. A tall scholarly-looking man was led in at tea-time, propelling himself like a walking toy, stiff in one leg, his right arm busy as an egg-whisk. A new part was added to the mealtime percussion band – a tremolo of knife and teaspoon.

After tea the ward sister came with a message for Edwin. 'Your wife's been on the telephone,' she said. 'She says she's caught a bit of a cold and is staying in bed. You're not to worry, she says. She'll be in to see you tomorrow.'

Just before dinner Dr Railton came in, very cheerful. 'Hallo, Doc,' he said to Edwin. 'They've done the lab test on your fluid. I checked the reading with the other ones that were done. It's gone up, if anything. There's a hell of a lot of protein there.' He rubbed his hands. 'But we'll push on. We'll find out what's wrong. We'll send you out of here a fit man.' And, himself a fit man, a robust trumpeter, he left, smiling.

There was no visitor for Edwin. R. Dickie had several. 'Here,' he said to a small boy, 'go and be a good Samaritan to that gentleman over there. Nobody's come to see him. Shame, ennit? You go over there and have a bit of a word with him, cheer him up a bit.' The small boy came to Edwin's bedside and was soon absorbed in the nude magazines, Charlie's present. He sniffed a good deal and tried to wipe his nose on Edwin's bedclothes.

When the visitors had left, R. Dickie said: 'He's a good little lad, enny? Gives no trouble to nobody. Any time,' he said generously, 'you've got nobody comin' to see you, you can always have one of mine. I get plenty.' He saw visitors and grapes as of the same order.

The new patient had a nightmare. 'Aaaaah,' he called over the dark. The sneering neighbour of Edwin obliged with fresh football results. The Punch-like young man coughed. Edwin lay awake thinking of the wonder of the word 'apricot'. 'Apricock' in Shakespeare, the later version due to confusion of stop consonants. 'Apricock' led back to an Arabic form, 'al' the article glued to the loan-word 'praecox', early, an early-ripe fruit. How charming

41

is divine philology. But did it really have any greater validity than the nightmare in the corner, the dream football results? Sheila ought to have come to see him, cold or no cold.

Chapter Six

Next day Edwin was called down to the cellars for an electro-encephalogram. 'Electro-encephalogram' was a pleasing scholarly word reduced, on the signboard outside the door, to EEG – a mean cartoon cry. Edwin was met by another crisp snowy girl who told him to lie on a table. He asked her, chattily, what she understood by the middle term of 'electro-encephalogram'.

'We just call it EEG,' she said. She fixed a net over Edwin's hair, pressing salted wet cotton-wool under each node. 'It's rather a long word otherwise. I don't know why they want to make them so long.' She was preoccupied with her preparations, a very red tongue-tip protruding as she wired Edwin to her machine. This machine was like an organ console with dials, a mile of paper threaded over its surface in a pianola roll.

'What exactly does this *show*?' asked Edwin.

'Sort of electrical impulses from your brain,' said the girl. 'I don't quite know what they do with them, but that's what it's for. Now all you have to do is to relax. Open and close your eyes when I tell you, and don't move.' The girl sat down at her console. Behind her was a glass panel, beyond that a man and a girl technician larking silently. Where, wondered Edwin, was the aquarium, this side or that? The couple looked at him as if he were a *thing*, laughed at their own joke, went off together. Edwin felt unaccountably angrier than he had felt for a long time. He said:

'I don't think you really believe we're human beings at all. A couple of X-ray plates, those bloody electrical impulses of yours – sorry, I apologize, for the swearing. What I mean is –'

'Do you mind?' said the girl. 'I've got my work to do.'

'That's just it, isn't it? You've got your work to do and you assume that you're doing it with something inert, something passive. You forget that I'm a human being.'

The girl looked at him in a new way. 'If looking at me excites you,' she said primly, 'you needn't look. You can keep your eyes fixed on the ceiling.'

Edwin was horrified. Was that, then, one of her professional hazards, or a carry-over from her social life, or some pose learnt from films or television? 'I didn't mean that at all,' he said. And, having made that disavowal, he felt a sort of rudimentary desire, or a desire for desire, stirring in him.

'We're here,' said the girl reasonably, 'to help. To make you normal again. Now keep your head still and your eyes open.'

What would the doctors say, he wondered, if he suddenly found sex flaring up in him again and attacked, like a satyr, one of these prim snowy nymphs of technicians, ravished her on her own machine, with the paper still flowing through, the ink-pens tracing madly away? They should really, he supposed, be pleased. He looked at the girl, whose eyes were down watching the electro-encephalic pattern pour steadily out. She lifted her eyes for an instant, caught his gaze, primly looked down again.

'Close your eyes now.'

His eyes closed, Edwin could feel more clearly the beat of the eyeballs, the blood coursing through. It was young blood still. He tried to fill the blank space with a harem – a languorous spread of haunches, navels, nipples, arms – but he sensed no response in his loins, only a slight constriction of the throat.

'Open them now.'

In hate Edwin stripped the girl of her stiff whiteness,

tore off the flowered dress underneath, crushed her against the glass panel. Primly she kept her eyes down. It was no good: the most violent act of the imagination could produce no response. He sighed, a mere lay-figure in striped pyjamas lying on a hard bed, a ridiculous hair-net with electrodes on him, feeding a machine.

'Do keep your head still. Now close your eyes again.'

Edwin thought of a little article he had proposed to a magazine on Popular English Studies, an article on the bilabial fricative and its persistence through centuries of colloquial English. Sam Weller did not, of course, interchange 'v' and 'w': he used a single phoneme for both – the bilabial fricative. But a recorder like Dickens, untrained phonetically, would think he heard 'v' when he expected 'w', 'w' when he expected 'v'.

'Now,' said the girl, 'don't open your eyes. Keep them tightly shut. I'm going to flash a very strong light on to them. Try and keep perfectly still.'

In his brain arms seemed to close round the bilabial fricative, to protect it from all these people with their white coats and lights and humming machines. Then the flash came: a sharp coloured pattern was etched on the inside of his lids, hideous and somehow obscene. 'Oh Christ,' said Edwin, 'that was horrible.'

'Was it?' said the girl. 'Now, once more.'

Again the obscene sharp pattern – cones, cubes, globes in malevolent colours which he could not define. The humming of the engine stopped. 'All right,' she said. 'That's the lot. You can open your eyes now.' She hummed as tunelessly as the machine had hummed while she took off Edwin's hair-net and detached the damp salt gobbets of cotton-wool. Then, with cool indifference, she said: 'You can go back to your ward now.'

Edwin stood outside in the corridor shaking with a rage which he found difficult to explain. 'Bitch,' he said under his breath, 'bitch, bitch.' But he had already forgotten the electro-encephalogram girl. It was as though

45

the obscene flash had engendered a sudden and rather surprising hatred for his wife. He felt insulted that she should have thought it necessary to lie, so as not to hurt his feelings. He looked at his wrist-watch: nearly midday. He would telephone her and make it absolutely clear that she was under no obligation whatsoever to visit him if she didn't wish to. Or, better, he would be greatly obliged if she would cease to visit him altogether. 'Leave me alone,' he wanted to say, 'with my disease and my bilabial fricative.' And then he saw that that, of course, wouldn't do at all. Moreover, the task of finding copper to make the telephone call would be, he foresaw, wearisome. Let it go, he decided.

She came that evening, alone, sniffing with a genuine chill, and he, as was inevitable, said:

'You shouldn't have come.'

'Yes, that's what I thought, too, but I felt – well, it can't be much fun for you, after all, not seeing anybody.'

'But it isn't just *anybody* I want to see, is it?'

'No, I suppose not. Oh, I do wish it were all over.' She spoke the words fervently, as though her involvement in his disease were more than the empathetic one of a mere loving wife. And he thought that she must have been entrusted with some secret about the disease and its prognosis. She could never keep a secret with ease: it was agony for her not to have the freedom to blurt everything out to the very person who must be the last to know; it was cognate, Edwin supposed, with her sexual incontinence. He said:

'If Railton's told you something that I'm not supposed to know – Well, you know me well enough. I can take anything. And I don't like secrets any more than you do.'

She got up from the bed's edge nervously. 'I've told you already,' she said. 'It was just nothing, just about everything being all right and I wasn't to worry, that's all. Honestly.' Her eyes had a pleading look. She said: 'I suppose I ought to go now, really. They'll be ringing that blasted bell any minute now, and I hate anybody *telling* me to get out.'

'But you've only just come. There's plenty of time.'

'Look,' she said deliberately. 'This doesn't do any good. I mean, it's so artificial. We've nothing to say to each other really, and we both keep looking at our watches in a surreptitious kind of way. It's true, isn't it? It isn't normal, this kind of thing – it makes me all jumpy. And you know I hate hospitals.'

'You mean you don't want to see me, is that it?'

'Oh, it's not that. While you're in here I get a feeling that it isn't really you at all. And it isn't, is it? It's you sick. It's you sort of suspended – you know what I mean, suspended animation. And I hate this lack of privacy and this clock-watching and the artificiality of it all. So would you mind very much if I didn't come in every night?'

'Well,' said Edwin slowly, 'if you really feel that way about it. I do understand, you know, don't think I don't. Could you,' he asked, 'possibly write me letters?'

'I could do that, yes. Yes, that's a good idea.'

'Although it does seem a bit stupid, doesn't it, when you only live a couple of hundred yards away.'

'And,' said Sheila eagerly, 'there are quite a number of people in the Anchor who'd be only too pleased to come and visit you. So you won't be too lonely.'

'All right, if you want it that way. You mean I can look forward to a procession of colourful low-life characters to cheer my solitude?'

'Well, it was kind of them to offer, wasn't it?'

'And when are you coming to see me again?'

'Oh, in a few days. At the week-end. Please, Edwin, don't tie me to anything. You know how I hate being tied. I'll come fairly soon, honestly I will.'

Chapter Seven

The tests that followed required more than a single white-coated operator, so that greater opportunities presented themselves for treating Edwin as a thing. Impotent on a cellar table, he could be discussed or, when a social mood prevailed, ignored. The tests were intimate and searching, so that he was fingered more, heaved about more, recalcitrant parts of his body were scolded more. But when he was particularly docile and plastic he was elevated to a pet's level and patted.

The doctors wanted an arteriogram. A pink vermilion-lipped pudding of a nurse squirted a tranquillizer into his buttock, then he was wheeled into a lift and carried below. Radiographers greeted him cheerfully – maturer women, and perhaps more virginal, than those he had met on previous occasions. He was slid on to an operating table under the nozzles and eyes of X-ray apparatus, and there was happy talk and bustle while the doctor, opener of arteries, was awaited.

'I've put a new cone in, Mabel.'

'Oh, good-oh.' A yell above Edwin's head.

Edwin saw faces, upside down, peering at him incuriously. The inverted human face is horrible: too many holes, far more monstrous than any monster from outer space.

'And what did she say then?'

'She said she wasn't going to wait all her life looking for the right man. By the time she'd found him, she said, it'd be too late anyway.'

'Who's she to go on about waiting for the right man? Have you seen that hair?' There was a puff of derision.

The inverted face
Of any given member of the human race
Is far more monstrous than

'Hiya, girls.' It was a Canadian doctor, keen-faced and with thick hair *en brosse*. He was young and evidently most accessible to the laity. 'This our patient? Hiya, Mister.'

'Doctor,' corrected Edwin.

'Yes?' said the doctor. 'That's right, I'm the doctor. Now I'm just going to give you a small local.' He grasped the artery on the right side of Edwin's neck and pumped in his anaesthetic. Then he sat down and waited. Two other young doctors, at a loose end, came in and joined him. There were friendly greetings, and the female voices grew louder, moved some way along the short female road to hysteria. *Hysterikos, hystera*, the womb. But Freud had shown that there was no connection, despite the etymology.

'And what sort of a time did you have in Italy?'

'It was all right, I guess. *Molto buono.*'

'Do watch those vowels,' said Edwin, almost automatically.

'We drank the *vino* and tried to make the *señoritas. Molto bella.*'

'It's in Spain they have the *señoritas*,' said one of the radiographers, 'not in Italy.'

'They're the same, whatever you call them, wherever you go. All women are the same, made to be made.'

'They're not all the same,' said a provocative radiographer, 'thank you very much.'

'Don't thank me, sister. Well, time to have a go at that artery.'

The small underground room seemed full of people, upside-down faces all round Edwin, jovial advice as the Canadian doctor tried to grasp the squirming artery. 'Like as if it's alive,' he said. 'Like a snake or something.

Now,' he said to Edwin. 'I've got a sort of dye in this syringe, a dye made out of iodine. When that starts circulating it'll colour the blood vessels, and when they take a picture of it that'll show what's wrong. Okay?'

But the artery had a life of its own. Edwin could see the eyes on it, fascinated, as though watching a death-duel of small fierce animals. 'Goddam it,' said the doctor, 'just can't get it in.' Then came a general shout of triumph as contact was made, the artery was pierced, and the dye was shot into it. A white-coated young lady with cool hands started to feed the artery with a saline solution. Preparations were made for the radiography.

'You'll feel,' said one of the loud women, 'a feeling like of hotness all along that side. Very hot. But don't move, whatever you do.'

The taking of the pictures seemed, to confused Edwin, to involve the shouting of signals. At the loud cry of what seemed to be 'Take' the heat came, and more. A pain that seemed green in colour and tasted of silver oxide, that, moreover, seemed to show, by some synaesthetic miracle, what the momentarily tortured nerves looked like, shot down his face, gouging his eyes out, extracting teeth with cold pliers. Again, it was not a matter of pain: it was a matter of the sick realization of what perverse experiences lurk waiting in the body.

'You're being very good,' said the saline girl. 'Really you are.' And his right arm was, for an instant, stroked. There was an interval. The other artery now had to be pierced and filled with colour.

The insignificant becomes, when doubled, the significant. A crude sprawling blot on paper makes, when the paper is doubled and opened out again, a pattern which, though still crude, is literate. And so the repetition of the processes on the other side of his neck gave Edwin a strange image of beauty. The test became a ritual. The snaking artery was caught, tamed, force-fed. Edwin's thing of a head was posed under the flying machinery, there was the hysterical cry from a distance, and again there was the complex of oxide taste, green pain – as though a tree were shouting out – and the tearing-out of teeth and eye. 'Good,' they all said. 'That's over.'

Edwin was slid back on to a trolley, wheeled to the lift and taken up again. The world never changes to greet the hero. The young man with the Punch-back was being pommelled and coughing up dislodged sputum. R. Dickie sat placidly like a king on a bedpan. The newcomer with the dragged leg and the egg-beater hand had had his head shaved; he roamed the ward, dragging and whisking, in a bobbed woollen cap. He came up to Edwin, looking down on him from thick goggles, his grey moustache quivering.

'Gest na var welch purr?' he said.

'I think that's very likely,' said Edwin.

'Gorch,' nodded the man and, seeming satisfied, moved out of the ward to the lavatories. R. Dickie said:

'Doesn't speak English like you or me. That's his brain, see. They'll put that right for him and then he'll be comin' out with the King's English – though it's the Queen's English really, ennit? – as good as you or I or anybody here. Poor old man. Mr Ridgeway his name is, and he knows some of the streets round where I used to work. He can't say the names so good, but you can see what he's gettin' at. Standin' here by my bed this mornin' he was, recitin' these names off. Thinks the world of me, you can see that. Marvellous, ennit?'

The drugged day went by, Edwin listless in bed. In the evening two visitors came for him. One, the big moustached man, he recognized: the belcher of Siegfried's horn call and crier of '*Nothung!*' Les, he remembered, was the name. With Les was an exotic woman Edwin needed time to take in. 'A letter,' said Les, 'from your missis. She asked me to bring it. Bruised you a bit round the neck, haven't they?'

Edwin read:

Darling,

Am writing as promised though nothing much to say of course. Hope you all right. Bearded man who is named Nigel and an artist is taking me to sort of wine drinking club this evening. Will try to come week-end. Be good, dearest.

Sheila.

'This is very kind,' said Edwin. 'Very kind indeed. But you needn't really, you know, have bothered.' Les's companion was a swarthy round-faced woman, obviously Mediterranean, in a blue jumper that strained at the breasts' heavy pressure, a skirt patterned with names of dishes – *kebab, risotto, pilaff, chow mien, nasi goreng*. She had sharp dark eyes, much blackbird-black hair, and innumerable warts. Her throat was tattooed with a cryptic sign. Edwin awaited an introduction, but Les said:

'There was nothing on tonight, so I thought I might as well come here as anywhere else. Last night was *Sieg* and tomorrow night's *Gott*, but there's nothing doing tonight. Heavy work, and you need a night off. Singers go on about what they have to do, but I tell them that they ought to try lugging bloody Valhalla about and making sure that you know where the bloody Rhinegold is, ready for throwing back into the water. Lost it once, and there they were frantic looking for it. That's why they took me off props and back on the heavy stuff.' He looked capable of coping with the heavy stuff, thought Edwin – massive oak shoulders, a neck like a chopping-block, a chest like two kettledrums. He had sat down on the bed's edge, but his lady remained standing, arms folded, smoking.

'There is, I think,' said Edwin, 'a chair somewhere over there.' The trouble was that R. Dickie had so many visitors: his bed looked like the bed of the dying Socrates.

'Carmen doesn't mind standing,' said Les. 'That's not her real name, Carmen, but I first met her when I was doing the opera, and it seemed to fit, somehow. A sod that is for changes – tobacco factories, bullrings, brigands' caves. But not as bad as *Aida*. You have to practically set up the whole of Egypt for that, pyramids, Suez Canal and all. This gentleman,' said Les carefully to Carmen, 'is ill. That's why we've come to see him.' Carmen bowed. 'She doesn't speak much English,' said Les. 'She'd been lured over from North Africa, you see, on the job.' He winked. 'I got her out of that, though. You'd think she'd be grateful.'

'*Yo hablo espanol, señora*,' said Edwin. Carmen now spoke. She showed a smiling mess of decay, gum recession and metal, and said:

'Blimey, you 'ear? 'E spik lak good man. Why you not spik lak 'im? You bloody zis fackin' zat all time. *Señora*, 'e say. Bloody ole bag an fackin' 'oor, you say. Why you not be good man? No money you give one day, two, sree. One day I go. Blimey, yes, get good man. Lak 'im I get.'

'She's a bit narked about not being really married,' said Les evenly. 'I've told her I can't, not in this country. Got one in Gateshead. Good thing, in some ways, to have one somewhere else. Keeps them on their toes.'

Carmen had picked up one of the nude magazines. 'Notty,' she said, giving Edwin a carious leer. 'You very notty.' And she performed a brisk sequence of thrust and recoil, giggling.

'Stop that now,' said Les. 'You don't seem to learn. This is England, not North Africa. We're civilized here. A child of nature,' he said to Edwin, 'that's her trouble.'

'Blimey, I not do dutty sing when I do zat.'

'No, we know you meant nothing rude, but there's times and places, you see, lass. At the moment we're here in this hospital visiting this gentleman whose wife we know and who you say you like. You savvy that?'

'Who wife? 'Im wife? 'E got wife?'

'Yes, yes, the one that bought you the double gin when you did that sort of fandango the other day. The one whose hair you combed.'

'Oh, 'er? Black 'air, but not very match. I got more

black 'air. I not lak 'er too match. She bloody ole bag too. She dance wiz Grik man.'

'Never mind who she danced with,' said Les, 'because that's her affair. And don't let's have any of this calling other women whores and bags just because you're jealous.' He rasped nastily at her. 'I didn't bring you here to meet a respectable and educated gentleman in order that you could insult him to his face. We're visiting the sick,' he explained. 'A corporal work of mercy, as they say.'

' 'Oor and bag you call me, yes. Blimey, I 'ear. When I get you 'ome I mek enough 'ell, yes. Oh blimey.'

'I did not call you a whore and a bag,' said Les, patiently but loudly. 'I said that that's what you're not to call other women, especially this gentleman's wife. She is a lady, which is more than what you are.'

'You call me not leddy? Oh blimey, I show you now.' She made for Les, but he, with an easy arm, an arm used to knocking down Valhalla and draining the Rhine, grasped her wrist. 'You stop zat now,' she cried in pain. 'Oh blimey.'

'All right, then, you behave a bit better. Sorry about all this,' he said to Edwin. 'I can't take her anywhere, as you can see.' Edwin observed that the ward was much interested in this pseudo-marital quarrel. He tried to dissociate himself from it by moving down farther in the bed, but the bed itself had become, appropriately, the battlefield. Carmen tried to bite. Les said:

'Biting, eh? Biting and scratching like a little puss-cat, eh? We'll soon stop that, won't we, my little passion-flower?'

'*Yo me voy cagar–*'

'And we won't have any of those rude Spanish words, either. This gentleman knows what they mean, being educated, and I've got a bloody good idea, though I'm ignorant. Ignorant, that's what you think I am, don't you, my little black beauty?' He turned her wrist like a tourniquet.

'Oh blimey, you bloody fackin' 'oor.'

'That very rude word might just about apply, but the last one will not, my African mountain-blossom. So I'll thank you to keep your dainty bloody dirty little trap shut, see?'

'I get you yet, you see I not.'

'*Not* is right,' said Les. '*Not* is the word. And now I'm taking you out of here before they throw you out.' There was no nurse to be seen, no sister, but the Negro orderly hovered, fearfully undecided. 'We'll come in and see you again,' said Les, 'if I can get her to behave. I'll get this bloody primitive wildness knocked out of her before she comes here again, you see if I don't.' Tougher, less neurotic, than Jose of the opera, he dragged her out. 'Hope you're better,' he called from the door.

Edwin thought that perhaps this delegation notion of Sheila's was not, after all, such a good idea. When all visitors had gone R. Dickie called across, chummily:

'Them relations of yours?'

And later Dr Railton came in, massaging his lips, to say:

'You're supposed to keep quiet after these tests, you know. Lie still, keep quiet, that's what you're supposed to do. I hear that you've been shouting the odds or something, at least that's what one of the sisters told me. Don't do it, don't upset yourself. You'll need every ounce of stamina you can find before we've finished with you.' He sat down on the bed. 'Well, we've all had a good look at today's pictures. There's definitely something there, we think. But we've got to make absolutely sure by looking a bit deeper. The day after tomorrow we're going to pump your brain full of air and take more pictures. That'll show, that'll be definitive.' He laughed boyishly and slapped Edwin's hidden thigh. Then he said good night and returned, as Edwin supposed, to his trumpet. Strumpet, trumpet, pump it full of air.

Chapter Eight

'I suppose,' said the voice at his back, 'you'll be getting to know this sensation pretty well by now.' Edwin sat in a kind of pillory, his buttocks bare, in another room of the cellar, attended on either hand by new, less boisterous, nymphs in white raiment. The doctor had already announced himself as a psychiatrist, here for a fortnight's brush-up on his neurology, and his tones were professionally soothing. 'A few c.c.'s,' he soothed, 'of cerebrospinal fluid.' The needle penetrated deep, Edwin's vertebrae collapsed as before, the floor became littered with knobs and discs tossed like chicken-bones at some heroic banquet, his life juice spattered everywhere. 'Nicely, nicely,' said the doctor. Soon a test-tube of spine-gin flashed by.

'And then we restore the balance. Having taken something out of your cerebrum, we proceed to put something in. Something quite harmless. Something that costs the hospital nothing. Air. Yes, air. This air will, after the manner of air, rise from its point of entry up to the brain, circulating freely. Then the work of these charming ladies commences.' The honied voice made Edwin drowse, while the charming ladies were heard, felt, to simper.

The air entered coyly, eased its way up the bony chimney, split up into quiet crocodiles tramping corridors they had never seen before. Suddenly Edwin felt strong thirst and nausea.

'Keep very still now.'

'I think,' he said, 'I'm going to be sick.'

'No, you're not. You've nothing in your stomach to be sick on. Now just keep that head-still.'

The nausea eased but the thirst persisted. Edwin had visions of the brown shaggy pierced breasts of coconuts, ice-cubes clattering clumsily into a pint of gin and ginger-beer, a running kitchen-tap and himself held under it, snow crammed into his mouth, his teeth crunching lemons. A picture clicked. Good, now another. Click.

'Now we pull your head upside-down. You'll be able to feel the air bubbling about inside. Can you? I believe it's a funny sort of a sensation.'

They resented his body, Edwin could tell that. It was in the way, a long clumsy shoot out of the potato they were trying to roll around. If only the head could be, perhaps painlessly, temporarily severed and then, with some epoxy resin or other, fitted back. The air hissed about in all the convolutions and curlicues of Edwin's brain, and the ladies in white, panting, coaxed it to the eye that would see everything. Click. And again click. It took most of the morning.

'You'll have a rather nasty headache for a couple of days,' said one of the ladies. 'You won't have to move around very much.'

'And what happens to the air?' Edwin felt unreasonably sorry for it, imprisoned in that labyrinth. 'Can it be sucked out again?'

'The air,' they said, 'will be absorbed.'

He and the air were trolleyed back to the ward, where a conference of clinical sneerers was in progress. Lying still in his bed, Edwin listened to his own dressing-gowned neighbour and the two youths in pullovers who had come up from the medical ward, their speech impeded by the set eerie grimace they all shared.

'I mean, if I saw you in the street, and we was both the way we are now, I'd think you was taking the mike out of me, wouldn't I?'

'It might be the other way round, depending on who looks first.'

'Dead sinister. Could make a packet in one of them horror films.'

Suddenly Edwin had the sensation that his own face had twisted and fixed itself, compulsively, in an *homme qui rit* mask. He felt each cheek in turn with his left hand, then reached over to his locker for his shaving-mirror. The air in his skull and his head seemed to split. He lay back again, convincing himself that, if he were to speak, the same flat sneering vowels he now heard would be emitted from his own spread mouth. He said aloud, loudly:

'Ye Old Tea Shop is a solecism. The "Y" is a mistake for the Anglo-Saxon letter called *thorn*, which stood for "TH".'

The conference was silenced. The pullovered youths said they thought they'd better be going down to lunch. Edwin was aware of being watched narrowly by those nearest to him. Oh well, if they thought he was mad – Anyway, his mouth was still mobile, as capable of rounding as of spreading; at least he'd proved that.

Another long yawn of a day, a huge mouth into which dull meals were thrown. At visiting-time a small man in an old baggy suit, cap and muffler, shambled in. He had a piece of paper in his hand. This he showed to an Italian ward-maid who was removing chrysanthemums. She pointed to Edwin's bed. '*Il dottore*,' she said, without satire. The man, still capped, shambled over.

'Told me to come 'ere,' he said, standing at ease. He was a youngish man, though lined, and his incisors and precanines seemed to have been yanked out as a single wedge. ''Er. She told me to come.'

'It's very, very kind,' said Edwin.

'Beat me at shove-ha'penny at dinner-time. Didn't think she'd beat me, I didn't, and I didn't 'ave the price of a pint on me. So couldn't buy her one. So she made me

58

come 'ere instead.' He continued to stand at ease, but kept his eyes at attention. They were pale blue eyes and they looked fixedly at the blank wall opposite.

'You needn't stay if you don't want to,' said Edwin.

'Got to. It's only fair. She beat me at shove-ha'penny.' There was a lengthy pause. Edwin said:

'What do they call you?' This, he was sure, was a man with no real name.

' 'Ippo.'

'Hippo? Why do they call you that?'

'That's what they call me. 'Ippo.'

'It's quite a distinguished nickname really, I suppose. Have you ever heard of St Augustine of Hippo?'

The man stood easy. He turned his eyes on Edwin with something like animation, saying: 'Funny you should say that. That was the school just round the corner from where we was. Sinter Gastin. We used to knock 'em about a bit comin' 'ome. Didn't stay there long, though.'

'No?'

'Up and down, we was, up and down for a long time. My old governor was very 'ard. Knocked 'ell out of us kids. So now I can't read nor write. Not proper.'

'What do you do for a living?'

'What comes in, you know. A bit 'ere and a bit there. Carryin' the boards about a bit just now. Advertisin'. One front, one back, as it might be a sandwich. Don't know what's written on them, though. Might be anything.'

'Yes, I see what you mean.'

'But that's the way it is.'

'Of course.' There was another very long pause. Edwin said: 'I've had rather a tough day, I'd like to sleep. You can go now, if you want to.'

'I'll stick it out.' He was grimly at ease again.

'There's no need to if you don't wish.'

'She said I'd got to.'

'I see. But I'm going to try and sleep, just the same.'

Edwin lay on his side, watching this conscientious little man through his eyelashes. But feigned sleep became real sleep: the dull headache was something to escape from. When he awoke all visitors had long since gone. He wondered what the time was and looked painfully towards the locker-top where he normally kept his wristwatch. The watch was no longer there. Curious. He sat up and looked again. Really anxious, for this watch had been a present from Sheila, an expensive present too, he opened up the locker's two compartments. It was not easy to search through the jumble of towels and discarded dirty pyjamas while still in bed. Very gingerly, Edwin started to get out. The air bounced all over his brain and the pain hammered excruciatingly. On his knees, he searched both locker-compartments, searched beneath the locker, behind it. No watch. Well, serve her damn well right. It was her idea, wasn't it? – sending in the odd disreputable characters she met in the public bar, thieves, adulterers, possibly murderers too. The pain in his anxious head was now nearly insupportable. He was just dragging himself back to bed when Dr Railton came cheerfully in.

'Good at disobeying orders, aren't you?' said Dr Railton. 'Sometimes I wonder how you managed to achieve the rank of doctor.' This was evidently, to this M.B., Ch.B., a sore point. 'It's a matter of elementary common sense, after all, to avoid pain if one possibly can.'

'It was my watch, you see. I was looking for my watch.'

'Never mind about your watch now. We've more serious things than watches to talk about. Perhaps we'd better have the bed-screens round.' He dragged the screaming curtains-on-wheels to the bed where Edwin now lay again, creating a sinister fragile little private room.

'You're not going to do anything now, surely?' said Edwin.

'Not now, no. I want to tell you about the results of the tests you've been having.'

'Yes?'

'There's something there all right. That's been amply confirmed. Now we know exactly where it is.'

'But *what* is it?'

'Never you mind what it is. It's something that shouldn't be there, that's all. That's all that you need to know. Something that will have to be removed.'

'It's a tumour, I suppose,' said Edwin. 'That's what you told my wife, I suppose. You shouldn't try and entrust her with secrets. It's not fair. Why couldn't you tell me?'

'Why upset you before it's absolutely necessary? Not that it's really anything to be upset about. The operation's a simple enough matter.'

'Supposing it's malignant?'

'I don't think it is that. You can never be sure, of course, but I don't think it is that. The layman,' said Dr Railton, depressing imaginary trumpet-valves on the bed-cover, 'the layman tends to get emotional about medical terms. Cancer, gastric, malignant. Just take it that there's something in your head which is doing you no good at all, and that something can be removed swiftly, simply and painlessly. I'm sorry,' said Dr Railton, 'that we had to burden your wife with our suspicions. She's a strongly emotional type. But there was the business of getting her permission to operate, if operating became necessary.'

'You got her permission?'

'Oh yes. She was very concerned about you, very anxious that you should be made well again.'

'And how about my permission?'

'Well,' said Dr Railton, 'obviously you can't be dragged into the operating theatre screaming your refusal to be operated on. You're sane enough, and you have the power to choose. But I think you'll see that it's very much in your interests to say yes.'

'I don't know,' said Edwin. 'I haven't felt too bad

61

really, despite the collapses, despite other odd things, sex and what-not. I have a feeling that I'll survive somehow without anybody mucking about inside my head.'

'You can't be too sure of that,' said Dr Railton, still depressing, with vibrant fingers, the trumpet-valves on the coverlet. 'I'd say it was dangerous the way you are. There's also the question of your job back in Burma.'

'I could give that up.'

'You'd have to get another job somewhere. That won't be easy. And do remember that you'll get steadily worse.'

Edwin thought for a minute. 'There's no doubt about its being successful?'

'There's always some doubt. There's got to be. But the chances are overwhelmingly in favour of this operation going well. I'd say about a hundred to one. You'll be a changed man when it's all over, you won't be the same person at all. You'll bless us, really you will.'

'A changed man, eh? A man with a changed personality.'

'Oh, not fundamentally different. Shall we say a healthy man instead of a sick one?'

'I see. All right. When?'

'Next Tuesday. Good,' said Dr Railton, 'good man.'

'Supposing I change my mind before then?'

'Don't,' said Dr Railton earnestly, 'don't, whatever you do. Trust us, trust me.' He stood with his arms out, a figure to be trusted, looking all too much, however, like a dance-band trumpeter who had put down his instrument in order to take a vocal.

'All right,' said Edwin. 'I trust you.'

Chapter Nine

On Sunday afternoon Sheila came, only a little tipsy, dragging in by the hand a reluctant young man with a beard. She looked younger and prettier, was smartly made-up, and wore her beige opossum coat swinging open over a new mohair dress. 'Darling,' she cried. 'Darling, darling.'

'Forgive me,' said Edwin, 'if I don't start out of bed to greet you. It's this air that's still buzzing about inside.'

'Oh,' said Sheila, 'of course you two haven't met. Strange, isn't it, really? Nigeledwin. Edwinigel. I'm sure you'd like each other a lot if you got a chance to meet properly.'

'How do you do.'

'How do you do.'

'Look here,' said Edwin, 'that awful little man pinched my watch. The one you beat at shove-ha'penny who calls himself 'Ippo.'

'Did he? That's annoying. I haven't seen him since, nor has anybody. He was passing through, resting his sandwich-boards, and the Anchor isn't his local at all. You *are* a fool, Edwin. You're too trusting, that's your trouble. We'll have to get you another, won't we? A good thing that one didn't cost any money.'

'Didn't cost –?'

'I got it off Jeff Fairlove. *You* remember. I bullied him into giving it to me. For a present for you.'

'And why,' asked the bearded Nigel, 'were you able to bully him? That is to say, what *hold* did you have over him?' Edwin grinned to himself at this sly glint of jealousy. Nigel was a young man untidily trying to make himself look not older but ageless – the ageless maned bearded painter.

'My beauty,' said Sheila, with Cockney vowels, 'my infinite attractiveness. No man can resist me when I bully him.' The painter nodded seriously. 'This afternoon,' said Sheila, 'Nigel proposes to draw me. Not paint, draw. I'm so glad, darling, that everything's fixed up at last. It'll be such a relief to get things over. You must be pleased yourself.'

'So they've told you, have they?'

'That man Railton was down in the hall. He said they're going to operate and that everything's going to be all right. It's such a relief.'

'A relief not to have to nurse that secret any more?'

'That too.' She smiled. 'We can be back in Moulmein for the winter. I hate the cold, you know,' she said to Nigel. 'I hope this flat of yours is warm.'

'If I were a painter,' said Edwin, 'one of the things I'd like to paint is the view you get from the air as you're dropping down to Moulmein. Beauty and utility. All those paddy-fields of different shapes and sizes, not a square inch of waste, a big collective artifact, yet not anything else that's human or even natural in sight. But I suppose it would be too easy to paint.'

'Nothing's easy to paint,' said the painter. He had a gobbly kind of voice. 'Take my word for it, painting is absolute hell. That's why I keep on with it.'

'And what modern painters do you most admire?' asked Edwin.

'Very few. Very, very few indeed. Chagall, perhaps. Dong Kingman, possibly. One or two others.' He looked gloomy.

'Never mind,' said Sheila. 'Don't worry so much about things. Everything will be all right.' She smiled reassuringly at him, patting his arm. He wore very tight trousers. 'Nigel,' she said, 'is really a very good painter. When

64

you're well you must see some of his things. Some of them are most effective.'

'Don't,' snarled Nigel, 'use that word. They're not effective. That's the most damning word you could possibly hope to find.' He raised his voice. 'Noise again,' sighed Edwin to himself. R. Dickie's squad of visitors looked over interestedly, assured that there would always be entertainment of some sort or another on Edwin's bed. 'To say they're effective is to lower them to the level of, to the level of, to the level of a cinema poster. It's bloody insulting.' R. Dickie's visitors nodded to each other, pleased at this fulfilment of the expected.

'All right,' said Edwin. 'Shall we say that they're not effective, then?'

Nigel glared at Edwin. 'You haven't seen any of them,' he said. 'You're not in a position to make *any judgement whatsoever*.'

'You must remember, Nigel,' said Sheila sharply, 'that you are speaking to my husband and that my husband is very ill. I won't have this petulance about your art.' Nigel sulked. 'That's better,' said Sheila. 'And, Nigel, remember your promise.'

'What promise?'

'Just like an *artist*, isn't it?' said Sheila. 'All take and no give. Your promise about Edwin's laundry.'

'Oh, that.'

'Nigel,' said Sheila, 'is a very lucky boy. There's a Hungarian woman who comes every week and does his washing for him. That's in exchange for English lessons.'

'What,' asked Edwin, 'does he know about giving English lessons?'

'He's learning,' said Sheila. 'Learning by doing. And one thing he's promised to do is to have all your dirty clothes washed. Where are they?'

'This,' said Edwin, 'is most kind.' He was growing tired of always sounding like Mr Salteena, but what else could he say? 'That locker's stuffed with dirty pyjamas and

65

towels and things, and there's a shirt in the big locker outside.'

'Good,' said Sheila. 'We're going straight to Nigel's flat or studio, or whatever he calls it, and we can take those things with us.'

'We'd better go now,' said Nigel. 'I've had no lunch, remember.'

'But you had breakfast.'

'That was a long time ago.'

'When I was a young girl,' said Sheila, 'I always believed that artists starved. *La vie de Bohème.*'

'Plenty of stuffing goes on in the first two acts of the opera,' said Edwin.

'Oh yes,' said Sheila, 'that reminds me. Les and Carmen are coming to see you again this evening. I, of course, can't make it. Carmen is coming to apologize.'

'No,' said Edwin violently. 'I'm very ill. I can't have visitors. Please tell them that.'

'We shan't be seeing them, shall we, Nigel? So you'll just have to put up with it. Les has a queer life really, doesn't he?'

'I should think so,' said Edwin.

'Yes. He works in one of the Covent Garden pubs early in the morning, and at night he works in the opera house. That seems to me to be right – unification in terms of place, or something. And for the rest of the time he has Carmen. You must get him to tell you about some of the things she does sometime.'

'Come on,' said Nigel. 'We ought to eat.'

'Yes,' said Sheila. 'She's very quaint. They did *Samson and Delilah* and she went to see it and a couple of days later they had a bit of a row, and he woke up in the middle of the night to find her standing with the scissors over the bed –'

Nigel was looking, suddenly very intently, at Edwin. 'I don't know about your brain,' he said, thoughts of food apparently temporarily forgotten, 'whether it's worth while saying that. But as far as heads go, it's a good head. It's a better head,' he continued, with the artist's impartiality, 'than hers. I wouldn't mind doing it. I think I'd rather do your head than hers, though she, of course, from my point of view, has by far the more interesting body. And, of course, soon you'll have no hair.'

'There's a long way to go yet,' said Edwin. 'My family is not a family that goes bald early.'

'No, no,' said Nigel. 'If they're going to operate on your brain they'll have to shave all your hair off. I think that I should like to have a go at it then. It would make a very nice and rather original study. A painting, I think. The tropical brown of the face and a sort of nacreous pink – I should like to try that.'

Edwin was pale, aghast. 'You know,' he said, 'I just hadn't realized. I just didn't think of that at all.'

'Never mind,' said Sheila. 'It will grow again, very quickly. And it will be just the opposite of Samson, won't it?'

'What do you mean?' asked Edwin.

'Think it over, darling. Look,' she said to Nigel, who had taken out a small drawing-pad and was sketching preliminary studies of Edwin. 'You put this idea of food into my head. Let's go and eat.'

'All right,' said Nigel. 'And let's not forget to collect the laundry.' He was a kind young man beneath the veneer of artist. He took up in his arms a bundle of socks, underwear, pyjamas from the bedside locker, with a faint *ça pue* wrinkling of his snub nose. And off they went to collect the dirty shirt from the outside locker used for outside clothes and suitcases. Sheila peered in again gaily when they had done this, waving the shirt, blew a kiss which also embraced R. Dickie and the sneerer, smiled brilliantly, lovingly, and sardonically at Edwin, then left.

'Quite a card, your missis,' said R. Dickie later.

Just before dinner Edwin told the ward sister that he wasn't feeling well enough for visitors and could he

67

please have screens put round his bed. This was done, and in the process of straightening his bedclothes the Negro orderly found the preliminary sketch that Nigel had discarded. It showed, thought Edwin, little talent.

'Dyin', is he, that one?' one of R. Dickie's visitors was heard to ask in a loud whisper palpitant with excitement.

'Naw,' whispered R. Dickie back, 'not him. I think his missis upset him a bit, that's all. If it is his missis, that is.' A softer susurrous of speculation ensued.

Chapter Ten

'This, my little friend, is clearing the deck for activity.'
The Negro orderly, shedding light from every facet of his
skin, his glasses splintering with light, giggled at the daring of the image and began to fiddle with his tray of
instruments. He had an apprentice standing by him, a
morose tall Italian who had just joined the service, and
to him he explained what the instruments were.

'Scissors.'

'*Si.*'

'Clippers.'

'*Si, si.*'

'Electric razor.'

'*Si, si, capito.*'

Sheila had had, apparently, no time for a letter, much
less a visit, but she had sent a telegram: BEST OF LUCK
WILL BE THINKING OF YOU LOVE. He had in the past
received such messages at commercial hotels in strange
towns, on the eve of an interview for a new job. Now he
was going to travel to the ultimate bourn of thingness
from which return was possible. A pilgrimage, but he was
to be turbaned before Mecca was sighted. The Negro
began his work. Humming nonchalantly he pulled on
rubber gloves. Then he said: 'Scissors.' Scissors were
handed to him. Whorls of hair began to fall. Edwin
said:

'What's your name?' The Negro said:

'Please be so good as not to be distracting.' But, as more
and more swathes drifted down, he relented and said: 'If
you must know, my name is Mr Southey. *Mister,*' he

69

emphasized, as if to disparage Edwin's own title, 'like Mr Begbie, eminent specialist.'

The rapid autumn continued, the deciduous down-drift of brown bunches and wheels. 'Very bad dandruff,' said the specialist. 'That way you lose your hair.' The Italian watched every detail of the operation closely, nodding frequently to show that, despite the language barrier, he understood perfectly what was being done. Edwin began to feel cool, light and lamb-like. 'Clippers,' said Mr Southey.

Here was a new and voluptuous sensation, a curious abandon as total nakedness drew nearer. Hair was coming down as a whole Koran of Arabic letters mingled with a Pitman manual. In broad mowing strokes Mr Southey drove his purring instrument over a hill which, for thirty-eight years, had hidden its contours from the air. Aware of achievement, he sang. In mid-strophe he said:

'Razor.'

Now came the final stages of depilation. The Italian's mouth was half-open and he panted a little. The razor maintained its irritable buzz, the Negro's song grew more exultant. Soon the song tailed off for the business of pausing to stand back to scrutinize – an odd buzz here, a short whirring passage there – and at last the sculpture was completed.

'That looks good, really fine.'

'*Bello*,' the Italian agreed.

'You wait,' said Mr Southey, 'and I bring you a mirror.'

'No, no,' said Edwin. 'No, no, no.' His fearful fingers roamed over his scalp, palpating, sliding. 'For God's sake cover it up.'

'Everybody,' said Mr Southey, 'appreciates a little bit of appreciation. That's nothing to ask. You have a look in a mirror.'

'You heard me,' said Edwin. 'I don't want to see it, I don't want to know anything about it. Just cover it up.'

'Ingratitude,' said the Negro. He brought a woollen cap that fitted snugly. Then Edwin risked a look in his shaving mirror. He saw little Edwin in his pram – the little Edwin of a photograph his mother had had framed for the front room – but little Edwin with sharp mistrustful eyes, a jowl, and a day's growth of beard. He clattered the mirror back on to the locker-top and lay still in bed. The Italian swept away a whole barber-shop-floor-load of hair; the Negro wheeled off the bed-screens. Edwin now felt himself at last a full member of this prone club of pilgrims.

The staff-nurse came round to say: 'Do you sleep sound enough?' She spoke in the comfortable voice of Manchester.

'Enough,' said Edwin.

'Eh, you don't sound too convinced. We'd better be on the safe side. Tomorrow morning we want you to be nice and muzzy, half-dead, if you see what I mean.' She emptied a generous helping of tablets out of her bottle. Edwin sluiced them down.

He was soon asleep. His dreams were polychrome, stereoscopic. Three big dogs couched in the wood he was walking through turned out to be the folds of a python. He smiled in his dream: that was meant to be sex. He dropped down well after well after well. At the bottom of one well he encountered the expected: large crawling insects, an animated drawing out of an 1860 *Punch*, a severed marble head out of a film by Cocteau which repeated monotonously the word *habituel*. He was sitting on Brighton sands, surrounded by smiling people, and was desperately trying to hide his bare feet. At the bottom of the final well there was only darkness, no more images.

Chapter Eleven

Edwin awoke with mechanical suddenness, with no hint of a margin between dead sleep and complete wakefulness. He even sat up, fully aware of where he was, what he was there for. He had no idea of the time, but it was full night, with brilliant plenilunar light washing London. He awoke with a very clear intention, feverishly sharp, of an acuity undoubtedly, he saw, induced by the large dose of sleeping drug: that nobody should cut his head open, that there should be no excision of any tumour, that he should live – however briefly – and die – however soon – as he was, whether sick or well. He felt wonderfully well, as a matter of fact.

Death, anyway, was in the hospital: you could hear it snoring in the ward. Life was outside. He must leave at once. For if he returned to sleep his intention might be blunted by morning drowsiness; there would be too many to fight; they would pump a deader sleep into his buttock before he knew where he was and have burly men wheel him off to the theatre. Then it would be too late. It had to be now.

Enclosed by her frail walls of bed-screens, the night sister sat at her desk with its dim light. She was, he knew, an American girl over on a year's exchange. From Missouri or somewhere.

How bloody stupid he had been to trust Dr Railton and everyone else. To them he was already a thing, could not be less of a thing if he died under the anaesthetic: regrettable: Dr Spindrift has changed into a mere chunk of morphology.

The bed creaked as he got out of it. He felt his head: the woollen cap was still there: the woollen cap was going to look a bit bloody stupid in the world outside. Never mind. There were hats, wigs, weren't there? The sister's ears were sharp. She peeked out, then walked softly and swiftly towards him.

'You all right? You want something?' She was a pretty girl with a becoming uniform, a film sister. Her voice was rich.

'I just want to go to the –'

'Oh. Sure you wouldn't rather I brought you a bed-pan?' That hated word for a clumsy intractable thing took on tones of irony in her accent. It was a word you never heard in American films. The two vowels retracted and prolonged: badepairn.

'No,' said Edwin. 'I'd rather – I'm not all that incapable, you know.'

'Okay. Put on your dressing-gown.' The moon shone full on her prettiness. It was an honour to be bossed by her, a film goddess. And now she was going to get into trouble. Edwin felt sorry for her, but not all that sorry. 'And don't be too long,' she said.

'It may be,' said Edwin, 'rather a long job, if you know what I mean.' He paused on the brink of fake clinical details. 'Something I ate,' he said.

'Okay, okay.' She went back to her sequestered light. Edwin, tremulous with excitement, padded rapidly out. Opening a steel door of the lockers in the corridor opposite the bathrooms, he suddenly realized how much this last week had stripped him of possessions: watch, underclothes, hair. No socks, no shirt, he realized: at Nigel's flat, to be washed by a Hungarian. He was going to be cold: no overcoat, no raincoat; both shed before going to Burma. In great haste he carried tie, jacket, trousers to one of the bathrooms. And this time he must not forget his shoes. He put everything on over his pyjamas. The striped, rather grubby, pyjama top did not look much like a shirt. He frowned at it in the mirror. He wound the tie under the collar and knotted it. From the shoulders up he looked, to say the least, eccentric. The inside of his shoes struck his bare feet coldly and he shuddered. He paused. Should he steal? The lockers, despite their name, were not locked. There were other clothes available – shirts, perhaps overcoats. And then he thought: no. To commit a crime, however minor, would be playing into their hands. Such petty thefts would be attributed to kleptomania, part of the complex syndrome – a very sick man, not at all responsible for his actions.

He had very little money (he would count it later) and nothing he could pawn or sell. His overnight case, he had noticed, had been taken from his locker; reasonably enough, of course, for Sheila and Nigel had had to carry the laundry off in something. In the inner pocket of his jacket he found private papers, put there undoubtedly when the case had been turned into a laundry bag, and he felt the folded parchment of his doctor's diploma. Why the hell had he brought that home with him? There must, he thought, be some reason. But now was no time for wondering what it was. First he had to get out.

Thankful for rubber soles he stole fearfully to the heavy swing-doors shared by both the male and female wards. (But that duality itself was called a ward, Philpotts Ward; was each unit then a sub-ward or demi-ward or something?) He made, he was sure, no sound that could be significant to the unsuspicious. On the landing outside the doors he found the macabre light of a blue bulb. Here was no window for the moon to enter. The blue dimness saw him down the first flight of stairs, and then the blue light was found again on the lower landing, and so all the way down. He was quickly on ground-level. Here his real troubles must begin. The corridors were shadowy, and shadows imparted to the busts of the great dead a factitious life – leers, winks, smiles of false complicity. His final corridor flowed into the vestibule, and there the night porter stood, not at all drowsy, spelling out notices on the notice-board. It was not conceivable that Edwin could get past him. Nor was there any guarantee that the outer door would be unlocked. Edwin saw the time on the vestibule clock – four-forty – and automatically he tried to set his watch. Bloody 'Ippo. He cowered in the corridor shadows, wondering.

There were, of course, cellars. My God, didn't he know there were cellars? He knew, too, where a stairway – grubby and unclinical – seemed to lead down to those cellars; it was a corridor or so back. Those stairs had become a mere appendix, an unwanted organ, for lifts were the order in descending to the torture-rooms. Edwin walked back to the shadows and found the stairway, found it creaked abominably. At its foot he found a closed canteen and kitchen doors. Of course. He had forgotten. There was more than one depth of cellar. He saw a window through which moonlight slanted; outside a squalor of garbage-cans; next to the window a door. Hopefully he tried it, but it was locked. Then he tried the window. The lower catch slid open; could he reach the upper one? He looked round – a box, a chair, anything to stand on? Amazingly, there lurked a small set of steps in a corner, of the kind that could be folded into a clumsy kitchen chair. Doubt swirled into his brain. Was this all a trap? Had they foreknown, with their long experience of head-cases, that he would try to get out of it, try to escape? Did this always happen on the eve of an operation, under the influence of a particular kind of soporific? Was it considered helpful to the patient to let him get so far, easing his claustrophobia, before leading him gently and humorously back to bed? Would Dr Railton and others, perhaps Mr Begbie himself, be waiting outside now? He would soon know. He lifted the set of steps and carried it to the window. He climbed up and undid with ease the top catch. The window opened gently and a still autumn night entered cat-like. Edwin smelt freedom and London autumn – decay, smoke, cold, motor oil. It was too easy. He clambered out, dropped a few feet into an area. Two cats ran away without noise, but another clattered a dustbin-lid. There was a spiked railing and a gate to match. The gate was padlocked, but the climb over was not difficult – foot on the dust-bin, foot up, he leapt to the street. The rip in his trousers was a nuisance, but not grave. Sheila would sew that up for him.

He could not afford to loiter in the street. Some nurse or orderly who knew him might be coming on duty: he was vague as to what time the day staff started. The night porter might appear on the front steps in the guise of an amateur selenologist picking out the Sea of Storms and the Sea of Tranquillity. A policeman might be suspicious. Edwin walked at a tangent away from the rolling façade of the hospital, skirting the railings of the square, finding a side street with shops and a genuine Tudor pub and ancient alleys branching out of it. He would be safe, he thought, round here, waiting for a safe time for decent people to be around. It was, he reckoned, now almost five.

Thank God he had taken the trouble to memorize the name of Sheila's hotel. The Farnworth. Fearful of losing the name, he had composed a rhymed mnemonic one night before sleep:

> Far north-west is the land of my birth,
> Far north-west in the north-west orth.

He could not in all decency go there till some reasonable hour, perhaps the hour of breakfast when, if the breakfast-room faced the street as in most small hotels, he might catch her attention as she crackled her toast. She did not eat much, but she was fond of breakfast. He did not fancy ringing the bell and confronting the management dressed as he was. But where exactly was the Farnworth? He could find out from a telephone directory. He might find a telephone directory in a telephone kiosk.

Wait! He could then, at a reasonable hour, ring up his wife and she could bring a taxi to collect him from an arranged spot. That would save a lot of embarrassment. But some tiny gnat-voice in his head told him that his wife was not altogether to be trusted. Why had he worried about having cash and something to pawn, when his wife had the sizeable balance of two months' salary? Why did he feel that his wife, humouring him over the telephone, would fetch not a taxi but an ambulance with strong men? But, he reflected, this distrust was natural: there were too many people seeking only his own good. His wife was his wife; Sheila was Sheila. She would understand, she would agree, she would help.

He walked down the side street to a wide thoroughfare of shop-windows and offices. This, he assumed, was one of the main arteries of London, a city he did not know very well. There were sodium street-lights, lights in windows. Occasional cars sped by. There was even an airline bus crammed with yawning passengers. Edwin saw himself reflected in a window full of tape-recorders – baggy, lean, a superior face between woollen cap and pyjama-collar, a viable get-up for a place like London. Then he sought a telephone directory. It was something to do. If stopped by a policeman, he could tell the truth and say he was hurrying to a telephone kiosk. Something urgent, as the pyjamas showed, if not the tie. The woollen cap? Something, perhaps, connected with the urgency.

It was some time before he came to a kiosk with even any single volume of the London directory, much less the one he required. But at last, near a statue on horseback and a shop with American suitings, he found this work in many volumes, a thesis for some super-doctorate. On the way he had met no police – only a strayed reveller, a hangdog workman or so, many cats. He reflected that not only was he unfamiliar with London: he had not been in England for over three years. This feeling of strangeness exacerbated his nervousness, his sense of being a quarry.

77

He groped in his inner pocket and felt reassured by the solid walls of his passport.

He had not thought it possible that there should be so many Farnworth Hotels. He chose one with the same postal district number as the hospital, but the name of the street meant nothing to him. Still, that would be something more to do, finding the place. Now he had many hours to fill in. This glass coffin on end seemed a fairly safe place in which to rest for a while. There were, he thought, few suspicious activities which could, in comfort and secrecy, be carried on in a telephone box. He took out his money, counted it as for a long-distance call, and found he had, in British currency, something over three shillings. He had also a few odd rupees and other foreign coins as well as a nail-file and a tiny pocket-knife. He was fairly sure that, despite the rise in the cost of British living that had taken place during his exile, it must be possible to buy a cup of tea and a few cheap cigarettes somewhere. Not yet, of course; at least, not in this district of shops and offices and late risers and arrivers.

Idly he pressed Button B. To his great surprise and delight four pennies chinked out gaily. This he took to be a good omen. It did not seem fair, however, that he should pocket this gift and spend it later on something atelephonic. Once, at the end of the war, he had proffered a ten-shilling note in a Berkeley Street tobacconist's and been given change as for a pound. He immediately bought further cigarettes to the amount of ten shillings. That seemed only right. Now he proposed to give the Post Office back its fourpence. Inspiration hit him. He looked up the number of the hospital and then, coppers already inserted, wondered what accent to assume. He decided on a stage Irish one, then dialled the number.

'Sure,' he said wetly, 'and there's some important information I'm wanting to be giving ye.'

The tired voice at the switchboard said: 'Yes? I'll put you through to the night porter.' There were windings and yawns. Why, wondered Edwin, the night porter? Why not some doctor or sister or other? 'Hallo?' said the night porter.

'Sure, and have ye a patient that's escaped from your hospital?'

'Escaped? Escaped? What do you mean, escaped?' It was the voice of one who didn't sleep enough during the day. 'There's nobody *escaped*, as you put it.'

'Oh, well now, there's a man here in Hounslow who says he's escaped, so if ye're wanting the spalpeen at all, ye'll know where to be finding him.'

'Where did you say? What are you talking about?'

'In Cockfosters, it is,' said Edwin. 'Sure, and I'll be mistaking my own name next.'

'It strikes me,' said the voice, 'that you're barmy. People don't *escape* from here. This is not a loony-bin.'

'All right, me boyo,' said Edwin. 'Don't say ye haven't been warned. May the blessed Virgin Mary and all the holy angels and saints guard ye and keep ye,' he added. Then he rang off. Curious. Did the American sister believe him to be still straining away there? Did she perhaps, being new to the country, think it possible that the British tempo of evacuation was different from that of the States? Curious that the whole hospital should not be humming with panic. He himself now hummed a little tune, hands in pockets, encased in this tiny pharos. He took one hand out to press Button B, but this time there was no free gift of coin, no – he laughed – metallic evacuation or numismatorrhea.

Chapter Twelve

It was still early, but there were purposeful people around rushing for tube-trains. Edwin had left his coffin because a woman, short, middle-aged, with a moulting fur coat, had come along to be a *bona fide* incumbent. (But could you say 'incumbent'? That meant a lier-upon. Perhaps 'instant' was more correct, and it conveyed also her urgent coin-tapping on the outer glass.) Edwin, evicted, wandered slowly along, thinking that, if William Barnes or the Nazis had had their way with the English language, there might now be FARSPEAKER instead of TELEPHONE; that closed butcher might be, as in old Scotland, a flesher; the tobacconist here would be a cigarette handler. Outside the cigarette handler's was a cigarette machine. Edwin had a florin, so he was able to buy a packet of ten. No human intermediacy. That was a help. Flat to the glass of the door of a stationer's he saw magazines. There was the one Charlie had brought him: *Brute Beauty*. And there were others he had never seen before: *Valour; Act; Oh!* He rubbed his eyes, which were troubling him with an odd impairment of vision. Were those really *Air, Pride, Plume, Here?* He lit a cigarette (five matches left) and tried to steady his eyes by reading the advertisement cards in a glass case. Exotic Coffee-coloured Model 41 – 24 – 39, Available Afternoons. Annette, Specialist in Correction. Janice for Leather. Baby's Pram Going Cheap. Flatlet Suit Business Gentleman, Regret No Coloured.

Round the next corner he saw a big white milk machine. He had sixpences. Excellent. An early breakfast, again without human intermediacy. He was delivered, to the flashing of lights, a clammy carton with a blue tear-off corner. He drank the cold milk gratefully, his eyes looking into the bitter morning sky which was still really a night sky. But the moon had set. A little farther down the street he saw a machine with six columns of chocolate. He fed in his last sixpence and drew out a block of Honey Nut Milkshake.

He chewed, sucking his clogged teeth. He had a three-penny piece and two pennies. That wouldn't get him far, would it? He couldn't even telephone without getting change. But, of course, he didn't want to telephone. Still chewing, an occasional milky belch rising (that, he thought, was appropriate to his woolly cap) he walked back to the wide endless thoroughfare. There were no art galleries or museums or libraries open at this time, were there? Bed was, at this hour, the only free entertainment for those who did not work. Lie-abed London. The cities of the East were aflame with life at this time of day. Edwin paused in his walk. He heard trains. One could wait warmly in a station.

He almost smelled his way towards the great terminus. The smell, he knew, should be of sulphuretted hydrogen, but his sick nose had sweetened it to something meadowy. He climbed a wide station yard to a Gothic cathedral skinned over with grime. Milkchurn-censers clanged; there was acrid incense; a hooter bellowed *Oremus*. In the huge hollow waiting-hall there were benches. He was glad to sit down. Thanked be Almighty God.

Angry people snarled out of local trains; there were a few, more placid, who meditated on the benches, awaiting longer journeys. Edwin felt his head and feet equally numb. There was a disarray of newspaper near him on the seat. He had heard that stuffed newspaper made for warmth. It was the *Daily Window*, and it screamed at him as soon as he picked it up: JIVE GIRL DROPS DEAD AT WEDDING. More sedately it whispered that a thousand

Japanese had been made homeless by an earthquake. Was it wholesome enough for improvised socks? he wondered. He thought he might kill his woollen cap with a thousand-a-week teen-age singer who had become engaged, but then thought better of it. He would be aware of the common little grinning mug pressed on to his baldness. He tried to make socks out of a page which gave advice on brassières to eleven-year-olds and another which was headed WE LIKE MUM AS SHE IS NO KIDDING. This he found too difficult, so he finally crammed cartoons into both shoes, thus making them a little snugger. But head and ankles were still cold. This was the great free world. He almost decided to return to the hospital.

He read his passport passeport 433045. Dr Edwin Cyril Spindrift, Lecturer, Born Whitby 25.2.21, Height 5 feet 11 inches, Colour of Eyes Hazel, Colour of Hair Brown. And there was a personable young man staring out at him, with a great deal of hair, a young man destined to go far, as far as Moulmein and farther. Edwin read all the visas with close attention, growing colder and colder. Then he noticed that there was, as an enclave of this terminus, a station of the Underground. It might, he thought, be warmer in there. As he walked across the waiting-hall he saw two elderly women look at his woollen cap and heard one say: 'Poor young fellow. Ringworm.'

Edwin had fivepence. He had more: he had fivepence halfpenny. The fare to the station nearest the hospital was twopence. The machine gave him his ticket without commenting on his appearance by look or word. He was made free of a platform and a bench and given advertisements to read. It was moderately warm. Trains rushed in, hissed open then shut, rushed out, and he caught none of them. There was all too much time. He even managed to doze.

At eight o'clock he thought it was time to go. Traffic was increasing: shaven men with newspapers; lipsticked girls. Most had a brief incurious glance at his ringworm top. He wondered if it might not be better to disclose the mystery, to whip off the cap and show a healthy baldness. But he decided against it. Standing on the train he tried to look foreign and turn his whole strange outfit into a national dress. Going up in the lift he said to the ticket-collector: '*Ashti vahrosch.*' He had always been good at improvising languages. Everybody looked at him. He bowed modestly, smiling in self-depreciation. Everybody looked away.

He had some difficulty in finding the Farnworth. It was in a street which specialized in private hotels, some of them squalid. From the doorways of the squalid ones uncombed sluts reached out for milk bottles, a man or two walked out looking ashamed and unshaven. But the Farnworth was not squalid. It was wanly respectable and had flowers in boxes. Edwin walked up and down outside, peering shyly into the breakfast-room. Sheila was not yet there, but it was still early. He noticed a young man in a pullover make a sandwich of his fried egg; an Indian girl ate dry cornflakes with her fingers; there was a man who looked Iranian wearing his hat at table. A typical cheap London hotel.

Breakfasters went and new ones took over their milk jugs. A grey-haired woman served – her spectacles blind, her mouth open, her soul withdrawn from her actions. Edwin waited. Soon a couple came down with a naughty child who would eat no breakfast. This child came to the window, pointed at Edwin's cap and began to cry for it. Edwin hurried down the street and inspected a wall of posters. An ersatz gravy shouted its virtues through the medium of a vast mixed grill, sausages three feet long, tomato slices like bicycle wheels, perpetually cooling in the London air. A model who looked not unlike that EEG bitch smoked a new cigarette called KOOLKAT. There was a sauce named MUSTAVIT, an imbecile husband spattering it on his plate, a rosy housewife telling the street: 'My hubby says he *must* have it.'

Edwin went back to the breakfast-room window. That child was now, apparently, kicking on the floor. Among the eyes that looked down frankly or were decently averted, Sheila's were not to be seen. It was time to be bold and inquire. He went up the steps and rang the bell. After an interval a fierce old man with white locks drooping from a middle parting, dirty-aproned, a fish-slice in his hand, came and said with no warmth:

'Ah?'

'Excuse me, I've just come out of the hospital round the corner, that explains my curious get-up, is Mrs Spindrift in, please?'

'Meesseess —'

'Spindrift. Rather a curious name, I know, but it is actually a name, believe me, it's my name too.'

'Here is staying nobody of such name. There was staying, but not now no longer.'

'Would you mind telling me when she left?'

'Yesterday, day before, who knows? Here today, gone tomorrow is rule of hotels. Excuse, fish is burning.'

'But did she leave no message, no address?'

There was a scream from the kitchen. 'I tell you,' said the old man, 'fish is burning. I go now, I know no more.' And he closed the door, nodding. Edwin stood on the steps, frightened, hesitating. This he had not expected. But the Farnworth Hotel had not yet finished with him. The grey-haired sleep-walking woman came, opened the door and said: 'What name?' She was evidently English.

'Spindrift.'

'Yes. A good name for a washing-machine, I thought when she wrote it in the book.' There was nothing somnambulist about her voice: it was commercial and bitter. 'But that's not the only reason why I'm not likely to forget it in a hurry. I wouldn't have her any longer, and you can tell her from me that it's no good her trying to come back under another name, because I shall know who she is. A man in the room with her, indeed, and her poor

84

husband a sick man in hospital. And if you're another of these men after her, I'm very happy to tell you that she's gone and I don't know where you'll find her. The things that go on.' The fish in the kitchen hissed loudly. 'So there.' And she closed the door.

Edwin stood for a short while in dismay. He would, of course, find her sooner or later, but it had been Sheila as a dispenser of cash or Sheila a hat-and-shirt-buyer that he had needed at once. And socks also. A bit of a *Daily Window* cartoon had worked its way out of his right shoe. The frame showed a generic tashed and sideboarded gangster with a striped shirt which Edwin envied. He was leering knowingly and saying in small capitals: 'I don't handle no dough, brother. You'll have to see the big boss for that.' 'You rat, Louie,' began the next frame.

That was not only a good idea but the only idea. The International Council for University Development had large funds. Its London offices were in Mayfair and full of marble and svelte secretaries. It could afford a bob or two. It was a pity it was such a long walk, though.

Chapter Thirteen

The question was whether to buy a box of matches or a threepenny tube ticket. Edwin felt pretty sure that it was not nowadays possible to find matches that cost less than twopence a box. Three halfpence, he was absolutely sure, could buy nothing except perhaps a cube of meat extract. It was better to walk all the way and be one's own Prometheus: to stop strangers and ask them for a light would be embarrassing and smell of real vagrancy. At the tobacco kiosk at the end of the street Edwin drew out his threepence halfpenny, put twopence on to the counter, apologized for his appearance, and came away with a box of fire. One always felt better for having an element in one's pocket.

He was already tired by the time he got to Tottenham Court Road. The traffic confused him and made him sweat – as good as a pullover. Oxford Street, Bond Street, an anonymous right turn, Berkeley Square. Bandbox Mayfair was all about him. In pyjamas and a night cap through brightest Mayfair. He watched with envy a man entering Trumper's.

The London office of the International Council for University Development was in Queen Street. Edwin hesitated outside, adjusting his cap, tightening the knot of his tie, smoothing his pyjama collar. The portals, a naked sculptural group above them emblematic of the Tutorial System, were designed to intimidate. The doors were all glass and hence appeared to be ever-open; this again must be emblematic of something. In the vestibule was a bronze bust on a marble pedestal: Sir George

Marple, great University Developer, a Sandow of higher education. Marple: marble. A pity they weren't cognate. The face of Sir George was veined, hard and insensible. High up on the wall that faced the entrance was the motto of the organization: SIC VOS NON VOBIS – Virgil addressing the bees: Georgic IV. A porter came up to Edwin. 'Have you ever thought about what that means?' said Edwin.

'What, sir? That, sir? No, sir.' He was a decent asthmatic old man.

'What it means is: "thus you work, but not for yourselves". I wonder who the "you" refers to.'

'Who was it you wanted to see, sir?' The old man, Edwin knew, had taken his measure. They must get a lot like that here: walking advertisements of the virtues of the higher learning – slovenly inarticulate pedants who had to be kept to the point. There were none about at the moment, Edwin noticed: the hall was warm with dark-skinned men flitting to and fro, high-voiced and able. Obviously able.

'I rather wanted to see Mr Chasper.'

'Mr Chasper, sir. And what name shall I say?'

'Dr Spindrift.'

'Oh, I see, sir.' The porter nodded and backed away slowly. 'Very good, sir.' He smiled kindly, backing to his glass box. 'I'll just give his secretary a ring, sir.' In his box he began, on the telephone, a longer speech than seemed necessary. Edwin wandered the hall, looking at recent publications of the Council – expensive free monographs and reviews of new architecture. They could certainly afford a hand-out of a couple of bob or so.

'What was the name?' A patrician voice, a blonde secretary of frightening smartness – tailored in black, her legs a *Vogue* stocking advertisement.

'The name is,' said Edwin, 'Spindrift. Dr Edwin Spindrift.'

'Oh. And what did you want to see Mr Chasper about?'

Edwin prepared a lecture on the idiomatic uses of the preterite. Its title should be: 'The Past Tense as a Lethal Weapon'.

'I still want to see him, if that's possible. I've been allowed out of hospital for the purpose of seeing him. That explains,' said Edwin, 'my rather curious get-up.'

'Oh,' said the secretary. 'I suppose you'd better come this way.' Which probably meant: 'I can't afford to be seen here talking to you any longer.' She led him down corridors and finally to a door which Edwin well remembered. Outside the door was a hat-rack with the curly-brimmed coke of Mr Chasper. A big-headed man. 'If you'd just wait here,' said the secretary. She went inside. After three minutes Chasper himself came to the door, loud-voiced and with a hearty handshake. 'Spindrift,' he said, 'Spindrift, Spindrift. The most poetical name in the whole department. Do come in, my dear fellow.' He was darkly handsome, as smart as his secretary, a Blue of some kind. Sitting at his desk, hands joined, he glowed muscularly at Edwin and said, with a falling intonation:

'Yes.'

'I've just come out of hospital, as you can see,' said Edwin. 'I wanted to have a word with you about money.'

'I take it the operation went off all right?' said Chasper. 'I suppose we'll be getting the report through shortly. It'll be up to our man, Dr Chase, to give you the all-clear for going back, you know. And how,' said Chasper, 'is Mrs Spindrift?'

'She's all right, I think,' said Edwin. 'What I really need at the moment is some money.'

'Hm. You were paid, weren't you?' Chasper frowned humorously. 'Two months' salary in advance. The bursar sent us a copy of the voucher. That means you're not due for any more salary until, let me see, yes, the end of November. That's quite some time off. I suppose,' he said mellifluously, 'you've found it pretty expensive living here. Or your wife has.' He smiled, as to say: 'Women *are* extravagant, aren't they? Mine too, old boy. I know.'

'Well,' said Edwin, 'to be honest, the whole trouble is that my wife has gone off for a little holiday and taken all the money with her, and I can't get in touch with her very easily. It's more a question of the odd quid or so, you see, to keep me going until she gets back.'

'But they're looking after you in the hospital, aren't they?' said Chasper. 'I mean, it's unusual to want extra messing and so forth, isn't it, in a hospital? And people bring you things, don't they? That reminds me,' said Chasper. 'I haven't been in to see you, have I? I must come and bring you some grapes or something. You like grapes, I take it?' He scribbled on his memo pad.

'If I could draw,' said Edwin, 'a couple of quid to keep me going. If you could give me a chit for the treasurer. To be taken off November's salary. That's all. A couple of quid. Pounds,' he translated, so that Chasper would thoroughly understand.

'I'll bring you some cigarettes as well,' said Chasper. 'I'm glad to see you looking so much better.'

'Better than what?' asked Edwin. 'Look, about this couple of quid. Pounds. One pound –'

'Oh, better than I expected you to look after all that probing about in the old grey matter. I suppose the hair doesn't take too long to grow?'

The secretary appeared. 'Professor Hodges to see you, Mr Chasper. He's a bit early for his appointment.'

'Show him in,' said Chasper. 'It's been delightful to see you again, Spindrift. I'll drop in during visiting hours. I should have done it before, but you know how busy we get here. My regards to Mrs Spindrift.'

On the wall was a map. Edwin stared at it open-mouthed. 'Zenobia,' he said. 'There's no such place as Zenobia.' A keen-eyed natty man came in, Professor Hodges. 'Look here,' said Edwin, 'what's all this about Zenobia? Whose leg are you trying to pull?'

'If you'd bring the file, Mrs Woolland,' said Chasper. The secretary went into an inner room. Edwin was left to see himself out. 'Good-bye, Spindrift,' said Chasper. 'Try and get plenty of rest.'

Outside Chasper's office there was now not only Chasper's hat but also Professor Hodges's. The professor's hat was very small. Chasper's hat was a little too big. It rested on Edwin's ears. The name on the band was of a reputable hatter. It could be returned, exchanged. That was the next job. Pawned? It wouldn't fetch much. Edwin went into the reading-room. Frowning Indians were reading *Punch* and the *New Statesman*. No *Brute Beauty* here. Edwin wrapped Chasper's coke in a copy of *The Times*. There was a rather handsome volume on Caribbean birds on the mantelpiece. That would fetch a little, though not perhaps enough for a shirt. 'Pardon me,' said a sudden Negro. 'That book is mine.'

Edwin came to with a shock. Stealing, eh? Real degeneracy. But it was all Chasper's fault. The mean bastard. Still, he couldn't very well sell this hat or exchange it. He would borrow it, that was all. Give it back when he got some money. *The Times*? Edwin decided to use one double sheet only for wrapping paper. That would come to about a penny. He left three halfpence, which was really generous, he thought. Now he was (lovely word) skint.

'Did you get what you wanted, sir?' asked the kind asthmatic porter, as Edwin walked out with his parcel. Edwin smiled.

The thing to do now was to walk back to the hospital region, to the Anchor perhaps, now – so a public clock told him – open. Sheila might possibly come in, though he somehow doubted it. His intuitions were working rather well these days, probably a consequence of his disease. But that was the best place to hang around. Somebody would know where she was; she might have given somebody a note to be taken into hospital to him.

Off Great Russell Street he saw a man in a cap carrying sandwich-boards. He shambled despondently along a grey street, under a grey sky. The fore-board said: MARVEL NOT, MY BRETHREN, IF THE WORLD HATE YOU. 1 St John 3. On the rear-board was written: THE FOOLISH BODY HATH SAID IN HIS HEART: THERE IS NO GOD. Psalm 53. ' 'Ippo,' said Edwin.

'Eh? What?' 'Ippo stared, lined and grimy, his upper lip sunk in where the wedge of teeth was missing. 'What you want?' he said.

'You know,' said Edwin, 'bloody well what I want. I want my bloody watch.' He held his hand out.

'Don't know who you are,' said 'Ippo. 'Never seen you before in me bleedin' life.'

'Shove ha'penny. Hospital. Watch.' A passer-by took this as an imperative. He stopped for an instant. 'A right bloody pair we must look,' thought Edwin. 'Ippo's voice began to rise in the bazaar whine of the Cockney.

'Never seen your bleedin' watch. Never even knew you had a bleedin' watch. Gettin' on to me.' He made Oriental gestures. 'Do a charitable bleedin' turn and that's what you get. I won't be got at,' he said, 'by the likes of you nor nobody.' He tried to collect a small crowd. 'Him here reckons I stole his bleedin' watch. Never seen his bleedin' watch. Never even knew he had one.' His biblical texts made him an object of sympathy.

'Shame,' said a woman in out-of-date tweeds, already genteelly tipsy. 'They ought to be kept in their own country. Foreigners doing our own people out of jobs.'

A man in overcoat and spectacles said: 'If you say that he stole your watch you ought to prove it. You ought to take him to the station and charge him in the proper way.'

'I don't want trouble,' said Edwin. 'All I want is my watch or the cash equivalent thereof.'

'They come here,' said a man carrying a wad of the

91

midday edition, 'learning our language. Too soft with them the government is, way I see it.'

'Sayin' I've pinched his bleedin' watch,' whined 'Ippo. 'What right has he got to go round sayin' that? I've done him no harm nor nobody. Tryin' to earn a honest livin' goin' round with these 'ere boards and he comes up and tries to get on to me. A bleedin' shame.'

'That's right,' said the tipsy tweedy woman. 'It's a free country, or was until these foreigners started pouring in. You can see them,' she said to a small chubby woman who had joined the group, 'living off the immoral earnings of white women. There's nothing lower than that.'

'Just goin' round advertisin',' said 'Ippo, 'as you can see from what's written here. Advertisin' some decent caffy I think it is where they wouldn't have johnsons like him comin' in. You can see I'm only tryin' to earn a respectable livin' keepin' a wife and seven kids.' The whine rose higher.

Edwin did not like the imputation, initiated by the tweedy woman, completed by 'Ippo, that he was a ponce. Moreover the fact of 'Ippo's illiteracy had dawned on the small crowd and made him a further object of sympathy. Edwin's intuition sparked up. He said to 'Ippo:

'I know all about you. You did a tray on the moor.'

Startled, 'Ippo waved his arms higher. 'It wasn't a tray,' he whined, 'it was only a stretch. And that's over and done with. I swear to Almighty God that I've gone straight. I'm not goin' to stay here and let him insult me. I'm gettin' out of his way,' he told his sympathizers. 'Gettin' on to me like that.' He prepared to shamble off, hoisting his boards.

'You have the police on to him,' said the tweedy woman. Dead on his cue, a policeman appeared at the far end of the street, looking. 'I think,' said the tweedy woman, 'we'd better not cause an obstruction.' Universal guilt, thought Edwin as, shamefaced, the tiny crowd broke up. The state's substitute for original sin. 'Ippo went off faster than any.

But the man with the midday editions dropped, in his haste, a copy of the *Star*. An autumn gust caught this and plastered a sheet of it on to 'Ippo's back-board. THE FOOLISH BODY HATH SAID IN HIS HEART was momentarily covered up, and 'Ippo proclaimed atheism to the London street. To him, however, it would be all one.

Chapter Fourteen

'Me and Carmen,' said Les, 'were to come in and see you tonight and give you this. But, seeing as you're here, I can give it you now.' He handed Edwin a note in an open envelope. It said:

'Darling. Am not staying in Farnworth now as too expensive. Don't yet know where but will write. So glad operation is over. Will come and see you when you are *really* better. Love. S.'

'Well,' said Les, 'they got everything over very quickly, didn't they? Wonderful what they can do nowadays.'

'Have you no idea where she's gone to?' asked Edwin. 'Didn't she say?'

'She was in here last night,' said Les, 'with this painter. I got the idea she was going over Earl's Court way. I can't be sure, of course.'

'I just haven't got a penny,' said Edwin. 'I've got nothing except this blasted hat.' This, in its *Times* wrapping, rested on the bar.

'You wouldn't get much for it,' said Les. 'Couple of bob perhaps. Money's always a problem. I've got Carmen out working now. A hamburger bar,' he added.

Les was, decided Edwin, a far nicer man than Chasper. Les had already stood two pints of light ale mixed with bitter. The people here in the public bar of the Anchor seemed all very nice people. The landlord and landlady seemed very nice, too. Very sympathetic.

'It's no good worrying too far into the future,' said Les. 'That's what you've got to learn. If you worry as far as the next drink, that's far enough. We could,' he said, 'if you like –' He belched and converted the belch into the opening of Siegfried's *Trauermarsch*. 'Marvellous,' said Les, 'that is. Carrying old Siegfried to the funeral pyre. Weighs a bloody ton. This one we've got now, Hans Wahnfreud, he slips each of the ones who carry him half a bar. So they can drink his health. A lovely fellow. What I was going to say was that, if we're worried about where the next drink's coming from, why don't we challenge those two over there to shove-ha'penny? When we win and they say what are you going to have, don't just say a half of mild. Say a gold watch or a vera lynn. They can afford it.'

'And if we lose?' asked Edwin.

'We won't lose,' said Les. His confidence was very large. He called over to two drinkers, one bloated, the other craftily thin. They sat on a bench by the great opaque window of the public bar, their pints behind them on the window-ledge. 'Larry,' called Les, 'Fred. Him and me will take you on.' He chinked the five coins in his hand. 'You Albert,' said Les, 'you take chalk.' Albert was an ex-bantam who had retired punch-drunk. He shook himself like a dog, sat down beside the shove-ha'penny board and waited, panting.

Les and Edwin won the toss. Les shot his three coins straight into the Scotchman, all three clean in the middle of the bed. Albert chalked the bed full. Larry got three out of his five, untidily. Edwin felt a sudden games-player's joy. Les was right: the end of this game was the only end worth worrying about. Edwin shot two into the top bed, one in a middle bed. The other two went on lines. 'Good,' said Les, quite loudly, 'we've got 'em.' Fred, with a stylish spinning style, got four in, but nothing near the top. Les placed all five. The top bed was full now. 'Lovely, lovely,' said Les. Larry went for the top two beds, placed three coins there. Edwin sent up four which sat on the lines. His fifth slid them clean into beds. 'Beautiful,' said Les, smacking his lips.

It was in the bag. The gap between the two teams was never narrower than five. Les filled the bottom bed, put two in the bed immediately above – all with insolent skill. It was up to Edwin to deliver the *coup de grâce*, somewhere in the middle. He faltered; he failed. The gap now narrowed dangerously. Both needed one only. A young voice behind Edwin said:

'Look here, whose is this hat?'

'Not now,' said Les. 'Just a minute, please.'

Edwin failed with three coins. He got the fourth in a good lay. 'Tickle it,' said Les. 'Just tickle it, that's all.' Edwin's heart beat fast. He touched the fourth coin with the fifth. The fourth slid in. Les was exultant.

'Bit tight for a last one,' said Fred.

'Tight?' said Les. 'Tight?' He appealed to Albert. 'You could drive a bloody coach and horses through it, man.' Albert said it was not tight. Larry and Fred ceded victory to Les and Edwin, whom they now asked what they would have. A light mit bitter and a gold watch. 'Look here,' said the young man, smart and citified, 'whose is this hat?' *The Times* had slipped away, leaving the coke sitting in curl-brimmed nakedness.

'It's mine,' said Edwin, 'more or less.'

'Lend it me,' said the young man, 'just for the afternoon. It's important.'

'I would,' said Edwin, 'but –'

'You shouldn't have said it was important,' said Les, 'because that puts the charge up. We'll say a quid deposit, returnable on return of the hat, and a straight charge of an Oxford for the loan. Right?'

'Right.' The young man handed over his Oxford scholar. 'And now perhaps you gentlemen –' A pound deposit; a pound on the counter.

'We'll have the same again,' said Les to the landlady, a handsome humorous woman. To Edwin he said: 'What did I tell you? Ten minutes ago you were worried about having no money to buy a drink with. Look at you now –

you're double-barrelled. *And* you've got something in your pocket.'

'I ought to buy a shirt,' said Edwin.

'Shirt? What do you want a shirt for? *I* never wear a shirt.' He plucked at his close-fitting striped garment. 'Not, that is, a real shirt that you have to wear a tie with. That you've got on is like a new fashion. Saves a lot of time in the morning. If you sleep in pyjamas, that is. And must save a lot of time at night. Here,' said Les, 'come the two erbs. They might know something about your missis.' But all Edwin saw was the dog Nigger. This dog put his paws up to the bar-counter and was given a pub sausage. 'You'd better pay,' said Les to Edwin. 'You've got the money.'

By the time Nigger had finished his sausage the Stone twins had entered the public bar. 'Look oo's 'ere,' said Harry Stone sadly. 'It's ve perfesser. 'At on an' all. If she was my missis, I can tell you, I'd 'ave 'er across my knee. You seen vat yobbo what she's been wiv? I wouldn't 'ave it.'

'Where is she now?' asked Edwin.

'I'll return it this evening without fail,' said the smart young man, waving Chasper's hat with grace. 'And thank you again.'

'No hurry,' said Les. The young man left, cramming the hat on to his head. It was a fair fit.

'She was in yesterday,' said Harry Stone, 'and she said she might be in again today. 'Arf a bitter, please, Leo.' Leo Stone was looking intently at Edwin. He began to speak what sounded like gibberish, rapid, rhythmical. Edwin was a philologist and knew that this was one of the *trompe-l'oreille* auxiliaries of old London. Syllables of genuine words were separated from each other by the vocable 'boro'. It was much too fast to follow, however. Harry Stone answered in the same lingo, looked at Edwin, made comments of his own. The twins grew Jewishly excited.

97

'What 'e wants to know,' said Harry Stone, 'is what you've got under vat 'at.'

'Not hair,' said Edwin. 'Not at present. Bald as a coot for clinical reasons.'

'Does it look 'orrible?' asked Harry Stone. 'What I mean is, is it sort of deformed an' 'orrible? I mean, is it sort of full of scars and cuts and fings what'd turn ve stomach of an ordinary person?' It was tacitly assumed, then, that nobody there was quite ordinary.

'No,' said Edwin. Two whiskies and a couple of pints inside him, he was losing his inhibitions. 'Look.' He whipped off his cap. Leo Stone said: 'Aaaaah. Bloody wonderful.'

'It's a nice 'un, right enough,' said Harry Stone. 'I fink we can use it.'

'I'll get on the blower right away,' said Leo Stone. Excited, he began to search for coppers. 'Lend us a couple of clods,' he said to his twin. Armed with fourpence, he ran off.

'What is this?' said Edwin. 'What's going on?' Harry Stone had started examining his nude scalp from all angles. 'If you think,' said Edwin, 'that anybody's going to start using me as a thing again – I've had enough of that, I tell you.' He put his cap on with dignity.

'Manny,' said Harry Stone with passion. 'It means manny. Everyfink means manny if you go abaht it ve right way. Vat bald 'ead means manny.' He struck Edwin with flailing arms in his excitement. 'Manny,' he repeated. Edwin admired that stressed vowel. 'Manny.' Centralized, lengthened, spread, so that Harry's mouth seemed to open greedily and yet contemptuously as to snatch at flies of money floating in the London air.

Leo Stone rushed in. 'You *are* under forty, aren't you?' he panted at Edwin. Edwin nodded, wondering what – 'And what name do you usually go under?' panted Leo.

'My own,' said Edwin. 'Spindrift. But what –'

'Spindryer,' said Leo. 'That's a gimmick, too.' He was off again, back to the blower.

'It's only right,' said Larry in the corner, 'that we should have us revenge.' He finished his pint and got flatly up.

'Sright,' said thin Fred. 'Albert take chalk again.' Albert was still sitting by the board, chalk in hand, mouth open.

Les nodded vigorous acceptance of the return challenge and began to sing disconcertingly the sailor's song which begins *Tristan und Isolde*. He sang it in a strange and apocryphal translation:

> 'The wind's fresh airs
> Blow landward now.
> Get up them stairs,
> You Irish cow.'

He won the toss and got his three in. Chalk, chalk, chalk. Fred got four. Edwin filled a middle bed and got two in the Scotchman. 'Lovely opera, that is,' said Les. 'This bloke goes to Ireland and brings this richard back for his uncle. Then they take a fancy to each other. What happens after that, you say? Tragedy. Stark horrible tragedy. He gets seen off and she dies on top of him. Sings before she snuffs it, of course. Takes hours to die.' It was his turn to play. Five coins found top beds without trouble. Edwin was aware of the Stone brothers breathing on his baldness.

'Bit of nap comin' up already,' said Harry Stone. 'Electric razor might be best. Needs careful tendin' till Fursday night.'

'What exactly –' began Edwin.

'Manny,' said Harry Stone, almost shaking Edwin. 'You're goin' to win lolly for us all.'

'I'm not, you know. If you think I'm going to be exploited in some bloody sideshow or other –' He settled his cap with dignity.

'Language, language.' There were shocked tut-tuts.

'It'd be a cryin' shame,' said passionate Harry Stone, 'for us to miss an opportunity like vis one. It's a competition, vat's all it is.'

'Your turn,' said Fred, nudging Edwin. Angry, Edwin scored four with dreadful ease. Larry managed three. Les placed the lot. Harry Stone said:

'A competition for bald 'eads. Best unnatural bald 'ead under forty. A special shaved bald 'ead, vat is. 'Andsomeness vey're lookin' for, too.' He shook Edwin. 'Judged by some of vem glamorous richards on ve telly.' Edwin was shaken from the other side: his turn. Zeds of chalk were coming up fast on the mark-beds: it was a rapid game. Les sang: 'Your tiny — is frozen; let me — it into life,' but gently, so that few could hear. He scored four with little trouble. Edwin said:

'That word you used has a most interesting history. You find the Middle English form *coynte*. Earlier forms have a more definite initial *kw*. Cognate with *quim*, of course and also, not perhaps as surprisingly as you might think, with *queen*. The quimtessence of womanliness, you might say.' He was pleased with his pun, but nobody seemed edified or amused. Harry and Leo Stone were listening intently to a voice outside the public-bar door.

'She's comin' in,' said Harry Stone to his twin. 'She's after you.'

'You be me for today, for God's sake,' pleaded Leo. 'I'm just not in the mood. Honest, I just can't face it.' The woman outside the door was now to be seen on the step, nodding to some one off-stage, finishing her share of the colloquy, with '*Ja, ja, ganz schrecklich.*' A monstrous lorry swerved and thrust at the narrow alleyway to the right of the pub, dislodging brick-fragments and medieval stone. She stood for an instant in the doorway, looking in fiercely, a clanging of mudguards behind her. 'One of vese days,' prayed Harry Stone, 'let 'er be knocked dahn and seen off by one of vem lorries. Let it be so, O

Gawd.' The woman was a stern tubby Hanseatic, well-corseted, in electric blue wool and low shoes, carrying a tapestry handbag. She looked from one to the other of the twins, deciding. She nodded, then waddled straight up to Leo Stone. 'Doppel gin,' she demanded.

Les and Edwin had three to get; their opponents five. Les missed a nice lay, cursed, scored two. Again it was up to Edwin to finish. Larry got four out of the five needed. Fred had only the easy bottom bed to complete, but Edwin had an awkward one in the middle. He had to get it this time. There was heavy breathing over the board, as over a pornographic portfolio. Edwin's first coin went nowhere. The second shot right to the end of the board, into the out-of-play area. 'Don't be nervous,' said Les. 'Take it easy now. Nice and slow. All the time in the world.' The third travelled to the bed above the one that needed filling. The fourth pushed the third up, but was itself too far down to make a nice lay. Edwin remembered that he had money in his pocket and it didn't matter whether they won or lost. He slammed his last coin. The fourth coin checked it just at the right point and the fifth lay in the dead middle of the wanted bed. 'Oh, lovely, lovely, lovely,' rejoiced Les. 'Done it again.' And he sang Herod seeing the seventh veil fall: 'Wonderful! Wonderful!'

A light mit bitter and a gold watch. Edwin was feeling that he had something to give to this little community, though not philology. Harry Stone said quietly: 'Listen to 'er, givin' 'im 'ell. She be'aves like she was married to 'im, instead of bein' what she really is. Too much oot altogevver.' The woman was scolding Leo Stone monotonously while Leo Stone made an endless meal of his lower lip. 'Doppel gin,' she said twice. Edwin said, not quite sober:

'If the idea is to use my bald head in order to feed that woman there with an endless succession of double gins, you've got another think coming.'

'Naaah,' snarled Harry Stone. 'Not all ve manny in ve world could make vat woman 'appy. Vis what you're goin' to win is only chicken-feed, not worf mentionin' to 'er. Need a fortune to keep vat woman in gin. Don't know why 'e puts up wiv 'er. I do, vough, in a way.'

'Why?'

'Guilt,' said Harry Stone surprisingly. 'Ve Germans gave ve Jews a bleedin' rotten time. So, when ve war was over, Leo over vere gave six or seven of vese German richards a bleedin' rotten time. You just 'ave no idea what a bleedin' rotten time 'e gave vem. It makes 'im shudder sometimes just to fink abaht it. So 'e puts up wiv 'er now. She's one what 'e wanted to give a bleedin' rotten time to, but she never gave 'im a proper chance to get rahnd to it. An' ven 'e started gettin' a bit guilty. Just you listen to vat moufful.' The woman was well-launched into a foul tirade in the language of Goethe. Leo Stone seemed to be replying in the same tongue. After a few phrases Edwin realized it was Yiddish. All the sorrows of his wandering, restless, tormented race were in Harry Stone's eyes as he said to the landlord: ' 'Ere, Jack, 'ere.'

'What is it?' The landlord was a compact man of good presence, kind shrewd eyes over a strong nose and a sardonic mouth.

'Give us a bottle of Gordon's,' said Harry Stone, 'and a bottle of Scotch. And 'arf a dozen tonics and a siphon.' He turned to Edwin while the landlord turned to his shelves. 'We've got to open up vis afternoon because we need ve couple of bob profit it makes. I 'ate ve place, but I'm tied 'and an' foot to it. But,' said Harry Stone, 'I'm not luggin' no beer over vere. Vey'll 'ave to drink shorts.' To the landlord he said: 'We'll settle up on Friday mornin'.' He looked up at Edwin's hidden baldness, nodding. 'Should be able to settle a few debts vat are aht-standin' after Fursday night.'

Chapter Fifteen

Closing-time and the prosaic street; a dull afternoon, broody with rain to come. They walked to the club – Les and the Stone twins in front, Edwin and the German mistress behind. The dog Nigger staggered in a course of his own, lurching from one delightful street-smell to another – merds, garlic, mutton-fat, urine, food-tins, dirty children. One dirty child adenoided something glottal at Harry Stone and Harry Stone squirted the child gently with the soda-siphon. The German mistress was called Renate. She waddled along beside Edwin and said:

'If you to him money going to give, don't give no money, my darling. Every pfennig I him give, so he spend. I come over here to England rich woman, now very poor. You think I to Germany can back get? Not on your nelly can I not. You think twice, you think a pair of times, before you money to him give. Not air-fare, my darling, no, not sea-fare save I can. Here,' she said, and she paused for much breath, stopping in her walk, stopping Edwin in his walk with a brown-wool-gloved hand, 'here am I without underclothes to my body, slave to a smutty Jewish man become.'

'Yes,' said Edwin, 'the eternal womanly us upward leads. I'm hungry,' he said, feeling little winds whine in various parts of his body, cramps creep, a heartburn with a spirituous taste ram at his breast-bone. 'I must eat something.'

'Eat, you say? Eat? No money for eat I in five days, a week, get. You have gold? Money you have? Eat shall we together now, give them three men the bloody slip already.' Saliva appeared at her mouth-corners. She could surely, thought Edwin, have asked for a pub sausage or two instead of doppel gins all the time. Perhaps, being of a famous sausage-land, she despised English pub sausages. 'Round the corner,' said Renate, 'is a small shop where man can swine-flesh and calf and ox with sour cabbage and black bread get.' It sounded delicious.

'The trouble is,' said Edwin, 'that the pound is a deposit, really, returnable when the man who has borrowed the hat I myself borrowed returns it.' He shook his head: he was becoming Teutonic and unintelligible. 'It is, you see, not my hat. If I cannot return the pound deposit I shall have to allow the man to keep that hat which is, after all, not my hat. That will be tantamount to stealing. Steal,' said Edwin, 'I cannot.'

Renate seemed to have absorbed the Christian philosophy of the public bar. 'Tomorrow you worry,' she said. 'If he the hat not back brings, then who is the thief? Not you, my darling. Perhaps when he it back brings you will money have.'

'Yes,' said Edwin, 'my wife. This afternoon. In the club. But eat first I must,' he said. That word-order was, surely, idiomatic?

Renate took him by the arm and walked him briskly across the street, away from the club. The Stone twins and Les had already opened up and entered: Harry Stone cursing and lamenting could be heard muffled within. Renate walked Edwin round the corner to a row of low shops, from one of which a powerful smell of violets was exuded. Edwin made the usual allowances for his sick olfactory epithelium and interpreted the spring odour as heavy hot fat. 'Or,' said Edwin, 'if I avoided the man, so that I was never present when he brought back the hat, how could that be called stealing?'

'You come inside, my darling,' said Renate, pulling Edwin along eagerly. 'Eat, eat, my kid.'

The eating-shop was called, to Edwin's pleasure, JUNG.

It had a counter and a coffee-machine and various arche-typal, though non-Teutonic-looking, layabouts at with-white-cloths-unbedecked tables. A cross fat woman with hair, once blonde, still Gretchen-plaited, presided. There was a harsh exchange of greetings between her and Ren-ate. From the colloquy that followed Edwin gathered that his woollen cap was not considered respectable. Renate explained, making scissor-noises and cut-throat razor movements. Mollified, the Gretchen woman nod-ded, giving Edwin a smile of brief honey and vinegar. Renate ordered, with articulation that sounded like a meal in itself, a meal.

It proved, when it came, to be a not very good meal – very fat pork chops with white salt cabbage, cheese and pumpernickel on the side. But there was a lot of it, and Edwin tore at his plateful like a dog. Renate shovelled in white cabbage, saying, *'Fabelhaft,'* and clenched her teeth on the black bread like one testing a coin, like one audi-tioned for the film part of Medea. Then Harry Stone stumbled in, panting. He grasped Edwin and tugged at him, as though he were imprisoned in quicksand. 'Quick,' he said, 'you've got to come quick. It's ve law. Ve law's comin'. Ve law's been spotted. You're to come and make a speech. It's ve law, I tell you.' His mobile face was agon-ized, his eyes were the eyes of every trapped animal in the world.

'A speech? The law? What do you mean?'

'You'll know when you get vere. You can ask questions ven.' Edwin rose and was dragged by desperate Harry Stone. Renate said: 'You pay, my darling. You leave money. Change will I bring when the meal ended is.' Edwin responded to Harry Stone's urgency, threw his crumpled pound on the table, and ran out. 'Vere vey are,' said Harry Stone. 'At ve end of ve street. Don't run. Walk sedate, like you was really a perfesser.'

'But I am.'

'Don't argue. Vis was Leo's bleedin' idea. Vat bleedin'

club. If Jesus Christ 'ad kept a club 'e couldn't 'ave 'ad no more agonies. Walk nice and slow, now. Like you was what you say you are.'

'How did you know I was in there?'

'You kiddin'? In vere on ve old sauerkraut ten times a bleedin' day she is. Knew she'd gone vere, fought she must 'ave taken you with 'er, you 'avin' ve odd quid to flash arahnd. 'Ere we are. 'Ere come vem two bastards.' As they reached the street door of the club Edwin saw two large men with heavy boots, wearing mufti as though it were a uniform, fifty yards off. 'After you, perfesser,' said Harry Stone. Once past the outer door, they scudded, disturbing old filth and newspapers, to the cellar steps, and Edwin was yanked, stumbling, down them. Then came the damp cellar with its two bulbs of low wattage, the club, but a club no longer. On the counter, resting against an empty mineral-water crate, was a child's blackboard. Facing the blackboard were a dozen or so disreputables, seated meekly in two rows of chairs. The jukebox had been covered with an old billiards-table cloth. There was not a drink in sight. Leo Stone clapped loudly at the appearance of Edwin and said, in his superior salesman's voice: 'So glad you could make it, Doctor. Your audience awaits you, all agog.' On the ceiling drummed clumping big crass boots. 'Cobblers to them,' said Leo Stone, looking up. To his audience he now said, seriously, in loud cultured tones: 'We have the inestimable and detestable honour' – it was evident that he had, at one time, been on the stage – 'of welcoming Doctor Livingstone I. Presume into our midst. That is to say, Doctor Spindryer of sacred memory. And he, my beloved brethren, is no pox-doctor, even though I do smell like a pox-doctor's clerk today.' He sniffed elaborately at his left lapel. 'Chance would be a fine thing, wouldn't it?' he leered. 'The doc,' he said, more seriously, 'is going to undress you, that is to say, address you, and I bet he's got some good addresses, too. He's performed his world-famous act before the Duke of Connaught, the Prince of Wales and other public houses. A little applause of both hands, or three if you've got them, for the doc.' A clumsy booted quadruped was now coming down the stairs, heavily hoofing. Edwin looked at his audience, recognizing the warted smiling Carmen, a loose-mouthed tow-headed girl who looked like a whore, a bemused lout or so, various carious mouths he seemed to recognize, an Alsatian dog, others whom one would not normally expect to attend a lecture on philology.

'Ladies and gentlemen,' began Edwin, clearly and confidently, 'is Cockney a dialect?' The Alsatian, whose tongue had been lolling, now closed its mouth and gave Edwin its full attention. 'It all depends, does it not, on what we mean by a dialect. By a dialect I think most of us would mean a form of a language assignable to a region, a part of a language as a region is part of a country, possessing features which relate it directly to the standard version of the language but differing from that standard in possessing a phonetic system, a vocabulary, and peculiarities of syntax and accidence which are hardly to be found reproduced in any other form of the language. Not, of course, that one dialect does not shade into another, as one region shades into another. Life, after all, is a continuum, and language is an aspect of life.' The eyes of the audience, which had been glassy, now looked sharply at the cellar door, on whose threshold two bulky men stood, chewing imaginary chinstraps. 'An important aspect of a dialect,' continued Edwin, 'is its claim to be considered as seriously as the standard version of the language, its equal antiquity with that standard, its development according to the same phonological laws and principles of semantic change. For what, ladies and gentlemen, gives the standard version of a language – say, for example, the Queen's English – its claim to particular esteem, its – shall we say – hegemony? Not any intrinsic merits, surely – only the fact of its having been used for a long time by the most influential people in the land.'

'What,' asked one of the policemen, a sergeant perhaps, 'is going on in here?' He was the bulkier and elder, breathed the more authority.

'A lecture,' said Edwin. 'On philology.' The Stone twins held their peace.

'It sounds fishy to me,' said the sergeant. 'And I wasn't talking to you, either. I was talking to whoever it is who runs this place, whatever it is.'

Edwin was nettled. This was his parade. 'At the moment,' he said, 'you are standing in a lecture-room and interrupting a lecture which I am giving. Will you kindly complete your official business, if any, and allow me to continue?'

'That,' said the sergeant, 'is no way to talk. It's very fishy, this is, and I'll deal with you later.' He pointed a finger in the direction of Leo Stone. 'You,' he said. 'I know you.'

'Are you referring to me or the dog?' asked suave Leo Stone.

'You know who I'm referring to,' said the sergeant. 'Don't act soft with me. We know each other too well.'

'Are you,' said Harry Stone, 'freatenin' 'im?' 'Keep your big trap shut,' said swift Leo. 'Yes?' he said to the sergeant.

'Information received,' said the sergeant. 'Which is to say that we have reason to believe that intoxicating liquor is sold freely to all here at any time, that these premises are moreover used for the illicit peddling of narcotics, for the sale and handing on of stolen goods and smuggled goods, and as a house of ill fame. There,' he said.

'We don't allow no murders 'ere,' said Harry Stone. 'Vat's somefink, anyway.'

'We won't have no lip from you,' said the sergeant. 'I'll

have you in charge for obstruction. What I want to know is, what's everybody doing here?'

'Education,' said Leo Stone. 'Education being the opposite of ignorance, and educated people being the opposite of ignorant ones, if you get my meaning.'

'I didn't come here,' said the sergeant, 'to have the carrying out of my lawful duty impeded, hindered and obstructed by the use of sarcasm.' He looked worried, and then at Edwin. 'Who's he, anyway?' he asked. 'I've never seen him before. What's his racket, I'd like to know.'

'My name,' said Edwin, 'is Dr Spindrift. Linguistics is my racket.'

'I don't like the sound of that,' said the sergeant. 'And you don't look much like a doctor to me. Pyjamas on and that cap thing on your head.'

'He's eccentric,' said Leo Stone. 'Being a man of learning, he has to be eccentric. That stands to reason, doesn't it? But perhaps the police don't come into contact much with men of learning.'

'That,' said the other policeman, speaking for the first time, 'is not a fair thing to say.'

'Let's see him prove he's a doctor,' said the sergeant. 'He's got no socks on, neither.'

'Just come,' said Harry Stone, 'from a sick bed.' He realized he had spoken the truth: his mouth remained open for some seconds.

'Here,' said Edwin, 'is my diploma.' He pulled out his parchment and the sergeant examined it sceptically.

'Could be forged,' he said. 'Doesn't make much sense to me.' He handed it back. 'Go on,' he said. 'Carry on with making your speech. Let's see how much you know.'

'Cockney,' said Edwin, 'is, phonologically, a dialect, and its peculiar phonemes have received close attention from phoneticians.' His audience sat quiet, but their eyes were on the law. 'But its structures and vocabulary do not differ materially from those of the standard form of the language. This is natural enough, as Cockney is the speech of part of the capital, and the standard form had its origins in the East Midland dialect which, of course, was spoken here in London. The peculiar forms of Cockney are not dialectal developments but deliberate and conscious perversions of standard forms. Let us take rhyming slang –'

'If,' said the sergeant, 'you're giving a lecture, you should give a lecture properly, and not bring slang into it. All right,' he said to everybody. 'We're off now. But there's something very fishy going on here. It's a very queer lot here to want education, and especially education of this sort.' He reserved a special look of suspicion for Edwin. 'It won't,' he said, 'be so easy next time.'

'*Arse,*' said Edwin loudly, 'will do for an example. *Arse* becomes *bottle and glass*. There is then a kind of apocope, intended to mystify. But *bottle* itself is subjected to the same treatment, becoming *Aristotle*. Apocope is again used, and we end with *Aris*. This is so like the word originally treated that the whole process seems rather unnecessary. Admittedly I've picked a rather exceptional case, but from this you can see –'

'You bet you've picked an exceptional case,' said the sergeant. 'So this is your lecture, is it? Dirt and obscenity. I thought there was something not quite right going on here. You lot have been warned,' he said. 'Just watch your step, that's all.' Heavily they left. The booted quadruped mounted the stairs, was heard on the ceiling again, then hoofed off. The audience breathed relief, then broke up into single foul-mouthed disreputables, howling for drink. Edwin called:

'Wait! Nobody gave you permission. I did not dismiss the class.' He banged on the plywood counter.

'All right, perfesser,' said Harry Stone. 'You take it easy now. You've done your bit, you 'ave. Alvough,' he said, 'you shouldn't 'ave said vat abaht *arse*. Vere are limits, as vat copper said. Vere were over words you could 'ave taken, instead of vat one. Vat was goin' a bit too far.'

Chapter Sixteen

A sentry was posted at the street-door – a small inarticulate man with a strained Duke-of-Windsor face – and interrupted drinking was resumed. But Edwin sulked. 'A thing,' he said sulkily. 'Something used, that's all I am, something used and then discarded.' Harry Stone punched him, saying with passion:

'You'll 'ave your chance again, vough we 'ope not. If ve law comes back we'll 'ave all vem yobs on veir arises listenin' again and you can carry on where you left off. In ve meantime,' he said, 'look at all vem drinks what grateful pupils 'as set up for you on ve counter. Drink vem up,' he said fiercely, thumping Edwin. 'Drink vem up quick. We don't want anybody should be standin' vere wiv all vat number lined up if we get ve signal.'

But the Stone twins tried, in a shy fumbling way, to show Edwin gratitude. They told doubtful tales and anecdotes, chopped off raw chunks of autobiography for his delectation. Both had been briefly East. Both had been dipped in the Merchant Navy. Neither had been anything for long. Leo had once been a child-actor, touring in *Peter Pan*, a catamite – till his voice broke – of the man who played Mr Darling. He had been a comic's feed, a soft-shoe shuffler, a bogus sanitary engineer, a waiter, a sailor, a market-seller of hair restorer, a quick-foot-jammed-in-the-door traveller in stolen encyclopedias, Japanese shirts and dog food, a fryer of potato crisps in engine oil, a runner of clubs, a bankrupt. Harry had been a bookmaker's runner, a ship's steward gladly bringing

111

sex with the morning tea, a scullion, a cook, a Christmas postal worker, a kept man, a greyhound trainer, a hawker of cheap summer dresses, a railway dining-car steward, an assistant in a fish-shop, a procurer of sausage-skins for shady sausage-makers, a stain-remover demonstrator. But, though each had mostly gone his own way, the calls of twinhood – which are deeper than love – had brought them together often in disastrous ventures at home and, on two occasions, abroad. When the rap had to be taken, Leo normally elected to take it. Prison life he found not uncongenial if the stretches were short and not too frequent – masochism aching back to the Land of Egypt and the House of Bondage.

Harry told of conquests of rich old richards when he had had a big head of curly hair and was handsome; of the revivifying of listless greyhounds by giving them a kill, of the dispiriting of lively greyhounds by giving them a big drink; of the time when he had been the only Yid in London to join both the Fascist and Communist parties at the same time; of brief morning tumbles with Australian nursing sisters in cabins of wartime troopships; of how to tell fresh herrings; of tic-tac technique; of the Somaliland hangman he had once met who had wept with thwarted revenge when his victim spat in his eye *in articulo mortis*. Leo spoke of amation, of the importance of afters and the special role of the man in the boat; of how to tell heads or tails by the sheer sound; of the private lives of Shakespearian actors; of perversions in Hamburg; of a Thai lady contortionist he had lived with; of a rich queer he had nearly lived with; of great gang figures like Big Harry, Tony the Snob, Quick Herman, Pirelli; of Qwert Yuiop, the Typewriter King. Meanwhile the drink ran out, bottles with unknown labels were obtained from a shady back door, and Sheila did not come. Renate waddled in, however, drunk on sour cabbage, plonking down Edwin's change on the counter and saying: 'Now I buy for myself. Doppel gin.'

Edwin grew angry and four different accents shrilled and rumbled at the bar.

It was at this moment that four members of the Kettle Mob – or ke'o mob, as Harry Stone whisperingly called it – came down the stairs and in, passed with no trouble by the sentry. Edwin, student of philology, knew what kettles were, cheap smuggled watches guaranteed to go for a day or two. The four men, though drunk, looked well on their racket. One was fair, big-boned, handsome as a film-star in tweed suit and a very good raglan, but with mad eyes and a thin mouth. One was large and tubby, seemed ready to cry, endeared to Edwin by the fact that he too wore pyjamas under well-creased strides (he had a pyjama-cord that seemed to spring from his navel), sports jacket, loose cravat, raincoat. One man, very saturnine, carried a large chinking gladstone. The fourth was called Jock, much disfigured through, evidently, Gorbals fighting. These four brought their own drink – whisky in flat bottles – and seemed to have come solely for the company. The fair handsome mad-eyed one called for music.

'Not today,' pleaded Leo Stone from the bar. 'We've had to kill it today, Bob. We've had a visit.'

'Cobblers,' said Bob, swaying handsomely. He looked at Edwin and said: 'You got up for a turn. You sing.'

But a small dark ugly man had appeared, soundlessly. He said to Bob: 'What did Nobby get?'

'Free mance,' said the saturnine gladstone-carrier.

'What? Not get fined nor naffin?'

'No.'

'Fackin' lacky he was.' And the dark ugly man left. Edwin said:

'What did Nobby get three months for?'

'He had a grand's worth of kettles when he was caught,' said Bob. 'There's where he made his mistake, see? Getting caught with them on him. No import licence nor

113

nothing. What,' said Bob, 'do you know about Nobby?'
He came closer to Edwin, suspicious but fascinated.

'Nothing, nothing. I always get interested when I hear
that somebody's copped something. That's all.'

'Why? What have you done?'

'A tray on the moor,' said Edwin, without hesitation,
smacking the words with pleasure, words being – to a
philologist – only a game.

'What did you do? What did you cop that for? What
are you, anyway? What have you got that get-up on for?
What name do you go under, eh?' Bob was excited.
'You're kinky, aren't you? I can tell from your eyes you're
kinky. I'm kinky, too. What is it you like best, eh? Go on,
tell me. What sort of thing do you like?' His eyes shone
with excitement. Edwin grew frightened. He was saved
by the lurching in between of the tubby man. The tubby
man said:

'Nobody loves poor old Ernie. Nobody talks to poor
old Ernie.' He had a pint Johnny Walker in his right
hand. 'Not even my mother won't speak to me now. Poor
old Ernie.'

'You keep out of this,' said Bob. 'Nobody asked you to
start shoving your fat belly in the way. You're a big slob.
We're talking, him and me. Where's your bleeding manners?'

Ernie screwed up his eyes for tears. 'There you are, you
see,' he said in a crying voice. 'Nobody wants me.'

'I want you,' soothed Edwin. 'There, there.'

'You do?' said Ernie, with a fearful joy. 'You'd be a pal
to old Ernie?'

'He's no good to you,' said Bob irritably to Edwin.
'He's no good at all. He's normal.'

'Him and me,' said Ernie with dignity to Bob, 'have
just got out of bed. You can see that, just by looking.
Only he's been in bed longer because his pyjamas is
dirtier than mine.' He put his arm round Edwin and
said: 'If you're a pal of old Ernie's you'll never look back.

I'll take you to my mum's house and if I say you're Ernie's pal she'll be your pal, too.'

'Why,' asked Edwin, 'won't she speak to you?' Ernie broke away, hurt. He whined:

'You shouldn't have said that, you shouldn't have reminded me.' He was, Edwin calculated, at least forty-five. Edwin suddenly remembered something A. S. Neill had once told him: the delinquent child stealing watches in order to open them up, to find out, symbolically, where babies came from. The Kettle as Mother – a good title for something. He said:

'Do you love watches?'

Ernie grew serious and tried to control his face. 'A good watch I love,' he said. 'A real good piece of Swiss workmanship with a lot of jewels and something like a real movement. But this crap,' he said, 'is something to get off your hands, that's all.' He dug into his raincoat pocket and produced a ticking handful. 'You can have,' he said, forgetting what he had previously said, 'any one of these for three nicker. Because you said you'd be Ernie's pal.' The Gorbals man, horrible to look on, came up and breathed, squinting, on the kettles.

'I haven't got three nicker,' said Edwin, 'nor one nicker, nor half a bar, nor a tosheroon, nor,' he added, 'a solitary single clod. I can't buy anything.'

The men of the Kettle Mob looked at him with sly interest, weighing, appraising. Bob gripped him by the pyjama-jacket and dragged him a little way off. 'Do you,' he said, his voice trembling, 'want to make a bit, eh? I'm loaded. I've got two whole smoked salmons in the car. I've got a bottle of *French* champagne. I've got this inside pocket stuffed with crispies. You come back with me,' he said, breathing hotly on to Edwin, 'and you see what I'll give you, you see what I'll do for you, if only you –' But the Alsatian, owned by the blonde with the bulldog face, had launched itself on Nigger, though in play. Nigger yelped, and the Alsatian made a noise like blowing across

115

the lip of a big bottle. 'Dogs,' cried Bob, drawing his raglan about him, tiptoeing like one avoiding incoming waves. 'I don't like dogs.' The dogs were around him, a small raging sea of brown and black, capped with the white foam of teeth, and Bob vented little womanish screams. He kicked, but his toecap connected with nothing. Harry Stone said:

'Don't you kick vat bleedin' dog. I don't want no trouble in 'ere, but don't you kick vat bleedin' dog.'

'Call them off, then. Flaming great brutes.' This time his toe caught the Alsatian's rump, a well-fed rump that felt nothing. But the bulldog blonde abused Bob with woman's foulness, to which man's obscenity is as baby-talk. The saturnine and the Glaswegian mobster looked ugly, ready for trouble. Then the sentry fell down the cellar-stairs and yelled:

'They're comin'! They're at the end of the street! Put them drinks away quick!'

'Chairs! Chairs!' cried Harry Stone. 'Get vem chairs lined up!'

Nobody in that cellar was as yet incapable. There was a rapid downing of spirits, a pocketing and hand-bagging of sticky empty glasses. The kettle-mobsters were stupid, they had to be pushed and brutally organized. Gin bottles, whisky bottles were hurled by Leo Stone at the bar to Les by the juke-box. Les caught them with 'alley oop' and hid them under the billiards cloth. The Alsatian cried dismally as it was dragged by its collar to its place in class. Nigger crawled on his belly through the flap-opening of the bar. Harry Stone fanned at the cigarette smoke furiously, using a copy of the *Ladies' Directory*. 'Right, Perfesser,' he panted. 'You do your stuff.'

'We consider now,' said Edwin, finding it hard to focus, 'what is known to philologists as folk etymology. I will write those words on the blackboard.' A piece of tailor's chalk was thrown at him. He failed to catch it, stooped and scooped it up from the floor. He felt faint and wondered why this should be somehow appropriate. He held on to the bar-counter an instant, then felt better. Somebody had scrawled a rude word on the child's blackboard. He rubbed this off with his sleeve. Then he wrote, clearly and carefully, FOLK ETYMOLOGY.

'Etymology,' said Edwin, 'is concerned with the origin of words, the true origin, that is, the Greek *etymos* meaning "true". By folk etymology we mean the attempt made by the unlearned to absorb a foreign or unusual word into colloquial speech by changing what is exotic in the word into something more familiar-looking. The unlearned thus try to convince themselves that what is really foreign is not foreign at all: they *explain* the foreign element *away* by imagining it to be cognate with something already well-known. There are various stock examples of folk etymology. Let us take, for instance, the word *penthouse*.' As he wrote this on the blackboard the booted quadruped could be heard again. As he turned to face his audience he saw all their eyes blearily turn upwards to the ceiling. The four heavy feet spondeed to the head of the cellar-stairs. '*Penthouse*,' said Edwin, 'contains a familiar element – *house*. But the original form was *pentice*, derived from the French *appentis*, itself derived from the Latin *appendicium*, which means "something added on, an appendage". The *-ice* ending was changed to *house*, so that the word should look more familiar.'

The feet clomped down steadily. Again on the threshold stood the heavy two in mufti-uniform, imaginary-chin-strap-chewing. 'In the same way,' said Edwin, 'the Middle English *primerole* was rejected in favour of *primrose*, because the second element of the word already existed in its own right as a flower-name.' The junior policeman laboriously copied in his notebook FOLK ETYMOLOGY, PENTHOUSE, PRIMROSE. Suspicious, this, suggesting call-girls. 'And,' said Edwin, 'we mustn't, of course, forget *Jerusalem Artichoke*. The *Jerusalem* is a folk-corruption

117

of the Italian *girasole*, which means "turning towards the sun". The plant is, in fact, of the same genus as the common sunflower.' He paused. At this point something should happen, something important. 'And there is also *causeway*, which is the Old French *caucie*, derived from the Latin *calx*, meaning chalk. Meaning chalk,' he repeated, 'meaning chalk.'

'Right,' said the sergeant. 'I think we've had about enough of this. We've been on to the L.C.C. and they say they've heard nothing about a class of this kind being run. I thought it was fishy.'

'Oh, shut up,' said Edwin. He sank neatly to the ground into sheer restful blackness. He came to to find faces bending over him, not delicate brown Burmese but hard London white. 'Let us praise while we can,' he quoted, 'the vertical man.' Then he passed out again.

Chapter Seventeen

Edwin's consciousness flickered on and off. He was carried up the stairs by the two policemen, the serge of whose suits had a smell of rain-wet mushrooms. There were voices and people pushing. He was laid on the doorstep and saw, to his surprise, that the pavement was rain-wet. Then they were talking about where to and how, cars, ambulances, hospital. Edwin came fully awake at that last word, feeling much better than he had felt since his escape, as if some deep process of healing had been accomplished while he was off his guard. The two policemen were considering using Bob's car, Bob was moving from its back to its front a big box from which a toffee-golden French loaf protruded, eyes were away an instant, Harry Stone was just coming down the passage to the street door. Edwin quietly and swiftly rose and raced round the corner. 'What ve bleedin' 'ell 'ave you done wiv' 'im?' wailed Harry Stone, his voice approaching. Edwin found an alleyway. ' 'E was your bleedin' responsibility, woznee?' DAN LOVES BRENDA SHERRIFF said a chalk *graffito*. A chalk man was hanging from a chalk gallows. Chalk, chalk, calx. There were dustbins in the alleyway. Edwin hid behind one, crouching very low. 'Maybe,' said the voice of Harry Stone, ' 'e's 'idin be'ind one of vem dustbins.' Edwin shot up and ran. At the end of the alleyway the street sounded with newspaper calls, people were going home from work, the blue of the Underground sign shone. The alleyway had a left turn – more dustbins and *graffiti* – and down this Edwin ran, arriving back on the street he had left, but this time opposite the Anchor. 'Oi!' he heard, and 'Come back 'ere, you bleedin' fool!' The lights of the Anchor were on but the doors not yet open. The alleyway to the left of the Anchor led, Edwin saw, to the disordered yard of a timber company. He hesitated, found himself closely followed by Harry Stone in duplicate, but more closely still by a lorry. This had just turned from the street of crowds and newspapers and now proposed to enter the yard. 'Arf a minute,' yelled Harry Stone to the driver. 'All right, mate,' said the driver. 'I've been this way before.' And he negotiated, with dislodging of bricks and torturing of mudguards, the alleyway entrance. Then he found himself stuck. Edwin was now protected from his pursuers for a space. He tried the saloon-bar door, but it was still shut. The lorry was finding more success: amid shouts from Edwin's hunters, the fall of masonry and the clang of metal, it was straightening up, was almost ready to enter cleanly. Edwin ran into the timber yard and looked around desperately. To his left a circular saw, planks, raw logs, an overalled workman with cap and Woodbine. 'Yes, mate?' he said to Edwin. Edwin looked right: a wooden hut as office, a light within showing clips of curling bills hung on the walls, an elderly man sitting at a table laboriously extracting an upper denture, then looking at it seriously, then fitting it back in again with a head-shake of resignation. To the right of this office was a yard-wall, low enough to scale. Edwin ran to it, fitted his toe into a shallow jagged hole, and heard the workman say: 'You can't do that, mate, not here you can't.' Edwin raised himself by his hands, kneed the wall-top, found an overgrown garden on the other side, then swung himself over. He rested a second or two against the wall. Ahead was a house of four storeys and a basement, one of a row. Dusk had almost become dark. He stumbled through rank grass and bindweed, nearly fell over an unaccountable coil of barbed wire, clinked several bottles together like a glockenspiel solo, then came to an open back door, a scullery with a very bright light bulb. A pale young man with very oily black hair was leaning over the sink, wearing a woman's apron with frills. He was peeling onions under water but blinded with crying. Edwin stole across the scullery, through a dark kitchen, into a hallway. From a room to the left of the hallway a voice called: 'Is that you, Mr Dollimore?' Edwin passed a card showing times of church services, another with the legend SINNERS OF THE STREETS (x), a map of London, a wall telephone, opened the front door on which a card – HOUSE FULL – was hanging from a tin-tack.

The street was far from empty – the tube station had just released a liftful of passengers – but nobody seemed to be looking particularly for an escaped patient in woolly cap and pyjamas and – Edwin saw clearly in the street lamp – a very long tear in his trouser leg. He felt in his right trouser pocket and found only twopence. That German bitch had spent the change from his pound on doppel gins. Where was Sheila? Edwin felt the fear and self-pity of the lost traveller who feels night not as a cloak but as hands waiting to strangle. And now across the street was a uniformed policeman who paused in his patrol to look at Edwin. Edwin walked sharply towards the Underground station, entered its hall, which was sharp with light and the clink of pennies, then followed ticket-holders towards the lift. Opposite the lift was a rank of telephone-boxes. One of these was empty. Edwin entered, saw on either hand silent talkers fishily gobbling into mouth-pieces, made sure that his glass door was tightly shut, then paused to think. Automatically he pressed Button B, but its mechanism gave a dry barren click, and, turning an instant, he saw a queue already beginning to form – a middle-aged woman, a rabbity man behind her. This was strange. There was nobody waiting outside the other boxes. What was that rabbity man after? Edwin picked up the telephone, dialled – remembering his James Joyce – EDEnville oooo, and asked for Adam. He gave nobody a chance to speak. 'You,' he said, 'got me into this. If you hadn't existed I wouldn't exist. How is the apple-woman your wife? How are your incestuous sons? Give my hate to everybody back there.' The dialling-tone purred away. Edwin asked to be put through to various other Biblical characters. The middle-aged woman rapped on the glass with her dog-head umbrella-handle. Edwin saw this, saw the rabbity man snatch her handbag and run, saw the woman's instant of surprise, saw her cry and stagger off, brandishing her umbrella, then saw that the head of the queue was now Bob, mad-eyed kettle-mobster, ready to wait long.

Edwin said a few words successively to Ezra, Habbakuk, Elijah, Jeremiah and Isaiah, then felt weak, hungry and tired. Bob banged hard on the glass. Edwin opened up. 'Yes?' he said.

'You'd better come with me. I've got the car outside.'

'I don't want to come with you.'

'You better had. It's either me or the law.'

'What's the law got to do with it?'

'The law thinks you're crackers. I know you're not crackers. I think you're kinky, just like I am. You'd better come with me.'

'Why, what do you want? What are you going to do?'

'I've got two whole smoked salmons in the car. Cost a nicker each. I don't think that's too dear, on the whole.'

'I don't much care for smoked salmon.'

'I've got one or two other things in the fridge. But smoked salmon's what they call a delicacy.'

'Look here,' said an irritable voice behind Bob. 'Go and talk about smoked salmon somewhere else. I want to get through to my wife, I do.' Bob turned in the lazy-eyed style of a mobster, saying:

'You go and get stuffed.' Then he gripped Edwin's right wrist and led him from the threshold of the telephone-box. Edwin saw that his best chance of escape was to follow unresisting. The station vestibule was crowded now, and the ticket machines were merry with the song of coin. Just coming into the station was the young city man who had borrowed Chasper's curly bowler. He was wearing it, but, on seeing Edwin, he doffed it, saying: '*There* you are.'

'I'm awfully sorry,' said Edwin, 'but I just haven't got your pound deposit. I spent it, I'm afraid. Perhaps you could return the hat tomorrow.'

'Oh,' said the young man. 'I particularly wanted that pound. Not for tonight, it's true, but certainly for tomorrow morning. I got the job, you see. This hat was a great help. I looked in the pub but you weren't there. I was going to come back later.'

'All right, all right,' said Bob impatiently. 'If it's a question of paying out one solitary nicker.' He loosed Edwin's wrist to get his wallet out. Edwin saw his opportunity and dashed. He pierced a slow-moving slobber of youths who were about to enter a *Ristorante Italiano*. These then became a curtain, indignant when Bob tried to part them. Edwin ran past the DISCBAR, a shop proclaiming TEEN JEANS, and turned the corner into a sloping side street with a pub. A taxi stopped, and its passenger opened the door. 'In, quick,' said Les. 'Come on, in, quick. I'm late already. Bloody curtain's gone up.' Edwin mounted, panting thankfully.

'The less you see of that bugger, the better,' said Les. 'I know what he was after. Where do you want to be dropped?'

'Take me along with you,' said Edwin, 'for God's sake.'

'You weren't too well, were you?' said Les. 'You passed out earlier on, remember. Tight, that was your trouble. You shouldn't drink like that when you're just out of hospital. Do you think you could do a job or are you still incapable?'

'When? Tonight? What sort of a job?'

'Crowd scene. End of the third act. Where they lynch this poor bugger. Sings all the time he does, while they're lynching him. See,' said Les, glancing out of the rear window, 'that's his car. He sticks to it, I'll say that for him. When he wants a thing he goes for it. If he doesn't get you it won't be his fault.' Edwin looked too, seeing only headlights. 'It's him all right,' said Les. 'That's his number. Right,' he instructed Edwin. 'You just dash in when you get there. You'll get in all right if you say you're from the University. That's where they're getting the crowds from. And I'll hold off this geezer. Bob Courage, his name is. Courage, eh? Don't make me laugh. That's the name of a good beer.' He dug in his pocket and extracted a mound of copper for the fare. 'Got this from the cardboard box under the bar,' he said. 'While the rest was following your corpse upstairs. Only a loan, of course. Pay it back tomorrow or the next day.'

The taxi had stopped among smells which, Edwin knew, should be of chrysanthemums and cabbage-stumps but which his nose swore were of mint-drops. The taxi was throbbing waiting while Les leisurely told the coppers in his hand. The following car seemed to have been delayed, probably by traffic-lights. 'You get in there now,' said Les. Edwin got in, explained his provenance and mission, and was thumbed uninterestedly onwards to stairs that led apparently to a cellar. Cellars were playing a big part in his life. Edwin looked about him, open-mouthed at the vast mechanics of opera. Men fly-walked high above on the grid; there were wheels being turned and cohorts of switches being touched. In the distance an orchestra played all out and a tenor yelled above it. An offstage choir waited to sing, its conductor squinting anxiously at the score, and a man sat, waiting, at an organ. 'Down there,' said someone peremptory to Edwin, pointing, and Edwin walked, it seemed, a mile, past huge walls of scenic flats to the cellar stairs.

Deep in the earth was a great cold tomb full of people

and property-baskets. The people were young and arrogant-looking; evidently students: 'You're late,' said a willowy man to Edwin. 'Come on now, everything off.'

'Everything?' Edwin looked anxiously about, but could see no women. They, perhaps, were herded together in a different tomb.

'Everything. Including that little woolly cap.' And, with a delicate pincering of thumb and finger, the man himself lifted off the cap, then started back on seeing Edwin's nude scalp. 'But,' he said, 'that really is marvellous. There was no need to go to all that trouble, you know, but that is something that really can be used. You must certainly go right at the very front. The trouble,' he said, glancing round disdainfully at the students, 'is that all these people have too much hair. That looks unnatural in a crowd.' The students began to titter, with students' bad manners, at Edwin's baldness, but the willowy man rebuked them in a schoolmasterly way. 'You,' he said, 'have nothing whatsoever to laugh about. You all look far, far too young. A lot of stupid callow youngsters pretending to be a mob.' The students pouted sulkily. They were all dressed, Edwin now had time to notice, in a variety of Victorian garments. Some wore artificial whiskers whose adhesive strength they ever and anon tested gingerly; some had Karl Marx beards; a few even had watch-chains across their waistcoats. All had hats.

'I don't see that about the hair,' said Edwin. 'I mean, they all cover it up anyway, don't they?'

'Yes, they do,' said the willowy man testily. 'But they have to uncover right at the end, don't they? When the news of the death comes through. But you,' he said, dressing Edwin skilfully, 'are going to be uncovered all the time. That head is much too good to be blotted out with a hat.' Edwin did not like to ask what the opera was called or what it was about. The music had sounded contemporary and, in a vague way, British – Elgarian themes

125

wrestling with discords. He would ask one of the students. Soon Edwin found himself in a gaffer's smock with a clay pipe and a crook and heavy boots that fitted ill. It worried him that his woollen cap had been tossed away somewhere. Apart from anything else, that cap was the hospital's property, not his. He was stroked with grease paint and liners and given white whiskers to stick on. Now he looked vaguely aged: he would, literally, pass as such in a crowd.

Edwin asked an Indian student what it was all about. This Indian had also been cast as a lowly farm operative and Edwin could see that he resented it as colour prejudice. 'It is called,' he said with some distaste, '*Presbury Newton*, and it is written by an English musician called Emery Turnbull.' He paused an instant. 'Or,' he said, 'it may be the other way round. It may be *Emery Turnbull* or even *Turnbull Emery* written by Newton Presbury.' He paused again, seeing other possible permutations, but went on to say: 'It is of no consequence, anyway. It is not very good. It is a piece of fictitious American history in which a state governor falls in love with the wife of another man. The other man is jealous and angry and he takes a shot at the governor while the governor is travelling in a train to make a speech somewhere. The governor's life is despaired of, and the mob, which is us, drags his – as it proves – assassin from the jail and lynches him to loud music. Then the governor dies, but a new railroad is opened up, and a treaty of perpetual peace is made with some Red Indians. The Red Indians also provide a sort of ballet. It is very dull.'

'But, surely,' said Edwin, 'peasants didn't dress like this in America, did they? I mean, America's never had any real peasantry, has it?' He brandished his crook and wondered if there had ever been sheep in America.

'The Negroes, yes,' hissed the Indian. 'A slavery, not a peasantry. And the frivolousness of the whole approach to the subject is shown by these costumes that we have to wear – costumes which have never, at any time, been worn in America. Frivolousness,' he said, in a more resigned tone, 'will be the death of Western art, such as it is. Then perhaps it will learn the sweetness and strength of Indian monody in music and of stylization in the representative arts that avoids the vulgarity of overmuch naturalism and the mistakes attendant on it. Like this,' he added, and he indicated his own peasant's smock, lifting his brown Aryan head disdainfully.

Edwin looked round at the discarded clothes of the lynch mob, which was about fifty strong. He licked his lips at the sight of all those shirts and socks and ties. There was even a soft hat or two. His imagination luxuriated at the thought of all the money that must be in those trouser pockets, the pounds and silver of fat student grants. With a shock he found himself no longer squeamish at the thought of stealing. Then he had a vision of wigs. This theatre must be full of them. He salivated with a profound hunger for, at least, the appearance of normality.

'Now,' said the willowy man, lifting a long forefinger. 'I shall be away for a little while. I don't want any of you people leaving this room and going out to get drunk and perhaps wandering on to the stage in the middle of any of the love duets. I want you to stay here and remain *sober*. Cards I do not object to, nor any other *quiet* pastime such as reading. But nothing boisterous or *hobbledehoyish*. Do I make myself clear?' He went off. Two minutes later Edwin also went off, quietly, with his clothes and shoes under his arm in a little bundle. The hospital cap had disappeared. Never mind. Wig soon. Nobody noticed him leave, as many became engaged in a kind of rugby game with something or other they found in the *Salome* basket.

Edwin wandered quietly round at stage level but saw Les nowhere. The orchestra was playing a kind of railway scherzo during a sweating scene-change, and various eminent Victorian Americans – people, Edwin presumed, with a separate line each in the vocal score – were coming from dressing-rooms and waiting in the wings. One of the male principals said: 'Bloody awful opera it is,' in a Welsh accent. It was certainly a very long opera if the first act was anything to go by. Edwin wavered like an old man, leaning heavily on his crook, towards the dressing-rooms. Most of the doors were open and all the rooms were empty, save where one tenor sprayed his throat and trilled abominably afterwards. Another room seemed inhabited by an ectoplasmic wraith of cigar-smoke. Edwin entered softly here and, to his delight, found a very good white shirt and a pair of nylon socks on a radiator. On the dressing-table, under hideous bright bulbs, was a small pile of signed photographs. Edwin could not read the signature, but he disliked at sight the podgy smirking face, consciously celebrated, and he looked for other things to steal. Money seemed somehow vulgar, barefaced, so he chose a ring from a ring stand and put it in his smock pocket. Stepping out of the dressing-room he paused, undecided. Then there was the fortissimo of a flushed cistern, a lavatory door opened, and a woman displaying opulent breasts, possibly from her largeness the heroine, came swinging out in a flowing robe. Edwin bowed low and took over the lavatory. He stripped himself, then put on the stolen garments. The shirt was somewhat loose at the collar, and Edwin saw in the mirror for an instant an ancient literary celebrity – Aeschylus head and tortoise neck, probably O.M. Still, it didn't look too bad. He left the smock on the lavatory seat, opened the door and peered out. Nobody there.

As he walked gently away from this star region he encountered, with a sudden shock, an ancient and formidable-looking woman, dressed in châtelaine black and trodden-down slippers. 'Well,' she said, chewing roundly, 'and what might you be after?'

'A wig,' said Edwin truthfully.

'Oh, a wig,' said the woman, mollified. 'What size and what colour, might I ask?'

'I take seven in hats, I think,' said Edwin. 'And, oh, any colour you like.'

'It is not a question of what you or I like,' said the old woman, 'but of what is wanted by them as knows. You don't know much about wigs, and that's a fact. You'd better come with me.' Edwin followed her to a store which smelt of matches, interpreted by him as human hair. 'An awkward sort of shape of a head,' said the old woman, still carrying on with her rotary chewing. She tried him with a full-length Adonis, Caroline ringlets, Jerry Cruncher spikes. 'How about this one?' she said finally. It fitted well, reddish Byronic curls. Edwin regarded himself in a fine old blue mirror. Quite the little poet. 'Thank you,' he said. 'Thank you very much indeed.'

He was now in a great hurry to get out, but the old woman was inclined to gossip. 'No tunes like the old ones,' she said, chumbling, 'either for sweetness or catchiness. Lot of noise it is nowadays.' To confirm this, the orchestra lurched into a long-held chord of twelve notes, all of them different, very loud. 'Mark my words,' said the old woman, 'the rot set in with them Germans – Andel and Waggoner and such. Sweet old airs there was before, as none of them nowadays could go nowhere near.'

Edwin excused himself and left. Suddenly he found himself caught up in a rather podgy gang of Red Indians, giggling before they made their choral entry. They waved tomahawks at Edwin, and one said, in a refined voice: 'How about a nice spot of scalping, old boy?' Edwin grew frightened. This, of course, was the medical staff of the hospital, all dressed up. There, surely was Railton, and that chief of many feathers was Begbie, all expert in scalping. 'How,' said the chief in greeting, now clearly not Begbie. But Edwin fled.

Outside in the street a car, familiar to Edwin, was

parked, a toffee-golden French loaf gleaming under the lamp. Bob was there, too. 'Thought you'd be out sooner or later,' he said. 'Now we'll go and really see about that smoked salmon. And the other things as well. I've got some lovely things to show you,' he said, gripping Edwin by the upper arm. 'Didn't fool me a bit,' he said, 'wearing that lot up there. I'd spot those eyes a mile off. Kinky, they are. We're two kinky ones, that's us.'

Chapter Eighteen

Weak as kittens and water Edwin let himself be led to the car. But he felt himself protected by an armour of shirt and socks, a casque of curls, the talisman of a ring. The ring, however, he at once remembered, was still in the pocket of the stage smock that lay, with the stage crook, in that lavatory. At the wheel, Bob said:

'You should eat smoked salmon with brown bread and have red pepper on it, really. Now, I could nip out on the way to the flat and get those things, I suppose, but I don't trust you, see. You might take a leap out and get lost again. I don't bear any ill will about it, but I'm not having that happen.' He spoke like a man whose time was valuable. 'So we won't be having brown bread nor red pepper with that smoked salmon. I hope you don't mind.'

'We could,' said Edwin with hope, 'go into a shop together, couldn't we? There'd be no chance of my nipping away then, would there?' Oh wouldn't there? he thought.

'Oh yes there would,' said Bob. He shook his head, sad, world-weary. 'And at traffic lights, too. That's why, as you see, I'm keeping to the side-streets. It's not very far, my flat isn't, that's one thing. We won't be long getting home now.' He spoke comfortingly, as though he were delivering Edwin from the frightful evil of freedom. Edwin looked out at freedom as the car sped on; pianos and candelabra in display windows; an illiterate milk poster; teenagers sitting over plastic coffee in a grotto, ill with ennui; the creamy square dead eyes of a television shop; people. 'Won't be long now,' Bob repeated, as if to allay a natural impatience. 'Just round here, see, and at the end there. There, you see.' Edwin saw: a block of flats built in pre-war days, when flats spelt somehow Teutonic vigour, now, in the dark, cheerless-looking as a great workhouse. 'I'm at the top,' said Bob. 'It's better up there, really. Out of everybody's way. They used to have lifts once, so they tell me. Not now, though. Funny how a lift could just disappear, isn't it? We've got to climb all those steps at the end.' Bob stopped the car near the foot of a topless configuration of iron stairs with iron rails, each landing lighted dimly by a swaying bulb. A long climb, thought Edwin, and anything could happen on the way – a lithe vault over the first banister; a frantic knock at somebody's door and a shout of 'Police, police'; Bob tripped up and sent hurtling down, the salmon leaping with him; Bob brained with his own wine bottle, cunningly nicked out of the box. But it was not to be. Bob said:

'You go first up those steps.' This was while they were still in the car, Bob's mad watchful eyes on Edwin, his long arms reaching at the back for the box. 'And I'll be following close behind and there's not to be any more funny business, see. Because,' said Bob, 'I carry a knife up my sleeve, and this time I'll use it. I *can* use it, too, mate, sticking or throwing. I'm on the look-out this time, so no more buggering about. I've had enough of that with you already, as well you know.'

At the fourth landing Edwin pleaded for a minute's rest. Just out of hospital, out of breath, condition. Ruthless Bob drove him up with the crusty point of the loaf. At the sixth and last landing Bob said: 'Here we are. I told you it wouldn't be long.' Edwin gulped in several chestful of the rarefied air, his hands on the railings, looking far below at the street lamps. 'You see this door,' said Bob. 'Had it specially fitted. Nobody can bash that one open, that's for sure. Came from a blitzed posh house, that did. Belgravia.' Panting Edwin saw a massive slab of oak beneath the swinging lamp bulb, the knocker a tarnished snarling lion-head. Bob fitted in a vast iron key. The ward squealed, then the whole door groaned a prelude to a stately home. 'You first,' said Bob. Darkness and the smell of somebody else's house, and then the light snapped on to disclose the squalor of Bob's tiny hallway. 'Six nicker a month,' said Bob, 'which is not too bad, all things considered.' They walked between two lines of empty gin- and whisky-bottles, a gleaming little guard of honour. Then Bob threw his living-room into the world of light. Beer bottles and sticky frothy glasses, a broken Victorian couch with dust lying on it, a record-player. Bob kicked the switch of his electric fire: mock coals and a hidden fan which pretended the movement of flames. 'Now,' said Bob, still with the food box under his left arm, 'don't you try to get this key.' He wagged it at Edwin. 'You're staying here for a bit, that's what you're doing, and I'm not having you trying to get out. You have a look round or a sit-down or something while I'm getting something for us to eat.' He went out, leaving the key on the chipped and kicked sideboard, a punished piece of furniture which aroused genuine pity in Edwin. Edwin went to the living-room doorway and saw, in the foul kitchenette, Bob's back, Bob preparing to prepare a meal. He still wore his raglan coat, smart amid the empty sardine-tins, cloudy milk bottles, and dry heels of bread. A little refrigerator sang quietly. Edwin stole softly with the key towards the front door of the flat. Not, however, softly enough. Bob turned, knife in hand, and came grimly. 'Look,' he said, his lower teeth showing, 'I won't bash you because, for all I know, you may like that. I don't know what you like and what you don't like, not yet I don't. That's what we're going to find out. But you're not getting out of here.' He snatched the key from Edwin and put it in his jacket pocket. Then he changed his tone and, leading Edwin back to the living-room, said plaintively: 'What's the matter? Don't you like me?'

'That's not the point,' said Edwin, 'liking or not liking. I don't know what you've brought me here for, but if you think I'm perverted you're completely mistaken. I'm quite normal.'

'Normal? You? That's a laugh. You're kinky, the same as what I am. I can see it in your eyes. Everything you've been doing points to it. And when we've had some of this smoked salmon we're going to get down to it seriously. I'm going to show you one or two things and then see what you say about it. But we're going to eat first. You come into the kitchen with me so I can keep my eye on you.'

'It's pointless, I tell you,' said Edwin. 'I can't think of anything we'd have in common. You might as well let me go. You're just wasting your time.'

'We'll see,' said Bob, nodding. He pushed Edwin into the kitchenette and took two smeared gin glasses from the draining-board. 'We've got this champagne here,' he said. 'See.' Edwin saw that it was a Veuve Clicquot 1953. 'You open it,' said Bob, 'and we'll drink it while I'm cutting this salmon. And if you hit me with the cork I shan't complain.' Edwin began to see more. He said:

'You're a masochist. Is that it?'

Bob looked suspicious. 'A what?'

'A masochist. You like to be hurt physically. Perhaps you go in for flagellation. Is that it?'

Bob apparently knew what this second term meant. 'Whips,' he said, excited. 'Whips. It's whips I like. Come and see my whips. Now. Now. We can eat later.' He dithered with excitement, breathing fast and shallow, and dragged Edwin out and across the hallway to another room. He fumbled at the light switch and then pushed Edwin in. The room, except for a cupboard and a phalanx of empty bottles, was quite empty. Bob, half-blind, trembled over to the cupboard, pulled at its door, and then said: 'Look at them. Mine, all mine, all the bloody lot of them. Whips.' And he took whips from the cupboard, throwing them on the floor at Edwin's feet –

stock-whips, a nine-tailed cat, a horsewhip, a long one for a mule train, one handled in mother-of-pearl, a child's top-whip, one cruelly knotted, a knout, a lash with spikes: whips. 'Take what you want,' he said to Edwin. He was on fire with excitement. 'Choose whichever one you like. Go on. Go on, blast you. I want to see you with one in your hand.' Edwin hesitated. 'Go on. Go on.' Bob was in agony, still wearing his raglan coat.

'No,' said Edwin.

'You will. You must. Look.' Bob began to tear his upper clothes off. 'I'll show you,' he said, muffled by his shirt. 'Now then,' he said, throwing the shirt away. 'Look at that. I've had fifty stitches in my back. *Fifty.*' He displayed a broad back gnarled and wealed with lashes. 'But I don't care. You can do it as hard as you like. I don't care. Go on. GO ON!' he yelled.

'I won't,' said Edwin. And then: 'If I do, will you let me go?'

'Yes, yes, yes, yes, yes.'

'Only one, though. Just one. And then you'll let me go?'

'Anything, anything. Come on, get on with it.'

Edwin chose a whip with a stout short stump and a long lash. He cracked it in the air and then on Bob's back. An angry photograph of the lash appeared across the tortured puckered skin. 'Harder, harder,' moaned Bob. Edwin felt the joy of the sadist arising in his loins. This would not do at all. Angry with himself, he cracked the lash again. And again. Then threw the unclean thing across the room, letting it clank the bottles and then lie a dead snake. Bob lay on the floor on his face, panting, quiescent. He had fallen on the heap of his outer clothes. Edwin said:

'Let me go now. Give me the key.'

'No,' came the voice from the floor.

'You promised. Let me go.'

'No. No. Stay.'

Edwin, mild Dr Spindrift, kicked Bob viciously, trying

to roll him off the jacket where the key nested. 'Yes,' said Bob. 'Do that again.'

'I,' said Edwin, 'will kick you to bloody death if you don't give me that key.'

'Yes, yes, do that.'

It was no good. 'You're a swine,' said Edwin. Bob started to cry. Disgusted with himself, Edwin went into the hallway and tried the outer door. It was certainly locked. He entered the bedroom and found it paved with bottles, its bed unmade and the sheets in need of changing, torn lurid magazines everywhere. The window opened on to six storeys of emptiness. Edwin came away from it and was surprised to find, on a chair, a magazine devoted exclusively to flagellation. Fascinated, he turned over the glossy pages, box after box of eager advertisements, fierce pictures of whips in action, a scholarly article on Babylonian torture chambers, a chatty editorial which mentioned the blood brotherhood of its readers. As he read, open-mouthed, he heard the lion-head knocker thud thrice. Groaning Bob went to the door in his overcoat, looking in calm-eyed at Edwin on the way. 'You,' he ordered, 'stay in there. This is business.' Edwin found a pack of lewd pictures on the dressing-table and flicked through them, amazed at the twisted variations possible on what, in his healthy days, had seemed so simple a theme. He heard a Scottish voice enter: the Gorbals man, presumably. He heard a conversation in the living-room.

'Witch the narnoth and cretch the giripull.'

'Vearl pearnies under the weirdnick and crafter the linelow until the vopplesnock.'

'Worch?'

'Partcrock mainly at finniberg entering. Word fallpray when chock veers garters home.'

'Wait. Weight. Wate.'

'Vartelpore wares for morning arighters. Jerboa toolings in dawn-breakers make with quicktombs.'

'Good.'

Bob came back to the bedroom as Edwin was examining from many angles a most complex multiple position. 'I'm off,' he said. 'Going to never-you-mind-where in the car. Business. I'll be back tomorrow. Say about lunchtime. You're going to stay here.'

'I'm bloody well not.'

'Oh yes you are. You'll be all right. You won't starve. Two smoked salmons at a nicker each. Now I'm going to get dressed.' He went back to the torture-chamber and could be heard kicking bottles around. The Gorbals man came in to see Edwin. He nodded, winked with his remaining eye, and leered knowingly.

'Yü,' he said, 'duckteer fellosserfee?'

'That's right,' said Edwin. 'Ph.D.'

'Deevid Hüme,' said the Gorbals man. 'Berrrrkeley. Immanuel Kunt.' It was not really surprising to hear such a parade of names from such a person. French criminals would, Edwin knew, quote Racine or Baudelaire in the act of throat-cutting; and Italian mobsters would at least know of Benedetto Croce. It was only the English who failed to see human experience as a totality. 'Metterfezzecks,' said the Gorbals man, and would have said more had not Bob returned knotting his tie. 'On our way,' said Bob, 'if we're to make it. You're sure he'll be there?'

'Süre.'

'You be good,' said Bob to Edwin. 'You have a nice kip. You watch the telly in the front room. Have some of that smoked salmon but watch your fingers when you're slicing it.'

'It's about watches, isn't it?' said Edwin, 'this business of yours.'

'Our business,' said Bob, 'that's what it is. Not yours. See you tomorrow.' And they went off, nodding. The door slammed and the key creaked. Then Edwin was left to what was, after all, his first night of freedom for a long, long time.

Chapter Nineteen

With a beer glass full of champagne and a wedge of smoked salmon on a tear-off from the loaf, Edwin sat down to watch television. The armchair, the only one, made a winging broken-spring noise and dust rose, making him sneeze. He switched the set on, and almost at once was plunged into a medical lecture so technical that he fancied he must, by a quirk of chance, have blundered into some hospital closed circuit. The white-coated lecturer looked fatly unhealthy and, because his spectacles were full of light, blind. 'The minimum identifiable odour,' he was saying, 'or MIO, is determined by means of Elsberg's apparatus. Olfactory testing methods have an obvious, though limited, application in clinical neurology. In about seventy-five per cent of patients with tumours in the frontal lobes, or about that area, the MIO was invariably found to be somewhat elevated.' He beamed at Edwin. 'Elsberg's methods,' he said, 'as well as Zwaardemaker's, only yield relative thresholds. As far as absolute thresholds are concerned . . .' Edwin depressed a white tab on the set and immediately a man with a hat on shot a man without a hat and said to a cowering woman: 'Don't worry any more. He'll never trouble you again.' To the most noble of processional music the names of the cast rolled up the screen:

Jack Fairfly	..............A. E. Maudlin
Brenda Pill	..............Mary Critchlow
The Bear	..............Bert Laidlow-Storm
Creep Vassalage	..............Herbert Rector

And then commercials came cheerfully on. 'Spindrift,' said a large-mouthed happy woman, 'washes everything, but everything, in the minimum of time and with the maximum of efficiency.'

'No, no, no,' said Edwin. 'I'm not having it, it's not fair.' A hidden trio sang:

> 'Spindrift, Spindrift
> Is so cheap yet so posh.
> For a snowier wash
> Get Spindrift, get Spindrift today.'

The cheap little waltz-tune accompanied the gyrating of a white square machine with Edwin's name on it. 'No,' he repeated. 'No, no.' And he switched off. In this home of a kettle-mobster there was no clock, so time shuffled round the room in bedroom slippers. Edwin, very much faster than time, began to look at things. Bob had one or two rather dull books with screams, stockinged thighs and décolletages on the covers. Edwin deliberately tore up one of these and scattered the flakes of paper on the floor, watching with satisfaction the spindrift of odd isolated words as they snowed to the worn carpet. Bob's whips had lashed his blood to a desire for violence. It was easy to manhandle the old couch and armchair, rip them open and scatter the stuffing. The sideboard, already much bruised, Edwin had pity on. He shattered the television screen without mercy, however, and tried to hurt, though with little success, the refrigerator. Ripping open a pillow in the bedroom he was surprised but pleased to find wads of five-pound notes, so he put several of these in his pockets. Opening the window, he threw out all of Bob's whips except one. This he proposed to use not as a device for pleasure, but as a surprise weapon as soon as Bob should return. The face, he thought, eyes, mouth. And then he paused, shocked beyond measure at his rapid degeneration. What on earth had got into him?

Words, he realized, words, words, words. He had lived

139

too much with words and not what the words stood for. James Joyce had been such another, with his deliberate choice of a sweetheart from a sweetshop, his refusal to correct a visitor who had called a painting a photograph, because 'photograph' was so lovely a word. But James Joyce at least had not told a gangster that he had done a tray on the moor just because he liked the sound of it. A world of words, thought Edwin, saying it aloud and liking the sound of it. 'A whirling world of words.' Apart from its accidents of sound, etymology and lexical definition, did he really know the meaning of any one word? Love, for instance. Interesting, that collocation of sounds: the clear allophone of the voiced divided phoneme gliding to that newest of all English vowels which Shakespeare, for instance, did not know, ending with the soft bite of the voiced labiodental. And its origin? Edwin saw the word tumble back to Anglo-Saxon and beyond, and its cognate Teutonic forms tumbling back too, so that all forms ultimately melted in the prehistoric primitive Germanic mother. Fascinating. But there was something about the word that should be even more fascinating, to the man if not to the philologist: its real significance when used in such a locution as 'Edwin loves Sheila'. And Edwin realized that he didn't find it fascinating. Let him loose in the real world, where words are glued to things, and see what he did: stole, swore, lied, committed acts of violence on things and people. He had never been sufficiently interested in words, that was the trouble.

And then all that business about resenting being treated as a thing. That was very much the pot calling the kettle black-arse, wasn't it? He'd treated words as things, things to be analysed and classified, and not as part of the warm current of life. Now certain lovely words like 'cerebral' and 'encephalogram' and 'neurological' were getting their violent own back. And in this foul flat flagellation had been real whips, not Roman *flagellum*, diminutive of *flagrum*, and look gentlemen, how fascinating this interchange of 'l' and 'r'. And what pleasant alliteration, he thought, that was: foul flat flagellation. And what interesting ambiguity. 'Oh, shut up,' he said aloud. Kinky, that was right, he was kinky. 'L' in Spanish was 'r' in Portuguese: *blanco, branco*. And 'glamour' was, ha ha, really 'grammar'. Remarkable. Oh, shut up.

He suddenly felt very tired. Perhaps those sleeping tablets were acting at last. He sliced himself another helping of smoked salmon and finished the bottle of champagne. Hiccoughing (stupid mistaken analogical spelling, that) violently, he lay down in his clothes on Bob's disordered and unclean bed. In his wig, too. A very well-fitting wig.

Chapter Twenty

Just before he awoke properly he knew that he expected that he would think he was back in the hospital, so he awoke properly to know exactly where he was and everything that had happened the evening before. He guessed from the light that this was a reasonable hour to wake – the hour of palpating the cheeks after shaving and hearing the dry rattle of cornflakes falling into a soup plate. Near him a magazine lay open at a pornographic picture – a fully clothed woman cracking a whip – and the room's general squalor, worse in this morning light, was mitigated only by the regimentation of empty bottles on the floor. Edwin gently raised from the bed his headache and champagne mouth and, having found a kettle in the kitchenette (if they called watches kettles, what did they call kettles?) put on water for tea. Then he went to the tiny dark bathroom with its bits of soap, many rusty blades and stubbly filthy ring round the washbasin. Bob's razor was a ghastly clogged engine, but he put it to his cheek and submitted to a half-hearted rough scrape. Back in the bedroom, looking down to the street, he saw naughty boys on the way to school, whipping each other. Bob should be pleased: who knew what convinced young flagellants might not emerge here?

Seeing these boys, Edwin had an idea. There was no stationery anywhere around in the flat, but there was plenty of toilet-paper and, in Bob's dressing-table drawer, a variety of lipsticks. Edwin took one whose metal tube was stamped *Orchidaceous*. Lovely name, lovely word. Orchid: a ballock. Crypt-orchid: a flower found growing in a church. On three panels of toilet-paper Edwin wrote redly and greasily: PRISONER TOP FLOOR FETCH HELP. He folded this message inside a five-pound note, went to the kitchen and wrapped both around a chunk of very hard bread. There was no string anywhere, but he secured all with a tie of Bob's and then threw the parcel out of the window. Two boys ceased their lashing and counter-lashing to run to the middle of the road after it. They ignored the toilet-paper, letting it fall again in their excitement at handling a five-pound note. They looked up at the window, waved to Edwin and danced off. What a morning: whips and money. Edwin saw the message blown across the road, plastered an instant against a lamp-post, then spun and whirled by wind about the whirling world. Wild and whirling words, my lord.

Then down the street, early on the job, trudged 'Ippo, the unsavoury meat of a sandwich. The agency he worked for had evidently transferred him to its secular department, for the front slice, as squinting Edwin could see, said SPINDRIFT MEANS CLEAN. And the back slice read: THINGS COME CLEAN WITH SPINDRIFT. What the hell was this Spindrift? A device for cleaning, true, but whether a machine or a powder had never been made clear. That would do for Dr Railton. Send in your suggested quiz questions on a postcard. What are you, Spindrift, a powder or a machine? Edwin shouted down, loud as he could with London morning lungs:

'Ippoooooooooo!'

'Ippo looked around, in a manner of this-isle-is-full-of-noises. He had imagined it only, he decided: ancestral voices in the London air thick with ghosts. He trudged on. Edwin, having coughed, called again:

'Ippoooooooooooooooo!'

'Ippo stopped this time, took in the cardinal compass-points and then, shifting dimensions, the heavens from housetop to zenith to housetop. At last he saw waving

Edwin and cheerfully waved back. He lived in a world of mainly phatic gestures. Satisfied, he trudged on.

Edwin sighed and went to attend to the kettle, which had rarefied much of its water to steam. He made tea and hacked smoked salmon and breakfasted in gloom. Was it for this that he had been reserved – a whipping-boy for a member of the Kettle Mob? It was not what his parents – the dead kindly parson, Greek scholar; the horticultural and crypto-theosophist mother – had ever envisaged for their only son. After breakfast, smoking a cigarette of Bob's, Edwin went to the living-room window and opened it wide. To his incredulous joy he saw Charlie the window-cleaner at work, three storeys down and two windows to his left. He called.

'Good morning,' said Charlie without irony. 'Get around a bit, don't you? Changed the colour of your hair, too. Still, that's your business and not mine.' He rubbed away with his squeaking washleather, frowning.

'Listen,' said Edwin. 'Listen carefully. I know this sounds romantic and Byronic and whatnot, but I'm a prisoner here. My jailor's gone away, having locked the door, and I just can't get out. He'll be back sometime this morning and then he'll probably try to kill me. Can you please help?'

Charlie thought a little, frowning, seeming to compute. 'That flat,' he eventually said, 'is Bob Courage's. He's a kinky sort of a bloke. And he's locked you up in there. That's it.' He thought further and said: 'It's no good. This ladder won't reach as high as where you are. We generally come in there and clean from the sills. Not that all that number has them done. Unclean lot of beggars, I'd say.' And he rubbed away again.

'Well,' said Edwin, 'could you tell somebody about it, please? There must be some way of getting me out of here. Somebody could blow the lock open, for instance.'

Charlie thought. 'You'd want a peterman for that,' he said. 'Don't think I know any as are free at the moment.

You could have the lock picked, of course. That's probably the best way.'

'Yes, all right, but who's going to do it?'

'Any of the lot round there,' said Charlie vaguely. 'I
haven't got time myself,' he said. 'Some of us has to work,'
he added with indignation. 'We can't all afford the luxury of being locked up waiting for a kinky bloke to come
back with a load of kettles. I know him well enough, Bob
Courage.' He resumed cleaning petulantly.

'Money,' said Edwin, 'I've got money. Please. This may
be a matter of life and death.' He flashed a bundle of
fives towards Charlie.

'I don't want your bleeding money,' said Charlie. 'You
know what you can do with your money. When I do a
thing I do it because the bloke I'm doing it for is *my pal*.
I don't know whether you're my pal or not. Not proved it
one way or the other, have you? But your missis is different, if you see what I mean. She's drunk with me and had
a game of darts and stood her round with her own
money. And I know she'll be upset to beggary if she finds
out that you've been carrying on with kinky blokes like
that. So I'll go and get Harry Stone and Leo Stone and
tell them what's happened, and between them they
should be able to sort things out a bit. Just wait till I've
finished this pane here and then we'll see what we can do
about it.' He flashed a somewhat theatrical smile up at
Edwin and then carefully completed the passage he was
engaged on. Edwin was now convinced that everybody
except himself was mad, but it afforded him little comfort. His thudding heart anticipated the return of Bob,
kettle-laden and kinky and not too happy about the
flagellation of his flat. But Charlie, fifteen minutes later,
said: 'That looks really nice, that does, nice and shiny,
but do those sods appreciate it? Not on your nelly they
don't. Satisfied with any amount of old dirt and tripe and
droppings and that, but art for art's sake is my line. Per-
fectionist is what I am. Such types should get head

145

trouble and that more than you lot, but there it is. Now I'm going ashore.' He whistled himself down the ladder, pausing halfway down to shout to Edwin: 'Look after this gear while I'm gone and don't let anybody mess about with it. Shan't be all that long.' At ground-level he stretched like a man newly arisen, not descended, and then ran athletically round the corner.

The wind blew paper and leaves about the street, and once Edwin thought he saw the brief return of his toilet-paper message. A car stopped outside the block of flats and Edwin felt very sick as he fancied a familiar look about it. But the man who got out limped and looked harmless as a rent-collector. Edwin went across to the other side of the flat and peered out of the bedroom window. The street basked in the week-day calm of a residential area, hardly disfigured by men or vehicles. Edwin picked up the only whip left and walked restlessly about the flat, cracking and swishing.

At the end of an immeasurable slab of time Edwin fancied he heard another car draw up outside the block. He went to the bedroom window again and, to a relief as immeasurable, saw a taxi spilling out Charlie, a black mongrel, and two identical men, though one carried a bag. He waved wildly and continued to wave as the party mounted the iron staircase and the taxi moved off. When he was clearly visible to his, he hoped, rescuers, Harry Stone gave him a full gaze and said insincerely: 'Jesus Christ Awmighty. 'E's grown 'is 'air again,' he added. 'Take a shufti at vat flamin' big 'ead of curly 'air.' Leo Stone comforted his twin with a very reasonable exposition of how such a thing could come about in so short a time, and Edwin confirmed this by doffing his wig an instant. Harry Stone seemed not altogether appeased. 'Vat nap on it's growin',' he said. 'Vat'll want a good going over before tomorrow night.' When the team reached the front door Edwin went into the hallway and waited, like one who sets the table when he sees the chicken going into the pot. For the job was a long one. The dog Nigger snuffled under the door and Leo Stone mentioned the word 'peterman' and Charlie said: 'That's just what I said, a peterman.' Instruments clinked and probed, and the lock always promised coyly to yield and always, at the last moment, refused. 'A right bastard,' said Harry Stone. 'Dead 'ard, vis one is.'

'How about taking it off the hinges?' said Charlie. Heavy breath came from the crouching Stone twins through the keyhole. 'I think she's coming,' said Leo Stone. 'Keep your fingers crossed. Sod it,' he said, as the coquettish ward resisted. 'A hairpin,' suggested Charlie. 'If this one won't nothing will,' said Leo Stone. A heavy ferrous noise ensued, a rape of the lock. 'Now ven,' said Harry Stone. Costive groans came from the operator and then an asthmatic crescendo led to the door's sudden swinging in, aaaaah's of relief, a dog's head, a lion's head, three human heads looking in at Edwin. 'You,' said Harry Stone, 'are bleedin' liberated.'

'Now you've got it open,' said Charlie, 'I might as well clean his windows. Don't think much of the niff in here,' he said, entering. The Stone twins were not impressed by Edwin's savaging of the living-room. 'Like a dog,' said Harry Stone. 'Like what our Nigger 'ere done once when we left 'im on 'is own.' 'He'll get you for this,' said Leo Stone. 'You'll have to go into hiding till tomorrow night.'

'My wife,' said Edwin. 'Have you seen anything of my wife?' There were sad brown-eyed headshakes.

'Tell you what we could do,' said Leo Stone. 'Serve him right too in a way. Who's that one in the protection racket, you know, Mantovani or Schiaparelli or whatever it is?'

'Perroni?'

'He'll do,' said Leo Stone, creative excitement bubbling in him. 'Leave a note from Perroni. That'll make him give birth to a set of Diesel engines. Where's something to write with?'

While Charlie gave the windows a compulsive wipe, Leo Stone wrote large in lipstick on the cream wash of the living-room: PERRONI'S MOB WAS HERE WATCH OUT MUG. It took three full ones: Coral Pink; Morning Rose; Forest Flame. 'But,' said Edwin, 'won't all this cause trouble? I mean, won't the Kettle Mob start beating up this gang of Perroni's?'

'Trouble?' screamed Harry Stone. 'Beatin' ap?' He pushed at Edwin with his right shoulder. 'Vat lot start trouble wiv *vem*? Perroni's boys is far above ve Kettle Mob, far above vem, no bleedin' comparison at all. Trouble, eh? Vat's a laugh, vat is.'

'Dead clean those windows are now,' said Charlie. 'He can pay me when he sees me. Filthy way of living he has.'

'Anyway,' said Leo Stone to Edwin, 'you'd better stay in today. You can't hide in our place because there's only two beds and Renate's two daughters are there in the daytime, so I think it might be better if you stayed with Les. You'll be all right there, I should think. Bags of fresh vegetables to chew at.'

Charlie returned to his ladder and Edwin and the Stone twins found a taxi round the corner. The dog, in the manner of dogs, got in first and took the middle of the seat, licking his chops after a fishy meal which had cost at least a nicker. They travelled to a dingy street not very far from the Anchor and drew up before a decrepit terraced house: there were chalk scrawls on the wall, cheese-cloth hung for curtains, snotty truant children bawled at each other and played with bits of brick. 'Les won't be back just yet,' said Harry Stone. 'But I reckon she'll be in. Comes back for 'is kip at regular openin'-time, Les does, 'aving been on Scotch and milk since long before dawn.' Edwin tried to pay the taxi-driver with a five-pound note. 'Keep the change,' he said.

The driver was a good-humoured man in late middle age, one who had seen the world. He chuckled and said:

'Shouldn't have tried that one on with me, mate, because that makes me suspicious, see. In a shop you might have got away with it, not that you'd deserve to. Look at this here note,' he invited cordially. It was like Mr Begbie showing a choice cerebral tumour. 'It's not even made proper,' said the driver. 'Look at the eyes on this tart with the helmet on who's supposed to be Rule Britannia or whatever it is. Crossed they are, see. And that sort of ring thing going through the nose of that lion. It won't do at all, will it? I've seen good jobs in my time, deceive anybody they would. But just look at this. Shows you,' he said. 'Nobody doesn't seem able to make anything proper these days. You can blame it all on the war,' he said, 'like so many things. Terrible scourge to humanity that was.'

Chapter Twenty-one

Carmen was delighted to offer Edwin refuge. 'Oh blimey,' she said, 'yes, 'e spik lak good man. *Caballero* 'e spik lak. 'E slip in ze middle of ze bed.' Her dental caries seemed further advanced than when Edwin had last seen her (galloping caries, perhaps?) but she gave him a wide smile like an illustration to a textbook on odontology. She still wore her blue jumper, its interstices widened at the chest to virtual holes, but the skirt that had borne the names of exotic dishes had been changed to one with a more sober montage – famous cathedrals of Europe. For some reason a Spanish folk song he had once heard on the Third Programme – 'Let me put my little saint in your chapel' – came into his mind, and he foolishly said the words aloud. 'Notty,' said Carmen with joy, and she swung her heavy body an instant so that the cathedrals wagged obscenely.

'We'll leave 'im wiv you, ven,' said Harry Stone sadly. 'And don't let 'im get aht, whatever you do. It's danger-ous for 'im, see. 'E's got to be kept 'ole till tomorrow night, vat 'ead 'as especially.'

'What is this business tomorrow night?' asked Edwin. 'You haven't made it at all clear.'

'Told you,' snarled Harry Stone. 'Competition for bald 'eads, to see which is ve 'andsomest. Vere's a sort of talent-spottin' fing in which Leo 'ere takes part, an ven vey finish up wiv vis bald-'ead lark, which is organized by vem as is responsible for a new film wiv one of vese bald-'eaded yobs playin' ve lead in it. It's on ve telly, too, vis is.'

'And what's the first prize?' asked Edwin.

'A ton,' screamed Harry Stone. ' 'Undred nicker an' a film-test. Fink of vat means to you, only a poor bleedin' perfesser. You seen vese stars? Rollin' in manny and lollin' round in Caddies and over big cars, and ve richards of all ages screamin' to get at vem. You should be in veir position,' he said Jewishly, with a brisk thump at Edwin. 'And you will be,' he added, 'if you don't let no 'arm come to vat 'ead between now and tomorrow night.'

'So I don't get any money?' said Edwin. 'I just get the film-test, is that it?'

The twins became loud and Oriental, speaking at once, thrusting their arms about, ready, if there had been ornaments, to knock ornaments on to the floor. What was money, compared to a chance to become internationally known as a great screen myth? they argued. The hundred nicker was nothing, they had confidently assumed that a man of his intellectual calibre would scorn a mere trivial bundle of greasy notes, for themselves as lowly Yids without a solitary talent between them it was very different, in any case whose idea had this been, anyway? They punched and thumped Edwin to convince him what great favour they were really doing him, the time, the trouble, the worry, and he wasn't helping much, was he, getting himself picked up by kettle-mobsters and being chased half over London by the police. No sense of responsibility, that was his trouble.

'But,' said Edwin, 'if the prize is so desirable, I don't see how I can possibly stand a chance. There must be millions of people prepared to be baldheaded for a hundred nicker and a screen test. I just won't get a look-in.'

That was a laugh, that was. Did he think in all sober honesty that these things could not be arranged? Was he so naïve as to imagine that contests of this kind could not be rigged? Let him then know now that the promoter of the competition should once by rights have done time and that they, the Stone twins, knew it, and that there were certain things connected with certain illegitimate imports in the past – no, not kettles, nothing like kettles, don't be silly – which could be made public still to the immeasurable harm of some as should be nameless. And the judges? There, again, was something to excite risibility. For contracts on a certain television network certain richards endowed with a certain generic personableness but little talent else would do much. Let him not make them laugh, then. But Edwin was not really convinced.

When the twins, still talking loudly, had left, and their dog too, juggling with a cabbage-stump, Edwin was able to examine the small flat which was now his sanctuary. It was furnished mainly with vegetables from the market. There were two or three marrows recumbent in an arm-chair in the living-room, potatoes in the hearth, broccoli and kale and cauliflowers and cabbages arranged neatly on the few flat surfaces, a powerful smell of bruised fruit in the bedroom. Carmen was feeding a great steaming pan with stick after stick of celery to make, as she ex-plained, a strong specific against rheumatism. Edwin noted, with interest and hope, that his kinked olfaction machine seemed to be coming right, for an odour of rum led him to a tin bath of decaying bananas.

And it was of milk and Scotch that Les smelt when he came in. Carmen said: 'I not ask 'im 'ere, zis one. I not fack abaht. Oh blimey, zey bring 'im 'ere, zem two.'

'I know all about it, lass,' said Les. 'And I'm not worried about him in that way, knowing all about it from his wife.' He looked coldly at Edwin. 'Made a nice mess of things last night, didn't you? Got yourself into a nice jam, eh? That'll teach you, won't it?' Edwin hung his head. 'Never mind,' said Les, more kindly. 'The world's a very wicked place.' He had brought with him a gunnysack which he emptied on to the floor – more fruit and vegetables. Potatoes rolled under the table and there was a frou-frou of green leaves, rustling cabbages and a squeak of sprouts. But when the three of them sat down to an early luncheon the platter was for strict carnivores: wormy minced meat that Carmen had brought from her hamburger bar. 'Don't you eat many vegetables, then?' asked Edwin. 'Not really,' said Les. 'See too many of them, really. Surrounded by them most of the time.'

After the meal Les retired to sleep and Carmen prepared to go to work, an unbecoming toque on her blackbird hair and a shopping-bag in her hand. This was not for shopping but for hamburger mince. Edwin said casually: 'I think I'll come out with you, just for the walk. Fresh air, you know.'

'Oh blimey,' cried Carmen in a transport of distress. 'You 'ear? Les, you 'ear? 'E say 'e go out.' Les thumped into the living-room in his socks. He looked sadly at Edwin. He said:

'Now, I shouldn't have to explain things to you, you supposing yourself to be more intelligent than me. But don't you think we've had enough trouble, one way and another? Don't you think it would be more sensible to stay here, not biting the hand that feeds you, and keep out of harm's way? I'm not proposing to lock you in, because I don't really hold with keeping anybody behind bars, but I'm asking you for everybody's sake to stay put in here. There's plenty of things you can do to pass the time. You can read, you can peel potatoes, you can feed celery into that pot there for the rheumatism. You needn't be dull. But don't start endangering your own life and putting us who are supposed to be your friends into the ess aitch one tea as well.'

It was a cogent speech, and Edwin felt, for a time, ashamed. Carmen left and Les snored, and Edwin peeled an iron pot full of potatoes. At dusk Les awoke, smacking his lips dryly, and came into the kitchen to find Edwin at work. 'Good,' said Les. 'Good. Best King Edwards those are, as fine a spud as you'll find anywhere. Not that I eat many myself. Fattening.' Yawning, head-scratching, he put on his shoes, saying: 'War awe warthog Warsaw. Yaw,' he added. 'I beg your pardon,' he said. 'I'm just wondering what's the best thing to do this evening. With you, that is. We've got this opera on again tonight, but it doesn't look as though you'll be safer there than anywhere else. On the other hand, you can't go on peeling potatoes all evening in here. Drive anybody mad, I can see that.'

'I'll be all right,' said Edwin, 'just staying here.' His secret intention was to go out looking for Sheila. He felt that his counterfeit notes would perhaps pass in the dark and he would have no difficulty thus in buying transport from place to place, as well as refreshment on the way. Really, things had improved enormously. He was decently dressed and haired and had money. Counterfeit hair and money to match. He was a lot better off than he had been trudging back from mean grasping Chasper. About Chasper's hat he didn't care any longer. He was at last finding his level.

'Well,' said Les, 'that's all right, then. See, there are plenty of things to read over there.' He pointed to a wretched tattered pile of Pans and Penguins. 'And there are one or two classics, too, but I keep those in a cupboard. Things like J. B. Priestley and Nevil Shute, and *No Orchids*. Those are not just for anybody to get hold of, when all's said and done. But you're a reading man, like me and old Charlie.' He happily got dressed, singing the Habañera from *Carmen*:

> 'I'm a bastard, and you're a whore.
> If you were mine I'd have you on the floor.'

He went out singing, and Edwin was left to the vegetables and the classics. It was early enough still, so he boiled himself some potatoes, not forgetting the salt, and ate these, following them with a rummy mush of bananas which he spooned in for their known sustaining power. While he was combing his wig he heard a knock at the door. Bob, would it be? He picked up the bread knife, waited till the knock was repeated more urgently, and then thought: 'It must be Sheila.' He took his bread knife to the door, opened and brandished, and found Renate on the step.

'*Na*,' she said, shaking her head. 'I will not intread. Here can I it say.' She swayed, full of doppel gins.

'Yes? What? What is it?'

'*Ungeduld*,' said Renate. 'Impatience. Now I tell you. With a young painter with a beard your missis has seen been. You give me money. I tell you where.' She held out a confident palm.

'How do I know?' said Edwin. 'How do I know *you* know?'

'I know,' nodded Renate. 'My darling, I know. Last night and the night before were they in this place seen.'

'Here,' said Edwin, giving her five pounds. 'Where?'

Renate kissed the note and folded it quarto, octavo. She leaned forward ginnily and whispered: 'Soho. Soho. For a place a very silly name.'

'But where in Soho?' asked Edwin. 'Damn it, Soho's a big district.'

'I have the name forgotten,' said Renate. 'Oh, yes. It is for painters. A club.' She raised her arms from her sides, becoming cruciform. 'Big pictures on the walls. But not very good. *Nicht so schlecht*,' she spat softly. '*Nicht so gut*.'

'Greek Street? Frith Street? Where?'

'Soho,' said Renate, nodding herself off to buy more gin. 'You go there, my darling, you poor kid.' Edwin slammed the door and dashed back to finish his toilet. It was a start, anyway, somewhere to start. He admired himself in the mirror, prototypical poet, and wondered whether perhaps he would not be better with a beard. The man of the future, infinitely plastic. Also, perhaps, Bob-detection-proof. But it was the eyes, wasn't it? He rummaged in the living-room and found in a drawer –

among bus tickets, hairpins, buttons, odd comb-teeth, bottle-openers, fuse wire, a ripening tomato or two, cornflake gifts, hanks of hair in rage wrenched roughly, dirty pictures, an army pay-book, an old denture, cachous, a scented devotional BVM missal-marker, a few unwrapped Mintoes, P. and O. cocktail tridents, four or five playing cards, dominoes, a die and a shaker – a dusty cheap pair of sunglasses. These were Carmen's presumably, or her predecessor's, being of narrow fit. They sat, however, comfortably enough on his own nose and ears. Thus armed, his kinkiness hidden, he was ready for any adventure.

After much searching, side-street wandering, passing of sinister fish-and-chip-shops, Edwin found himself on a fine wide London thoroughfare, the very one he had haunted the foredawn of the day before. He glanced inside several tobacconist's shops and at last saw what he wanted: ill service from a gawky chewing girl who had more time for her waiting friend – an also chewing, plastic-raincoated, puddingy little bitch – than for her customers.

'Twenty Senior, please,' said Edwin, proffering a note.

'Haven't you got nothing less?' crossly chewed the girl.

Edwin removed his sunglasses to show sincere, though kinky, eyes, saying: 'Sorry.' And he suffered the girl to tell out his change with petulance. 'You'll have to have nearly all silver,' she said. This was his punishment. Edwin was profuse in his thanks. Out in the street, enjoying a free smoke, he hailed (Icelandic *heill*: health; hence a greeting; hence a call) a taxi. Real money for this, no free ride. But it really would be free, wouldn't it? How does one know, where does one start, what are really *meum* and *tuum*? 'The Soho Square end of Greek Street,' he told the driver. That seemed a reasonable sort of starting-point. Edwin, so much himself a sham, felt a sort of kinship with the sham pleasures of Tottenham Court

Road and Oxford Street as they travelled painfully towards Soho. When Crosse and Blackwell glowed on their left the driver said: 'This do, guv?' The square was a mess of cars, parked and crawling. Edwin paid him and but meagrely tipped him, then he walked into Greek Street. A club with paintings on the wall. How did one get into a club if one happened to be oneself not a member? One waited outside perhaps and asked a member to sign one in. Rather like the days when he would wait outside a cinema and ask any entering adult to be the accompanying adult without whom no child under sixteen could be admitted when it was that sort of film. *The Dangers of Ignorance. The Miracle of Birth. The Man Whose Nose Dropped Off.*

Edwin walked a long way without finding a club for painters. There were restaurants offering everything in the world but roast beef and Yorkshire. There were coffee-bars with gimmicks: Heaven above, Hell below and the W.C. called Purgatory; Necrophiles' Nest; The Vampire, with bloody lighting to encarnadine the coffee. There were pubs in plenty. Growing thirsty at last, Edwin entered one of these, decided he did not like the landlord, and tendered five pounds for his double scotch. 'What's this, what's this?' said the landlord, holding the note to the light. 'They've done you, that's what they've done, a real fake this is.' 'The swine,' said Edwin, offering good silver. 'You can't trust anybody, can you?' The landlord went to telephone, so Edwin gulped his whisky and left.

At length it seemed that he had found what he was looking for. THE CHINESE WHITE. About right for Han Su-yin, he thought nastily. A Negro with a small beard was just about to enter, so Edwin said politely: 'Excuse me, sir. There's somebody I'm looking for. It's a matter of buying a picture, probably. If you would be so good as to –'

'If you want to buy a picture,' said the Negro, 'I've got

pictures. Affluent patron of the arts, eh?' He both
sneered and smiled – the artist's age-old dichotomy showing through. 'You come in,' he said. 'I've got paintings
hanging up inside.' He opened the door, disclosing a shirt-
sleeved corpse of a man presiding over a visitors' book.
Edwin wrote down his name and was signed in. The
Negro, whose name seemed to be F. Willoughby, thrust
aside a curtain. Edwin took off his dark glasses and saw
what he had expected to see: shabby hirsute men and
girls in coloured stockings. The room was long, narrow,
noisy and smoky. There was a bar at the end, and the
walls were covered with canvases. Of Nigel and Sheila
there was no sign. Perhaps they would come in later.
Plenty of time, after all.

'I don't suppose I, as a non-member, am allowed to buy
drinks,' said Edwin. 'So perhaps I could give you this
money and you could do it for me.' He tried to fold a five-
pound note into F. Willoughby's large painter's paw. But
F. Willoughby said:

'Anybody can buy a drink in here once they get in
here. I'll have a large Pernod.'

'And so you shall,' said Edwin, seeing with joy that the
barman was busy and that he didn't like the look of him
anyway. He squinted a bit, just like the pseudo-Britannia
he was going to get. But when Edwin had just about
caught his eye, there was a general shushing and a temporary cessation of trade. Edwin looked round from the
bar to see that a lank young man with glasses, turtle-neck
sweater and hair geometrically straight, was sitting on a
stool in the middle of the floor, tuning unhandily a
Spanish guitar. After one or two sour and simple chords
he began to recite, chordally emphasizing his cadences in
the supposed manner of the Psalmist:

'For them that looked for the way out and found it:
   This.
 There were holes that grew as doors with looking for
   them,

158

And for those that walked through with their heads
    high as kites,
This.
Where were the holes?
In man, in woman, in bottles, in the tattered book picked
    up from the mud on the rainy day by the railway junction.
But the whole of wholes, the holy of holies, where was,
    where is
This?'

There was a great deal more, so old-fashioned as to
have become up-to-date, and Edwin thirsted, but most
listened with respect. 'That,' explained F. Willoughby in
a whisper, 'is *This*. Poetry,' he added. 'But those are
mine, those over there.' He pointed, and, seeing him
point, someone went shush. Edwin saw a series of small
canvases, and each one was of a circle. Some were bigger
than others, and the plain painted backgrounds varied in
violent poster-colour, but every one of F. Willoughby's
pictures was a portrait of a circle. 'They're only circles,'
whispered Edwin. 'Circles, that's all they are.'

'Shhhhh.'

'Only?' said F. Willoughby. 'You say only? You ever try
to draw a circle with your bare hands?'

'Shhhhhh. Shhhhhhh.'

'Through the ultimate hole is reached
This:
What mouselike becomes lionlike when the hole is seen not
    just as a door in but a door out,
A door out of
This:
Cage. Cage.' (And CAGE went the guitar-chord.)

'But surely,' whispered Edwin, 'all painting is done
with the bare hands, isn't it?'

'See here,' said the psalmist. 'I'm very nearly finished.
Do you mind?'

'Best line of the lot,' said Edwin.

'Shhhhhhh.' The girls looked prettier, pouting shhhhhh. The psalmist ended, postluded:

'The holy, the whole, when seen through the hole
Not seen wholly, but only whole holy deliverer
    from
This.'

His right chording hand plucked, withdrew from the strings, and poised in a plucking posture in the air. Edwin clapped as loud as any, ordered two large Pernods and whatever the barman wanted, and received lots of change in real money. 'About this circle business,' he said.

'There was a big painter in the past,' said the Negro, 'an Italian, and he could do that. Nobody else since. Only me,' he said, and sipped.

'But does that make it aesthetically more valid?' asked Edwin. 'The viewer doesn't know whether you've done it freehand or used a compass, does he?'

'Look as hard as you like,' said F. Willoughby, 'and you won't find any compass pin-prick in the middle.'

'But suppose I were to put a pin-prick there as though it had been done by a compass,' said Edwin. 'Would that make any aesthetic difference?'

'See here, brother,' said F. Willoughby, commercially candid, 'I just make them. I don't argue about aesthetics, see? Ten guineas the set.'

'Done,' said Edwin, handing over fifteen pounds. 'I want four ten change.'

'For four ten,' said F. Willoughby, 'you can have that canvas over there.' It was a not unpleasing pattern – whorls in puce and lemon and jade.

'Sorry,' said Edwin. 'In any case, it's your turn to buy a drink.' F. Willoughby fought his way through to the buying of two flat light ales and brought back also Edwin's change. Edwin became aware of a quickening beat of interest in him, speculative bright eyes on this munificent patron who, if he would buy a set of circles for ten guineas, would undoubtedly buy anything. 'I'm rather fond of Nigel's work,' said Edwin. 'Is there any of it around?'

'Nigel?' said F. Willoughby. 'Which Nigel? Nigel Crump? Nigel Meldrum? Nigel Mackay-Muir? There's a fair number of Nigels.'

'Nigel with a beard.'

'Bless you,' said F. Willoughby Dickensianly, 'they've most of them got beards. And there's none of their stuff round here.' He gazed somewhat gloomily at the mostly deplorable pictures on the walls: old-style Chirico pastiches with broken columns and arthritic horses; a portrait or two of the artist's commonplace friend; lifeless still-lifes; a kind of Klee with a stick man and a chunk of bread moon.

As the evening progressed Edwin bought most of these pictures. He thought it a pity that so many of the artists who eagerly accepted Bob's fake notes had been so little trained in visual observation, but that, after all, was their business. Edwin began to feel mature and gangsterish. The painters promised to arrange delivery of their works and, after some thought, Edwin gave his address as the hospital and his name as R. Dickie. There was still no sign of Sheila and whichever Nigel it was, but Edwin began to care less as the drink flowed. To give the young painters their due, they were quick to change their five-pound notes into wine, spirits and genuine currency. Ultimately, too, it was not the club that seemed to suffer: a painter who, from his lack of beard, seemed relatively prosperous, came in to cash a cheque, a fairly large one. He walked out head high, his nose splayed in the insolence of success, with a fair number of fake notes. So everything was really all right.

The young man with the straight hair and Colin Wilson turtle-neck took his central stool again and struck a lumpish bass E and a neuralgic treble one, a flat A, a tinny D, a fair G and a sharpish B. Then, to a bigger crowd than before, he began to sing a song very popular at that time with young England: an historic American ballad about the discomfiture of the British at the Boston Tea Party. But F. Willoughby, F. Primum Mobile Willoughby, still moved, like owls, in circles.

'You've got to admit,' he said, 'that that's the real test of draughtsmanship. Could Rubens do it? Could the one with one ear do it? Could that big Spanish painter with the astigmatism? No. But I've done it, haven't I? I let you have those too cheap,' he said.

'You can have another pound,' said Edwin, reaching for five.

'And so these Boston citizens, still with their feathers on,
    Staggered from the hold with the chests upon their backs.
Cheer, boys, cheer as the tea hits the harbour:
    Davy Jones can drink it and the devil pay the tax.'

'It's appreciation that's important, too,' said F. Willoughby. 'You need two kinds of patrons really. Those with the money and those with the taste. That might be a good sort of argument for marriage.'

'Shhhhhhh. Shhhhhhh.'

'But,' said Edwin, 'if a machine can do it better –'

'A machine can't do it better.'

'It's like photography really, isn't it?' said Edwin. 'What you don't get in a photograph is the human vision. But the human vision is essentially imperfect. That's why a perfect circle –'

'Shhhhhh. Shhhhhhhhhhhh.' Edwin pouted his lips in kisswise answer to a tousled shushing girl. A kiss? Was sex returning?

'Look,' said the singer. 'I've had about enough of this. It was just the same when I was reciting the poem. It's sheer bad manners. Either he shuts up or I shut up.' His guitar twanged agreement.

'I'm sorry,' said Edwin, ready with a five-pound note.
The singer glared and continued:

'That was the beginning of the famous Revolucyon –
Fight, boys, fight till America is free ...'

At the curtains of the club Nigel and Sheila had
appeared, Sheila in green with a hat like a leaf. 'Sheila!'
called Edwin, trying to break through the crowd.

'Shhhh. Shhhhhh.'

'Sheila! Sheila!' But Sheila acknowledged this call
with a mere formal wave. A man with unknown hair,
seen her before sometime. Must be so, for he knew her
name. Edwin pushed but was counter-pushed.

'May I,' asked the singer, 'be allowed to finish the song?
A few more lines, that's all. May I crave the indulgence of
a modicum of bloody courtesy?' There was a buzz of
angry approval.

Sheila and Nigel spoke silently to each other: too
crowded, too uncomfortable, too difficult to get a drink,
go somewhere quieter. Too many patrons tonight. (Too
good a patron in Edwin.)

'... Hang King George and roast his ruddy lobsters;
The devil is a-waiting to invite them all to tea.'

Sheila and Nigel were leaving. 'Sheila!' called Edwin.
There were claps and commiseration for the singer, hard
looks for Edwin. He tried desperately to carve a path to
his departing wife. 'Sheila!'

'Won't I do?' said a brassy woman. She was no artist: a
tradeswoman merely, driven to the membership of many
clubs by the Home Office ban on street peddling. She had
flesh – better than paint – to offer to rich Edwin. The
singer, grasping the neck of his guitar, came up to Edwin
and said:

'Bad manners are something I can't stand. I can stand
deliberate insults even less.' He gripped Edwin's jacket. 'I
want an apology.'

'Why? What for? Look, it's my wife out there. I've got to get to her. For Christ's sake –'

'You called me a sheila. I heard you distinctly. You've been getting at me all evening. Well, I won't have it.'

Edwin tugged his coat loose and tried to get away. The singer went for Edwin's collar. Edwin grew angry and hit out. The singer made a grab for Edwin's hair. To his horror it came away sweetly in his hand. 'Now see what you've done,' said the brassy woman. 'You ought to be had up for that.'

The Byronic wig now began to travel swiftly at head-level through the club, as in a forfeit game where, everybody fearing that the music will suddenly stop, there is a psychotic passing on of the balloon. Edwin chased it. F. Willoughby was no help; he laughed niggerishly, showing tombstone teeth. The wig reached the bar and rested for a brief space above the barman's squint. Then it swiftly completed the ellipse, returning, amid much applause, to Edwin via a woollen-bodied girl who clumsily curtseyed.

'You don't want to take too much notice, dear,' said the brassy woman. 'Let them laugh if they want to. I think bald-headed men are attractive.' Not unattractive herself, though brassy: a brassbold face, the curls of her brass-coloured hair set hard, breasts that seemed to promise the hardness of brass under the mustard sweater. It was nice of her to say that. Edwin went outside and looked left and right. No sign of either of them. They'd probably picked up a cab. Or were in some pub or other near here. It was a wearisome and drunken business, looking for one's wife.

Chapter Twenty-two

Time was the trouble, so far as pub-searching for her was concerned: there was so little of it left. Soon, when the barman of his fourth pub called it, there was none of it left. Edwin had a double Scotch and twenty Senior Service in each of the first three pubs, as well as four pounds twelve and a penny, looking round all the time for a sign of Sheila. Fondling the mounting tide of real money in his trouser pocket, he began to wonder why he was searching for her. Then he remembered: love. That was it, love. He knew there was something.

'Do take that thing off your head,' said the brassy woman. 'You look ever so much nicer without it. Honest. I love bald men.' The barman had called last orders, and there she was at the bar. 'Thank you, dear,' she said. 'I'll have what you're having, and you'd better buy a bottle to take away.'

'I've had enough,' said Edwin. 'Enough's as good as a –'

'Never in this world,' she said. 'The night is young and you're so beautiful,' and she performed one of those subtle ritual hip movements that women sometimes make.

'I should be saying that,' said Edwin, 'really.'

'Never mind,' she said. 'Plenty of time for compliments. And,' she said to the barman, taking her double Scotch, 'this gentleman wants a bottle of Martell Three Star to take away.' Edwin handed over another five-pound note.

'You've got plenty of those, guv,' said the barman humorously. 'You make them or something?'

'Yes,' said Edwin. 'Pretty good for an amateur, eh?' All

laughed heartily at this facetious exchange. The woman said:

'What's your name, dear?' Edwin thought quickly and answered:

'Eddie Railton.'

'Whose leg are you trying to pull? Eddie Railton's a trumpet-player on the telly. Was, I should say. A doctor now. But he's on tomorrow night, so they tell me. Smashing-looking he is.'

'All right,' said Edwin. 'You win. My real name's Bob Courage.'

'Oh, that's a sweet name. Like a big sheepdog or something. Now isn't that really sweet? You ought to have your hair over your eyes, really.' Edwin obliged, tipping his wig low. She laughed gratifyingly loud, so he said: 'What's your name?'

'Coral,' she answered, not without a simper. Funny, thought Edwin, how a woman can partake of her name, while a man's is just something he owns. The name made her hardness less metallurgical, drew attention to mouth and nails; its marine associations turned her eyes sea-green. But then, of course, it probably wasn't her real name.

The barman called time and a soggy towel draped the beer pumps. 'It *is* all night you want, isn't it?' said Coral. 'It isn't just one of those quickie larks before the last train?'

'Well,' said Edwin, 'I've nowhere to go. I mean, I'm not going back there to sleep three in a bed with all those vegetables. I did think of going to a hotel or somewhere.'

'And I know the very place,' said Coral, taking his arm.

'But,' said Edwin, 'I ought to explain. Don't think it's a matter of money or anything, because you're welcome to anything you like, but, you see, it's a bit difficult.'

'What is? Christ, it's freezing out here.' It was certainly cold; cold sat in the streets like a personification of cold. 'Taxi!' called Coral. Edwin swung his bottle of Martell like a truncheon, not liking the look of some Italianate young anthropoids ahead. 'Taxi!' called Coral again, and a taxi drew up. 'You, is it?' said the driver. '*You?*' mocked Coral. 'Who's You when she's at home?' and she named a hotel off Tottenham Court Road.

'The point is,' said Edwin, as they moved off, 'that there's a certain difficulty. A failure of the libido, they call it.'

'That's all right,' said Coral. 'I've had all sorts in my time. As long as you're not kinky I don't mind. But I knew when I saw you you weren't kinky. You can always tell from the eyes. You'd never believe what some of them ask for, never believe half of it.'

'The point is,' said Edwin, 'that I can't really ask for anything.'

'There was one of these,' said Coral, 'and he had me at his place and the place was full of coffins. But one of these had a side-door you could slide out of. Weird? I've never seen anything like it. But it was five nicker a nail, and things weren't too good after the Yanks left. There he was, hammering them in, shouting "Prepare to go and meet thy God," and me trembling like a bloody leaf inside, hoping that trap-door was going to open all right. It did, or I wouldn't be here to tell you, would I? And there are some who'll give anything to be whipped. *Anything.* Thank your stars you're not in my profession, coming up against all these kinky types, that's all I can say. Straightforward's good enough for me, with a bit of a cuddle before and after.' She gave Edwin a bit of a cuddle.

'The point is,' said Edwin.

'We're there,' said Coral. 'Don't tip this one too well, he's a bit saucy.' Edwin paid with real money, for which the driver evinced little gratitude. ('A five-pound note's what you deserve, my lad,' thought Edwin.) And he paid real money in advance to the reception clerk of the hotel, an hotel that did not seem to be merely functional: there was a tiny television room, and the clerk sped them upstairs with no wink or leer. The bedroom had a homely double bed with a chamber-pot gleaming glacially beneath; there was an electric fire with a shilling meter. 'It's bloody freezing,' cried Coral. 'Open that bottle and give me a swiggy.' Edwin laid his silver on the bed, looking for shillings. 'And ten quid on the mantelpiece,' said Coral, 'while you're at it. Then we can forget about the money side, see.'

They sat by the fire on a couple of bedroom chairs, drinking brandy from the one tooth-glass. 'I like a good talk,' said Coral, 'before getting down to it. It makes it more human, somehow. And it's nice to talk to somebody educated, the same as you are.'

'The point is,' said Edwin.

'I always had leanings that way myself. Books and music and so forth. But where does it get you? Where's it got *you*? Bald-headed before your time, with study, I dare say, studying away at books, as I can see from your eyes. Not that I don't like bald heads. I like bald heads very much. Do take that thing off,' said Coral. 'That's right. That's lovely. That's really attractive.' And she gave Edwin's scalp a sticky kiss. Then she raised her skirt unseductively and began to unfasten her stocking-tops. 'Warmer in bed than out,' she said.

'The point is,' said Edwin, 'that I can't.'

She paused, fingers at rest on a suspender. 'Can't what?' she said, her eyes on him. 'You had something shot off in the war or something?'

'No, no, it isn't that, that's all right. It's just that I can't. Failure of the libido.' Edwin gulped. 'That's what they call it.'

'That's what you said before,' said Coral. 'Whatever part of the body that is.'

'It's not a part of the body,' said Edwin. 'I just can't work up any interest, not in any woman. That's why my wife's gone off with this other man, a painter with a beard.'

'They're no better for having beards,' said Coral, shaking her head. 'Hair doesn't make them any better at it. That's where the Bible goes wrong. I don't care much for hair, anyway. Anyway, what do you mean by that remark? About no interest in women?'

'Please,' said Edwin, 'don't get angry about it. It doesn't mean that I don't think you're attractive. You are, very. But I don't want to do anything about it, that's all.'

'Would you rather be with another man, is that it? You're queer, is that it? Well, what the bloody hell did you start on me for?'

'I didn't start anything,' said Edwin, 'as you well know. And you haven't got anything to complain about. There's your money on the mantelpiece. You can just go, can't you? Ten quid for doing nothing.'

'That's right,' said Coral. 'Send me out in the cold. Make me look a bloody fool down there at the desk. I've got my pride, haven't I?'

'But surely,' said Edwin, 'you only regard this as a means of making money?'

'Oh, money,' she sneered. 'Money's all right, I suppose. But life can't be just money and nothing else, can it? I mean to say. It gets me, that does. Gets me where it hurts most. I mean, there you are, and you're not a queer, and you're not kinky, and you've had nothing shot off in the war. And then I strip off and lie down on that bed or in front of that fire and all you can do is say you're not interested. And you with that bald head as well.'

'Is that honestly all that you people sell?' said Edwin. 'Passivity? Just becoming a thing, a temporary receptacle for dirty water? That gets *me* where it hurts most!'

'Do you mean to say,' said Coral in wonder, 'that this is your first time? You've never been before? I'm your first one?'

'Well, you're not going to be,' said Edwin, 'as you know. But,' he said, 'I suppose yes, you are. There was never any need to. I married young, you see. What I mean is, I've never paid for it before.'

'And you needn't pay now,' said Coral, 'if you're going to use that tone of voice. I have my feelings, the same as anybody else. I'm not going to be insulted.'

'Please, please,' said Edwin, 'I'm not insulting you. Please. I like you. I think you're nice. But I just can't do anything. That's all there is to it.'

'Oh no,' said Carol, 'that's not it.' She rose from the bedroom chair and took off her jumper militantly, her suspender-belt as if she were buckling a belt for offensive action. 'You get stripped off, too,' she said, 'and get in there and warm it. We'll soon see whether you can do anything or not.'

Chapter Twenty-three

Edwin woke up guiltily late. He knew it was late, because he could hear the loud sounds of London at work. The loud sounds of London, anyway. Coral had gone, leaving the wig to curl like a cat on her pillow. Edwin was exhausted but had a large appetite. He called in the dispersed fragments of the night and roughly pieced them together, like a torn document. She had worked hard, that girl. She had earned her ten pounds, which, he saw, had left the mantelpiece. He hoped she would have no trouble with them. Naked Edwin got out of bed shivering and switched on the electric fire. There was no glow, and he then remembered that they had not troubled to switch it off the night before. He searched his pockets for a shilling and was interested to find that all his silver was gone. All his notes had gone too, the counterfeit as well as the real. Oh well, she had earned it all, he supposed. Still, he would have liked to be able to buy some breakfast. She had left all his cigarettes, spoils of several duped pubs and his matches. That was kind of her. Edwin put on trousers and shirt and socks and washed desultorily in the basin, wiping himself with the bedsheets. She had worked hard, that girl: a procession of many traction engines to crush a peanut. No, that was going too far. There had been an establishment of definite proof that rehabilitation was possible: a speck of gold in the river. Edwin completed his dressing and, before donning his wig, examined the stranger's bald scalp with care. Something was growing there, too: a kind of fluff sensible to the touch. He turned himself into quite-the-little-poet with a flourish and then prepared to go, not altogether displeased. His pockets were stuffed with cigarettes. He had matches. As that girl had sagely said, money wasn't everything. But he was so bloody hungry. She might at least have left him a pound. Two pounds.

Edwin went downstairs and into the entrance hall. There was a different reception clerk on duty who greeted Edwin with cheerful familiarity. 'The lady left a note,' he said, handing him a folded piece of toilet-paper. The message, unsigned, was TWISTER. She had a lot of room to talk, hadn't she? Twister, indeed. 'We get a lot of people like that here,' said the cheerful clerk. 'Takes all sorts to make a world.' As Edwin walked down the busy street towards a large chain restaurant whose directors had fed him with individual fruit pies during the war, he composed a litany to himself:

> Ineffectual fornicator,
> Purge of poor publicans,
> Kettle-mob catamite,
> Cheater of Chasper,
> Furniture-fracturer,
> Light-hearted ligger,
> Counterfeit-cashman,
> Free meal filcher,
> > Prey on us.

He was surprised to see, from a clock outside a watch-repairer's, that it was nearly eleven-thirty. He hurried to the great restaurant and was fascinated to find that a mad sort of compartmentalization had made – for the literal-minded – a full and balanced meal impossible. For there was a coffee-bar, a steak-house, a chicken grill, a potato parlour (Steaming Jumbo Murphies Slashed And Buttered), a yumyum pastry shop, and even a jungly-looking place called Lettuce Land. Edwin eventually found a Pickwick Breakfast Bar, sat on a stool of contrived discomfort at the counter, and looked at the menu.

'From six a.m. for Early Birds till Noon for Lie-abeds,' it said. Charming. A tired girl (no Pickwick Breakfasts for her) wearing a tall chef's cap took his order. He proposed flapjacks with maple syrup, haddock with two poached eggs, pork sausages and bacon with *rognons sautés*, toasted muffins, marmalade, much coffee. Various Pickwickian characters looked down from the wall in approval. Seeing Sam Bilabial Fricativeeller reminded him about his little popular article. Later. Plenty of time for that. Meanwhile there was a great deal to be said for sexual exercise, promoting as it did such appetite. Edwin was pleased to see a brisk trade in breakfasts and a Gents W.C. conveniently placed. Charming.

He ate like a raven, belching a rich counterpoint of flavours at the end. He finished the coffee, lit a cigarette, and saw that the serving girl was busy with a huge urn that made a strangled sound. He got off his stool and went to the Gents. There he took off his wig and his tie, stuffing them under his shirt. He limped out, gormless and aged, carrying a lavatory brush. He took his time, even pausing to throw glances of hungry censure at the breakfasters. Then he limped to the door, looked right and left in tremulous indecision, and shambled slowly round the corner. Easy, all too easy. And now it was time for the Anchor, wearing dark glasses to hide himself from possible Bob, and there undoubtedly at last would be Sheila, anxious and loving, having heard all, but now perhaps pleased to know that he was cured. Cured? He could prove it. The return of desire. Restoration of normal olfaction. No more syncopes. The future? Don't be silly, the future doesn't exist. Living for the day was most stimulating and remarkably easy, he thought, tonguing out sausage gristle from a back tooth.

But he needed a little money: enough for a pint if Sheila were late showing up or, perhaps, did not today show up at all. There was no particular hurry about Sheila, when all was said and done. Edwin saw a public library, pigeon-soiled soot-gnawed Ruskin, and went in. In the entrance hall were lavatories to right and left, so Edwin proceeded to one and voided a pint or so of diuretic coffee, fitted on his wig, tied his tie, and was ready for more petty crime. Or was it going to be that, really? For, though he was to take, he had given: the Gents now had two lavatory brushes.

The Reading Room he entered was raftered and grim. Shabby men stood at the newspaper-lecterns as at the treadmill; here the rarest wit of the feuilletons must crumble, the news of divorced earls became obscene. At rows of factory benches old men were reading in tough cloth cases, prayer-book-coloured with faded gilt titles, *The Nineteenth Century and After*, *The Poultry-Fancier's Gazette*, *Chambers' Journal*, *The Seventh Day Adventist's Quarterly*, *Blackwood's*, *The Church Organist*, *The Home Pig-Breeder*. One old man vented a loud bark of laughter at, improbably, something he had seen in *Punch*. Edwin went over to the shelves where mouldered the Encyc. Brit. and Grove and Jane's *Fighting Ships*. He chose a rather recent and still clean-covered book on heraldry, its pages not at all disfigured by the library brand of ownership. The flyleaf had an accession number but there was no book-plate. Edwin openly tucked this book under his arm and, humming quietly like an old man in the sun, strolled round the daily papers to see the headlines. Another teenage male pop singer, he noted, had been torn by girl admirers; a vendor of smuggled watches – not Bob, unfortunately – had been arrested; a fierce winter was forecast; the American President wanted peace. Interesting. Leisurely and still humming quietly, Edwin walked out of the Reading Room and back to the lavatory. There he very carefully tore out the flyleaf and made sure, by slow examination, that the book now looked an orphan. He walked out of the building, heraldry under his arm, and sought a street of secondhand books. The shadiest-looking shop had a twitching shifty man with three pairs of glasses. Edwin asked for fifteen shillings. 'I find,' he said, 'that I already have a copy in my library. Not even the most insatiable amateur of the subject needs more than one.' He demurred at the offer of five shillings but finally accepted it.

What an easy world it was to live in, this big innocent trusting London. Back to nature, with fruit growing everywhere for the plucking. Only a fool, really, would return to the hard graft of teaching linguistics under a Burma sun. Whether he was completely a fool he hadn't yet decided.

Chapter Twenty-four

''E's 'ere,' cried Harry Stone, punching Edwin hard as soon as he set foot in the public bar. 'Where ve bleedin' 'ell you bin? Buggerin' off like vat wivaht permission, ve 'ole of bleedin' town bein' scoured for you.' Leo Stone and Les looked reproachfully, as did various others outside the circle whom Harry Stone infected with his bitter wail. 'You're avin' one 'arf,' said Harry Stone, 'one 'arf only, and ven you're goin' to be locked up in our place, whever vose two little German bitches are vere or not. You see,' he said to Les, 'you couldn't be trusted. Give 'im you to look after and ven what happens? 'E's gorn, 'e doesn't come back till bleedin' near free o'clock frowin'- aht time.'

'Look here,' said Les, 'I'm not having that. Man is born free and is everywhere in chains, as J. B. Priestley says. It's downright indecent to lock a man up against his will. It's up to the man's own common sense, the way I see it. If a man can't see reason about it himself, then there's nothing that anybody can do about it.'

'Vis,' said Harry Stone, passion in every limb, 'is exceptional. 'E won't or can't see bleedin' reason. 'E can't see ve importance of keepin' vat bald 'ead safe till after to-night. Cor,' he said, looking up at Edwin's wig. 'Jesus Christ alone knows what 'e's been lettin' appen' to it. Let's 'ave a shufti.' He whipped off Edwin's curls and walked like a panther round the naked head. 'Needs a good goin' over,' he said, 'but otherwise it looks all right. Bleedin' wonder, vough, considerin' vat 'e's been aht all night doin' 'oo knows what. Come on,' he said bitterly, thumping Edwin, 'knock vat back, and ven you're comin' wiv Leo and I.'

'Leo and me.'

'Leo and I. I'm bleedin' comin' as well.' And Edwin was at once escorted from the public bar by the Stone twins, one gripping him hard at either side, and the dog Nigger prancing and barking all about.

'My wife,' said Edwin. 'What about my wife?'

'We've 'ad to tell your wife a bleedin' lot of lies,' said Harry Stone. 'To keep vat 'ead pertected for tonight.'

'You've seen her, then?' said Edwin, struggling to get free. 'Where have you seen her?'

'She's in the saloon bar right now,' said Leo Stone, 'drinking with that yob with the beard.' Edwin struggled harder and the dog snarled at him.

'You shouldn't 'ave said vat, Leo,' said Harry Stone. 'Now you'll 'ave 'im agitated and it won't do vat 'ead any good. Listen 'ere,' he said bitterly. 'She's no friend of yours, your missis isn't. You know what 'appened? She went to ve 'ospital, see, to see 'ow you was gettin' on, and vey told 'er vere vat you'd done a bunk and vey was all very worried. So she's goin' to get in touch wiv ve law and 'ave a bleedin' cordon of coppers all rahnd ve town closin' in on you. She's goin' to tell vem you're dangerous and 'ave got to be picked up and shoved back in vere.' He let his right shoulder shiver in the general direction of the hospital.

'Oh,' said Edwin. 'She did that, did she?'

'Yes,' said Harry Stone, and, with a toxic essence of bitterness – gall, wormwood and aloes distilling their innermost heart in a single word – he said, his teeth clamped: 'Women.'

'But she'll never know where you are,' said Leo Stone 'not till it's too late, that is. And she can't get out of the saloon bar of the Anchor, not for a long time.'

'Why? How?'

'Do you fink, said Harry Stone, 'vat me and 'im is

177

brainless, like you, even vough you are a bleedin' perfesser? Don't you use your bleedin' eyes? Didn't you see
vat lorry jammed in ve alleyway vere, and nobody not
able to get neiver aht nor in, so vat all ve saloon bar
customers is trapped in vere for a 'ell of a long time?
Vat's where ve door to ve saloon bar is,' he shook Edwin,
'in vat alleyway. Vere's some as won't get to work vis
afternoon,' he said sadly, 'if vat driver does 'is work
proper.'

'But,' said Edwin, 'if I could explain, if I could show –
I'm all right now, you see. I'm cured. I always knew that
the operation wasn't really necessary. If I could just explain to her –' But he was being led farther and farther
away from his wife. 'Is there a telephone there?' he asked.
'If I could speak –'

'Vere's no telephone vere,' said Harry Stone. 'Vere's only
ve box across ve road, and nobody can't get to vat. Now
don't you worry abaht anyfink till tonight's over, see.
Vere'll be plenty of time for worryin' when you've won
vis prize, and ven you won't 'ave to worry.'

'What were these lies you told?' asked Edwin.

'Nothing much,' said Leo Stone, shrugging his left
shoulder. 'We just said you were living with an old bag
somewhere near Stepney. A motherly old bag, we said,
who'd taken a fancy to you. But we said you came up for
air now and again and she wasn't to worry too much.
That's when she started on about getting in touch with
the law.'

They had arrived at a high Regency façade, noble in
decay, its former family unity now meanly nibbled into
innumerable rented cells. 'Vis is it,' said Harry Stone
with distaste. 'Vis is where we 'ang aht in ve utmost
discomfort.'

After two flights of naked stairs, the original Regency
paper on the well-wall scrawled on and peeling, they
came to a door that had long lost its paint. Inside was a
large high room with two beds in it. In one bed lay

Renate, in the other two flat-chested girls whom Edwin remembered from that Sunday afternoon in the club, the German girls who had found his bedroom slippers. They were silent in calm efficient sleep; she snorted and bubbled in irregular rhythms. 'Look at vem,' said Harry Stone in disgust. 'Wake up,' he cried, 'you bleedin' German sow,' kicking, with a foot held athletically high, the breech presentation of Renate.

'Don't do that,' said Leo Stone. 'Remember that it's me who's living with her, not you.' But his tone was not harsh.

'You kiddin'?' said his twin. 'We bofe live wiv 'er, God 'elp us, but you can do ve kickin' if you want to.' He turned away as to vomit.

Renate woke, bleared, with much mouth-smacking. '*So*,' she said. '*Wieviel Uhr?*'

'Time you got out of vat bleedin' bed,' said Harry Stone, 'and got somefink goin' on vat stove. None of us 'ere 'asn't eaten since last Sunday's breakfast.' In the case of the Stone twins, Edwin thought, that must be literally true; but, being hungry again, he did not dissociate himself from this general cry of famishment. Renate sat on the edge of the bed in an agony of yawning, her large Teutonic breasts lolling and wobbling, horny feet flat to the bare floor. After her yawns she seemed to recognize Edwin. 'You, my darling,' she said, nodding. 'Five pounds doppel gin yesternight have I yes drunken.' She shook her head as though bemused. Then she put on shoes and a man's overcoat – probably interchangeably both Leo's and Harry's – and quite amiably began to see about a meal.

Edwin sat on the now free bed and looked around the room. There was a fair Regency window giving on to television aerials and the autumn sky. There was a chest of drawers and a wardrobe, both of the kind seen flanking, outside junk-shops, an opulent radiogram at seven pounds whose bleat is that of an old woman trying to talk young girls' language. There was a gas-fire and a gas-ring and a meter. Renate turned on the ring, but there was no hiss; struck a match, but there was no flame. 'Schilling,' she said, 'is needing.' Leo Stone turned on her like a man whose neck is broken, and said:

'A pile of shillings was there yesterday. What you done with them, eh? What you done with that pile of shillings that I gathered, often begging on my hands and knees in this district that's so hungry for bloody shillings for old maids' bed-sitters, with agony and humiliation in the face of frequent refusals, eh?' This was a new Leo Stone without thespian and commercial voice-masks. He approached his mistress like an ape with a broken neck, his arms stiff with hooks at the ends of them. 'Shillings, shillings, shillings,' he said in crescendo. 'What should go for power and warmth and nutriment goes for gin. That's it, isn't it, eh? Gin. How many times have I not come home here weary and longing for the comforts and nourishment that are a man's right, regardless of colour and creed, and found instead the gas dead and no money for it? Is this the reward I get for the pampering and fattening of one who is, by rights, the enemy? The enemy, yes, by God. For the house of bondage in modern times was bloody Deutschland. Ah, *ja, ja, richtig*. And there's the bloody defeated, eh, in the lap of luxury, fattened and coddled by Jewish sweat, all the shillings for the gas dispersed and converted into gin for a bloody gin-soaked sauerkraut-guzzling apology for an old bag of a bloody bastardizing inefficient apology for a no-good layabout of an unsavoury and unappetizing sort of a whore.' He took breath. Harry Stone said:

'Vat goes for me too.' The two German daughters slept deeply in a bliss of myth: the ring in the forest and the guardian dragon and the shining hero with the sword. Renate said loudly:

'Ach, Jew. Jewish pig. Fat of Jewish pigs to make fat German land. No good else.'

'You'll take that back,' said Leo Stone, coming nearer. 'You'll take back that bloody slander or I'll cut your throat with this bread-knife here.' Renate grew visibly frightened. 'Now,' said Leo Stone, gripping the lapel of the overcoat, 'take it all back.'

'Jewish pig and hound,' persisted Renate. 'Jewish fat for soap to wash swinehouse.' Leo Stone, his face alight with the long hates of his people, said:

'The only good ones you ever had in Germany were Jews? Yes?'

'No, no. Jews pigs. Oh,' said Renate, strangling hands upon her. 'Yes, yes. Jews good, very good. You stop now, Jewish pig. Jews very good.'

'You,' said Leo Stone fiercely to Edwin. 'You're educated. Who were the big German people? Writers and whatnot?'

'Oh,' said Edwin. 'Look, I've got two separate shillings here. Let's have that fire on, for God's sake.' Harry Stone came and collected the coins bitterly. He lit the gas-fire. Its miniature pillars of fire hissed and glowed comfortably. 'Well,' said Edwin, 'there was Goethe and Schiller and Heine. And Kotzebue and Wagner and Schumann. And Nietzsche and Kant and Schopenhauer and Beethoven. And Hans Sachs and Martin Luther.'

'And they were all Jews, weren't they?' threatened Leo Stone. 'Everyone of those German bastards was a Jew. Say yes, blast you, or I'll do you in.'

'No, no,' said Renate. 'Yes, yes,' she amended. 'All Jew. And Hitler dirty bloody swine. He Jew too.'

Leo Stone dropped relenting hands. 'As long as you know,' he said, 'who's the master. We want no trouble, really. We want love and peace and harmony, as was taught in olden times. We want shillings in the meter and a hot meal ready when we ask for it. Now get cracking on that.' The gas-ring was hissing its poison. Renate lighted the jets. Leo kissed her on the cheek. All was forgotten.

'I was finkin',' said Harry Stone, 'vat we could use vem two.' His sad eyes of speculation were on the sleeping sisters. Edwin said:

'Isn't the club open this afternoon?'

'You kiddin'?' cried Harry Stone. 'After vose visits from ve law? And you passin' aht and makin' vem get suspicious? We got to lie low for a time.'

'I think I see what you mean,' said Leo Stone. 'Dressing them up and using them as a sort of pair of bridesmaids. And he could have a sort of stick in his hand and a train behind. Like the Coronation.'

'Vat's right,' said Harry Stone. 'Vat curtain vere might do ve job.' And indeed there was a fine moth-eaten length of what looked like red flannel bunched at one end of a runner at the top of the window.

'These girls,' said Edwin. 'What do they really do?'

'Well,' said Leo Stone, 'it's a night job, you see. We don't quite know what it is, but they do it together. Two nice girls they are if you get to know them. We call them Lili and Marlene.' Their mother meanwhile was frying some garlicky mess, singing:

> 'Mit blankem Eis und weissem Schnee
> Weihnachten kommt, juchhe, juchhe!'

And at the very mention of Christmas she began to cry gently, tears sizzling in the pan, thinking of the Christ-child and the candles, the silent snowy night and the tingling heavens. Evening came, cosy with only the two foci of burning gas. Leo Stone said: 'Christ, I nearly forgot. I've got to rehearse. Not a bad idea really, trying it out on him.'

'Just ve song?' said Harry Stone, handing his twin a walking-stick.

'Just the song. I can ad lib the rest. You know: sorry I'm a bit late getting here, but I just got blocked in the passage. That kind of thing. That comes easy enough. Lights,' he called. 'Music.' No music sounded, but Harry

Stone switched on the one bare bulb and the room became less cosy. The sleeping sisters stirred, groaned, frowned. Leo Stone sang in raucous old-style Cockney:

> 'Every night my old man
> Goes aht to ve boozer.
> Vere 'e drinks ve night awye,
> Spendin' all is 'ard-earned pye.
> Muvver knows when 'e comes 'ome
> Vat 'e will abuse 'er.
> 'E'll 'ave a crack at little Jack
> Across ve kitchen tible.
> 'E'll 'ave a go at Uncle Joe
> And also Auntie Mibel.
> Us kids is up in bed
> But know what 'e's abaht.
> And when we 'ear is tread
> We all begin to shaht:'

'And now,' said Harry Stone, 'we've got to join in ve chorus.' Leo Stone sang, at the same time performing a rudimentary stick-dance:

> ''E's got 'em on, 'e's got 'em on,
> 'E's got 'em on agyne.
> Just been to ve boozer
> At ve bottom of ve lyne.
> Oh, now e's 'ere wiv is belly full of beer
> And 'e's laughin' like a dryne.
> 'E's got 'em on, 'e's got 'em on,
> 'E's got 'em on agyne.'

And then, for want of a shilling, the light went out, and there was Leo Stone, a shadow against the gas-fire, leaping and shouting in the repeat of the chorus. 'Eat,' called Renate. 'Eat is ready, my darlings.'

''E's got to 'ave vat 'ead gone over wiv ve razor,' wailed Harry Stone. 'And vere's no light. Light, light,' he moaned. 'Oh, bleedin' 'ell.'

Roused by the smell of the nearly invisible food that

Renate slopped on to four plates, the dog Nigger crawled out from under the girls' bed, groaning and stretching. The girls turned over together, like another comedy turn, and the bells of their Eskimo hair could just about be seen, shaking. They slept solid. But Nigger wagged his tail at the complicated aroma of garlic, tomato sauce, burnt fat, baked beans, fried stale bread, bacon scraps and crumbled cheese. He put his chin to Leo Stone's knee, as to a fiddle, and looked up in firelit worship. Those bitter words of his master and master's mistress had been to him but as the sound of flutes and viols.

' 'Ave vem two vere in bed got any manny for ve light?' asked Harry Stone. 'Aht all ve bleedin' night and fetchin' no manny in.' He forked in food from his dark plate, standing by the mantelpiece. 'What in ve name of God is ve kind of work vey do, bringin' no manny in to ve 'ouse?'

'Their day,' said Renate, 'is sleep-time. Money in sleep-time man spends not.'

'But what kind of work do vey do?' Harry Stone insisted.

'For their mother they work,' said Renate, and she spoke, wiping her plate with bread, with pride. 'Hard work, small money, but I am not angry if they enough each night for one bottle gin bring. That is enough, for I am no cruel mother.'

'WHAT DO VEY DO?' cursed Harry Stone, and he pronged the wall with his fork.

'What could they do?' said their mother. 'No education because of the cruel war they have not. Little English speak they. But there gives work for girls with willing body in night-time London. They work hard, and some-times in schillings only the money to me they bring.'

'Shillin's,' said Harry Stone bitterly. 'Shillin's for ve light and ve gas, and you 'as to spend it all on gin.' But he groped about for a razor, fetched a tin mug of cold water from the landing, and then ordered Edwin to come to the gas-fire. The shaving was done carefully, though both patient and agent had to crouch by the glowing gas-columns. A pleasant domestic evening: two German prostitutes in bed, their mother sucking her teeth, Leo Stone audible from the landing lavatory, Nigger washing plates and frying-pan, Edwin becoming smooth as an egg by the fire. 'Lovely, vat is,' said Harry Stone at last, his phrenologist's fingers feeling Edwin's scalp. 'You'll walk away wiv it tonight if you don't do nuffin' stupid.'

Chapter Twenty-five

Out of his five shillings Edwin now had left only four-pence. Three men and a dog with only fourpence be-tween them had to reach a cinema on the other side of London. They must walk, then, but there seemed to be plenty of time, and Edwin had plenty of cigarettes. It was decided that the fourpence should be spent on some little treat for Nigger. After some argument and peering into cheap butchers' windows they finally bought a few bones with rags of meat on them. These Nigger refused to touch. Hard-faced Harry Stone returned the bones to the butcher with disparaging remarks on their quality, was given back the fourpence, and then bought an old fish head from a fishmonger's that was just closing. Nigger played with this for much of their journey.

There was a fine moon rising. As they walked east-wards they talked of many things. Legitimate ways of making money: a small cigarette factory fed with picked-up dog-ends; conducted night tours for American tour-ists; Leo put out to stud; old bedsprings sold as radio aerials; home-made potato crisps; face cream made out of horse fat; Nigger taught to do tricks; palmistry; Leo back on the boards; dust sold as snuff; ideas sold to great firms (a refrigerator with a back door, double-headed matches to save wood, a tickling machine, warm water sprays in W.C. pans); Renate deported and her two daughters on the bash for the Stones alone; a sixpenny soup bar with bread unlimited; miniature plaques of the Golden Hind ($\frac{1}{2}$d) sold in envelopes for ninepence to Westminster tour-ists; street-singing as blind and cripple respectively;

lonely girls met at King's Cross and sent out on the bash; expensive scent-bottles filled with Soir de Stoke-on-Trent; Edwin as the starving man in a sideshow; a cure for smoking (unlightable cigarette); Leo's body sold to queers; good honest work. Old London: the gates of the City from western Lud to eastern Ald; Finsbury Fields; St Olave's; Thames Street and Fleet Ditch; gas-flares and jellied eels; Jack the Ripper; Sweeney Todd; the Princes in the Tower; the difficulty of stealing the Crown Jewels. Classical murders; the old-time crook as gentleman; travel for broadening the mind. And all the time Nigger danced his fish head along, happy as the moon in the sky.

It was Nigger, through no fault of his own, that precipitated the trouble which almost wrecked the night. He and his masters and Edwin were only a street or so off their goal when it happened. They had reached a region already well known in the world's press as a cockpit of racial dissension, a curiously policeless district with static mobs lounging in doorways and at corners. 'Now ven,' said Harry Stone to his companions, 'go easy 'ere. Don't say nuffink, don't do nuffink. We don't want no trouble, not tonight we don't.' Edwin looked with interest at a lounging group of youths, simian-browed with horror-waxwork faces, their clothes and coiffures most, by contrast, civilized. Each jacket was as long as a British warm, the trousers were almost Second Empire, the shoes rose in layer after layer of sole. The hair of the head was piled up dramatically but was not balanced by a poetic cravat; instead, the tie was vestigial, a mere string. This was collective dandyism, thought Edwin, a crazy synthesis of rebellion and conformity. 'Stop lookin' at vem like vat,' warned Harry Stone. 'Vey'd fink nuffink of doing ve free of us.' And then happy prancing Nigger danced a little too close, fish head in his jaws, and one of the youths kicked out. Nigger, though untouched, yelped with surprise and fear, dropped his fish head and ran. 'Vat,' said

Harry Stone loudly, 'was a bleedin' filfy fing to do, dead bleedin' cowardly vat was. Vat's abaht your bleedin' mark, I reckon, a poor bleedin' defenceless dog.' Meanwhile Leo Stone, disturbed at the dog's panic, ran after him, shouting:

'Nigger! Nigger!'

It was unfortunate that three genuine Negroes from the West Indies should at that moment leave their exile-crammed house and see a white man now standing in the middle of the pavement and hear him calling gratuitous abuse:

'Nigger! Come here, you silly bastard!'

Edwin saw the three Negroes – smart men in raincoats and trilbies – advance on Leo Stone. They had had enough of white derision; they had learned that to ignore it was but to fan it. They were joined by two others of their race from another house: their ears had pricked at Leo's call. Meanwhile the seven loutish dandies were more slowly and with far less grace preparing to liquidate Harry Stone. 'And,' said Harry Stone, 'vis is just as bleedin' cowardly goin' to 'ave a go at me. I'll take any one of you 'ere on but not ve bleedin' lot of you, vat stands to reason.' It didn't, however, not to these; it was an out-worn code, the law of the fair chance. Leo Stone was explaining, genuinely shocked and apologetic, that he'd merely been calling his dog, that was all, named Nigger because of his colour. That didn't go down well. 'See,' said Leo Stone, 'I'll show you I'm telling the truth. I'll call him again. See, there he is down there.' And Leo Stone desperately, wildly called the hated name again. But Nigger did not respond; he loked back hang-dog, his tail between his legs, a nice hound but not very bright.

Edwin looked from one group to the other, bewildered. The twins were converging and their respective pursuers with them. West Indians and white louts were perhaps now smarting in an uneasy truce. Now they found themselves face to face, not really ready for battle, and suddenly they turned in surprise at the mild professorial voice of Edwin saying: 'This is so obviously pointless, isn't it? There's just been a couple of mistakes, that's all. I suggest that everybody concerned forgets all about it.' Harry and Leo Stone exchanged nods, Leo made a dash for it, and both whites and blacks found themselves preparing to kill or maim or otherwise discomfit the same man. Had it been a collective dream, that conviction of this man's being in duplicate, just for a second or so before that other man there starting talking? 'Vat's right,' said Harry Stone in a sort of loud fearful glee, 'you bleedin' lot of cowards. Not satisfied wiv 'avin' a go at each other, so now you bofe 'ave to get togever to do in a poor bleedin' Yid. Go on,' he said. 'Black unite wiv white for vat purpose.' A white lout pulled out a bicycle-chain and a quick Negro responded with a knife. In half a second they were at each other. 'Right,' said Harry Stone to Edwin. 'Leave vem to it.' They ran, shouting battle proceeding behind them, and then Nigger suddenly became brave again, barking loudly. He had lost, but perhaps now forgotten, his fourpenny fish head.

When they had run a block they stopped, winded, and there they found Leo waiting for them, his breath just about coming back. 'Vat,' said Harry Stone, 'was bleedin' lacky. Teds against Yids and Spades against Yids and nah Spades against Teds. Poor bleedin' Yids,' he said. 'Ve ole world's been against vem ever since vey started. Ve Egyptians and ve Babylonians and ve Philistines and nah vis bleedin' lot.' Harry Stone held out his arms like a Hollywood prophet. 'What 'arm,' he asked Mount Sinai, ' 'ave we done to vese bastards? When are ve Yids goin' to be bleedin' delivered from ve 'ouse of tribulation? 'Ow bleedin' long is it goin' to be?' The dog Nigger grew skittish, meeting Leo Stone again, barked and begged to be chased. Leo Stone called:

'Nigger! Nigger! Silly bastard!' Dead on cue a Negro

appeared in a cap, swaying, throwing the breath of rum before him like flower petals. 'Man,' he said, 'you got no right to say what you said just then.' A *corps de ballet* of Negroes was, Edwin was sure, about to appear in the wings. Edwin said:

'He was calling his dog. He bought this dog for a pound or quid or nicker. Hence the name, Nicker. When he utters the name he shows a slight tendency to voice the velar plosive and this makes for a certain phonemic ambiguity. He meant no harm. He did not even say what you thought he said.'

The Negro was rummily unconvinced. In the near distance the groans and thuds of inter-racial battle continued. 'I don't like all them long words,' said the Negro to Edwin, speaking as through a lamp-chimney. 'If I'm not educated whose fault is that? There was no education in them slave ships, man. Who sent us out there in them slave ships?'

'Oh, come on,' said Harry Stone. 'On our bleedin' way. All ve sins of ve bleedin' world bein' brought up just when we're on our way to a nice bleedin' innocent bald-'ead competition.' But the dog Nigger seemed to have been pursuing thoughts of a similar nature to this man's whose colour he shared. Dogs persecuted, dogs kept down, dogs chained in kennels. He lightly jumped at Edwin, caught Edwin's trouser tear in his teeth, and pulled. The trouser leg at once became a sort of slit skirt. 'Nigger, you bastard,' called Edwin as the dog raced off, a waving pennant in his jaws. 'There you go again, man,' said the rum-flavoured West Indian. 'You just asking for trouble.' And he lurched off, singing a sad slave song of the sixteenth century.

'Vat's what 'appens,' said Harry Stone, 'when you concentrate on one fing to ve detriment of anover. You bleedin' bad dog, Nigger,' he parenthesized mildly. 'We'll 'ave to knock off somebody's strides when we get vere. Can't 'ave you marchin' rahnd wiv all vat leg showin'.

Indecent, apart from anyfink else. What a bleedin' evenin' vis is turnin' aht to be.'

A few more blocks and a right turn, and there, at the end of the street, was a shining cinema called the PANTHEON. They yearned towards it as to the light of their own hearthstone. Above the cinema entrance was a huge portrait of a bald actor with sensual lips and the sardonic eyes of a Mongol, presumably the prototype of all the vying hairless of this evening. 'Take off vat wig now,' said Harry Stone, 'to show vat you're a bonified competitor.' Edwin doffed the curls and thrust them for safe-keeping inside his shirt; thence a curl or two peeped out in a hint of virility. TONIGHT, yelled a floodlit streamer, MAMMOTH CONTEST. BALD ADONIS OF GREATER LONDON. WHO? 'Only one answer to vat,' said Harry Stone confidently. They made their way, Edwin's heart pounding with misgiving, towards the stage door.

Chapter Twenty-six

On his second day in the army Edwin had attended a sort
of spiritual parade at which the C.S.M. had said: 'C. of E.
this side, R.C. that side, fancy buggers in the middle.' A
fat man in a phosphorescent dinner-jacket now conducted
the same kind of segregation behind the cinema screen,
and Edwin found himself a member of a suspicious-eyed
male herd. It was not possible to see very much of these
other competitors, because the screen was gigantically
preoccupied with a cosmically panting struggle in a dark
cellar. Speech, too, was impossible because of the Brob-
dingnagian stereophonic nightmare of the music. When
colossal horses finally earthquaked over a sunlit plain,
Edwin was able to appraise his rivals. They were not
impressive: many looked as if baldness came naturally to
them, part of the syndrome of decay; there was a bald boy
of about ten who could make his scalp-skin creep, horribly. During a long silent interlude of huge kissing, a
thin artisan-type of about Edwin's own age said:

'Right lark this is.'

'Yes.'

'Not right, really, the way I see it. But somebody's got
to do it, I suppose.'

'That's right.'

'My missis'd go mad if she found out. It's the other one,
see, that made me do it.' The vast osculation suddenly
unleashed a flood of thundering horse-monsters, and
Edwin was able to hear no more. The man in the dinner-
jacket, glowing like a high herring in the dark, came
round fussily with number-cards, mouthing silently

against the noise. Edwin hung a big black 8 from round his neck. Then in a pride of trombones that was louder than any dream of Berlioz, the film came to its end and lights came up. Harry Stone appeared in underpants, thin-legged but, surprisingly, wearing sock-suspenders He handed a crumpled bundle to Edwin, saying:

'You'll 'ave to take my strides. No bleedin' good, I've looked everywhere, but I can't find one solitary pair to knock off. 'Urry up and change into vem.'

An old-time jazz band had started playing, greeted with much applause. Harry Stone performed a brief hairy-legged cakewalk, his eyes sad and grim. Nigger could be heard barking in the distance, presumably locked up in some lavatory. The trousers, Edwin found, were too short: a lot of sock was visible. Still, they would have to do. The jazz band, having given each instrument a vir-tuoso chorus, now crashed into its shipwreck climax with every man for himself. Teenage screams laced the ap-plause. Harry Stone went back to his twin, and Edwin watched from the wings the turn that followed. A sloppy young man was greeted with ecstasy. He sang of teenage love, how that and that alone was the real thing, and how life ended at twenty. He treated the microphone as a very thin teenage girl and, after bestowing various caresses upon it, he threw it to the floor and lay on the long rod of the stand, kiss-singing into the mouthpiece while his body made perceptible rutting movements. The girls' screams became orgiastic, orgasmatic. An austere age, thought Edwin, an age of economy. The opulence of *Tristan* had once been required to produce a like effect in an older generation, though a tactile effect only.

The fat phosphorescent man went on to the stage to announce that all performers tonight were strictly amateur, but some of these amateurs – who knew? – might well become professionals. The next turn, how-ever, was, he said, one that had once been professional, a long time ago, and he was to be given a big hand accordingly. The teenagers howled, left in the air in mid-orgasm, and greeted Leo Stone as if they would like to crucify him. 'Listen to vat bleedin' lot,' said Harry Stone's voice in Edwin's ear. But Leo Stone grinned, a Semite who had wandered through the buffeting world, and said that he was sorry he was late, but he'd just got blocked in the passage, that a funny thing happened to him on the way to the theatre tonight, he'd met old Abie Goldstein on the way to the synagogue with little Izzie, and old Abie said he was going to get his hair cut, that he's been out with many girls in his time, even a nun, yes a nun, she'd have nun of this and nun of that, would you believe it? He prattled on, and there was little laughter. He sang his song, which the pianist accompanied from memory and clumsily, and few joined in the chorus. Finally he said he would like to do a little monologue called 'Laugh And The World Laughs With You, Snore And You Sleep Alone'. 'Wrote vat 'imself, 'e did,' said Harry Stone with twin's pride.

'Life's a funny thing, my friends. It brings both joy and
  tears;
A fact that I've discovered as I've travelled down the years.
Life's an April day, my friends, where sun is mixed with
  rain –
A laugh or two, a joke or two, a little grief and pain.'

At this point Nigger appeared on the stage. 'Owwwww,' squealed Harry Stone, strangling his voice with clenched teeth. 'Oo ve bleedin' 'ell let 'im aht?' Nigger recognized his master and approached him with every sign of joy. 'Bugger off,' Leo Stone could be seen saying from the corner of his mouth. The unkind audience now laughed, but Leo Stone's wit was quick. He picked up Nigger, improvising slowly and loudly:

'And so through life we travel on to reach our journey's end,
  But life would be just nothing if we did not have a friend,

A friend, my friends, a little friend, as on through life we
   jog.
A girl's best friend's her mother, but a man's best friend's
   his dog.'

He bowed himself off to a ragged chord from the band,
clutching Nigger who now, with dog's perverseness, was
struggling to get away. The audience booed and cheered
ironically. Edwin was angry.

'And now,' said the phosphorus-man, 'another newcomer, who has not brought his dog with him: Lennie
Bloggs from Bermondsey, who will sing for you "A Teen-
ager's Heart".' There were fresh screams of abandon-
ment. Edwin was angrier. But Leo Stone said:

'That's all right, really. I've been seen, that's the main
thing. They've got television cameras out there. I've been
inside millions of homes tonight, that's what you've got
to remember. There'll be offers of contracts galore before
the week's out, you just wait and see.'

After Lennie Bloggs had been screamed off, the main
event of the evening was announced. 'The Bald Add
Honest of Greater London,' said the compère. 'This competition has been organized by Megalopolitan Pictures
Incorporated in connection with their film sensation
Spindrift featuring Feodor Mintoff, bald-headed heart-
throb of the silver screen, on general release next Monday.'

'What is this?' said Edwin. 'What's going on? How did
my name get into it?'

'You get in vere and win,' said Harry Stone. 'Ve name's
neiver 'ere nor vere. A cohen sidence, vat's all. You play
your cards right and you'll win.'

'But,' said Edwin, 'I thought you said that had all been
fixed. I thought you said it had all been arranged.'

'As good as,' said Harry Stone. 'Look at vem over yobs
takin' part. Vey don't stand an earfly compared wiv
you. You're 'andsome, you are. Look at vat 'ead. You
'ave confidence in vat 'ead and you'll win. Go on, now.

Vey're all marchin' on.' And he gave Edwin a push stage-wards.

'Twisters,' said Edwin, 'a pair of twisters. I'm not going on.'

'You're on, boy,' said Harry Stone. 'Bester lack.'

Edwin found himself in a circle of baldheads, marching round the stage as at prison-yard exercise. The audience cheered. Television cameras were trained on them and, on a small monitor screen, Edwin saw himself in miniature trudging round and round looking angrily out at several million viewers. In the orchestra pit the jazz band was slowly surfacing on a hydraulic platform, playing an old music hall song called 'Hair, hair, hair, he's got none on his noddle'. The leading trumpeter looked suspiciously like Dr Railton. On stage, on a rostrum with a table and mark-sheets, sat three silly beauties of television fame. An even sillier man with a floppy evening tie ran on, acknowledging the cheers of the audience with extravagant waves. 'Sorry I'm late,' he said, speaking somewhat adenoidally, 'but I just got blocked in the passage.' The audience roared. 'I've just been out with a girl,' he said. 'She was a nun. Yes, a nun. She'd have nun of this and nun of that and nun of the other.' The audience collapsed. 'Some lovely bonces here tonight,' he said. 'Real skating-rinks for flies. Look at that,' he said, slapping Edwin's like a bottom. The audience nearly died. 'Now,' he said, 'march round, you lot. Here,' he said, 'we have three lovely pieces of homework who are going to judge – Ermine Elderly, Desiree Singe and Chloe Emsworth. First of all, we eliminate the duds. Right, girls? Write down the numbers that don't stand a chance. March, slaves, march. Music, maestro.' And he lashed the competitors with a whip of air, the while the band played and the audience cried its glee. Round and round shambled the bald. 'Stop!' yelled the flop-tied man. The silly pretty judges giggled and presented their consensus. 'Fall out the following,' he cried, in a mock sergeant-major's woof that had the audience helpless. 'For'y. Firty-free. Twenny-six. Noin'een. Twelf. Foive.' Off went the eliminated, hairless to no avail. 'And,' yelled the flop-tied man, 'WE SHAKE THE BAG. Too many still in,' he said, sad. 'A lot of zombies. March, clots, march. Lefrye lefrye lefrye.' He whipped the shambling circle again, the drummer adding the synchronized crack of a rim-shot. The audience wiped streaming eyes. At the next elimination the flop-tied man dismissed two little ducks, legs eleven, doctor's chum, Downing Street, Kelly's eye, and various others. Edwin was still in. 'It's in ve bleedin' bag,' called Harry Stone from the wings.

The final elimination left Edwin and four others still circling on the stage. Now it was to be a matter of placing in bald merit order. The flop-tied man raced around as if ready to expire with excitement. The audience was ready to expire with joy. 'Here it is,' he cried. 'It's coming up now.' The melodic instruments ceased playing and only a drum rolled in slow crescendo. 'I can't see,' said the man, tottering round with a paper before his twitching eyes. 'Sure and it's a terrible thing for Oi'm bloind intoirely.' The audience micturated in mirth. 'Now,' he said in a cavalry officer's voice, 'it has all come cleah. And the winner is the winner is the winner is Numbahhhhh EIGHT.' In his excitement Harry Stone ran on to the stage and into the camera sights, trouserless. He ran off again. The band played 'Why was he born so beautiful?' with zest and some accuracy. Edwin was led downstage, linked by the flop-tie man.

'What's your name, son?' he asked Edwin. 'What did your mother call you?' Edwin told him. 'Isn't that lovely?' the man told the audience. 'Doesn't he speak posh? Ever so soup-and-fish. Now have you, as Mr Bald Adonis of Greater London, any message for the great viewing public?'

Edwin saw the first trumpeter, now clearly revealed as Dr Railton, leave the stand quickly and go off. 'I've nothing to say,' said Edwin, 'except that the sooner I get out of here the better.'

'Oh, so that's the attitude, is it?' said the flop-tied man in mock indignity. 'What's the matter, I smell or something? Well, here's somebody you'll like, son. Isn't she lovely, eh?' On came a gold lamé vision with nacreous shoulders, bosom, smile, to the noise of music, cheers and whistles. 'Here she is, your sweetheart and mine, if we were lucky, that is. RAYNE WATERS,' he announced. The audience went mad. Rayne Waters kissed Edwin's baldness then put her arm in his. Edwin saw a cheque in her slim flame-tipped fingers: for ten pounds only. Surely the Stone twins had insisted it was a hundred? Rayne Waters spoke in a mid-atlantic accent, cunningly designed to give no offence to Americans.

'This must be a very big moment for you,' she said. Edwin was sure that he saw men in uniform in the wings, institutional men impossible to resist.

'Not really,' said Edwin. 'I've known bigger moments, much bigger. As a matter of fact, I feel somewhat ashamed at having been a party to all this. So typical, isn't it, of what passes for entertainment nowadays? Vulgarity with a streak of cruelty and perhaps a faint tinge of the perversely erotic. Shop girls blown up into Helen of Troy. Silly little men trying to be funny. Stupid screaming kids. Adults who ought to know better. Here's my message to the great viewing public.' He leaned forward and spat full into the microphone a vulgar, cruel, erotic word. There was a sensation. History was made. Edwin ran to the prompt side wings and quite certainly found strong men, directed by Dr Railton, ready to take him. On the O.P. side were the Stone twins fighting ineffectually with other institutional toughs. 'You'll 'ave to make a bleedin' jump for it,' said Harry Stone. 'Give me vem bleedin' trousers back first.' Edwin ran back onstage, took a jump from behind the floats and landed on the musicians' hydraulic platform. Stands and music collapsed flutteringly and tinnily, and a piano-accordion played a dismal chord as it went over. Edwin leapt into the audience, hearing anger behind him and a dog's bark. The audience were frightened and held back their skirts as Edwin raced up the rake of the auditorium. But one member of the audience stopped him in his flight to say: 'May I just briefly express my entire agreement, sir, with what you said just then?' From the stage it seemed that a voice cried: 'Stop him. A danger to the public. A cerebral tumour. May run berserk at any time. Don't let him get away.' This encouraged the audience to give Edwin plenty of room for his escape. A woman screamed and shouted: 'Come over here, Alfie, stay with me, Alfie, it's a bogeyman, Alfie.'

Edwin reached the top of the mild hill and looked down at the stage. He thought he heard Harry Stone's fighting voice above all others crying. 'Take vat in ve bleedin' cake-'ole.' Nigger was giving a growl preludial to trouser-ripping. There was a certain well-lighted confusion on the stage and somebody trying to apologize to the television audience. Edwin escaped through curtained EXIT and found himself in the vestibule among yearning cut-outs of film stars. He ran panting across the soft-footed carpeting, the colour of digestive biscuits, to the great glass doors and the street. A known voice greeted him.

'Got a little bone to pick, haven't we?' said Bob Courage. 'You and me, eh? And perhaps the boys. Very annoyed they were about what you did. Come on, get in.' A cruel grip braceleted Edwin's right wrist, Bob administered a token backhanded slosh on the nose as an earnest of things to come, and then Edwin was shoved into the front seat, licking a spurt of nose blood.

Chapter Twenty-seven

'This time,' said Bob, as they sidestreeted west, 'there's no smoked salmon in the back of the car. This time there's nothing for you except what you've got coming. And have you got it coming? I'll say you've got it coming.'

'It was your own fault,' said Edwin. 'That's what comes of being kinky.'

'Don't try and annoy me,' said Bob, as comfortably glowing pubs flashed into the safe and happy past. 'Don't think you can make me stop the car to give you another one on the snout and then you nip out smartly. Oh, no.' They passed a building site with cranes dipping and hammers knocking at night work. 'Sold five kettles there,' said Bob with pride, 'only the other day.' He turned fiercely on Edwin. 'Don't think you can get round me that way, because you can't. I know you for what you are. You kicked my telly in. You threw my whips out of the flaming window. You pinched my money. But I'll have it all back, never fear, in one form or another.'

'That was fake money,' said Edwin.

'Oh, fake money was it?' said sarcastic Bob. 'Shows how much you know about it, doesn't it? Well, if you want to know the truth, only part of it was fake. The rest of it was real. You always mix up the bad and the good, the fake and the real, just like in real life. As it might be you. Because a fake is what you are. That's what you are, a fake. Just like some of those fives that you pinched.'

'At least my eyes aren't crossed,' said Edwin.

'Trying to be funny, eh?' said Bob. 'Trying to draw me out, eh? I know what you're referring to, never fear.

You're referring to that bird with the helmet on pretending to be Rule Britannia. Well, he was very sensitive about that, him that did it. He was past his best, let's be honest, but there was nobody who could come in a mile of him once upon a time. Very funny,' sneered Bob. 'You know the truth about your eyes? They're false eyes, that's what they are. Just like that hair you had on. False eyes, pretending to be kinky, but no more kinky than my bottom. A deceiver, that's what you are. A snake in the grass. But you'll get what's coming to you, never fear.'

'What are you going to do with me?' asked Edwin. He was indifferent, really, to the prospect of pain, having suffered an arteriogram and an inflation of the skull. But he was intrigued by the notion of a masochist devising as a punishment something that would hurt and, by solipsist logic, thus give pleasure.

'I haven't quite made up my mind yet,' said Bob. 'But I'll think of something that the boys can do to you. Some real sort of torture that'll make you yell blue murder.'

'So the boys are there, are they?' said Edwin. 'This is going to be fun.'

Bob gave him a long sly sidelong look, driving with speed still down a back street free of traffic. 'That's where I think you're a liar,' he said. 'You won't think it's funny at all. You don't like that sort of thing. You're a pretender, that's what you are.'

'How would it be,' asked Edwin, 'if I were to give you a good going-over, with whips and everything? Great big whip-lashes on your back, with the blood pouring out all over the floor and you howling for mercy. That would be lovely, wouldn't it? And it would be a real punishment for me, seeing that I'm not kinky.'

'Don't,' said Bob, clenching his teeth and raising his shoulders in response to imaginary back-blows. 'Don't tempt me. You've got to have your punishment. That's

201

only right and fair and just. You've got to suffer. Don't mention things like that,' he warned. 'It's not fair to try that on when I'm driving.'

'Do you think,' asked Edwin, 'I could put my wig on? I feel very sensitive about this bald head, you know.'

'And you'll feel sensitive somewhere else,' said Bob, 'before the boys have finished with you. Keep those hands down where I can see them. I'm not having any more funny business from you, not likely I'm not.' He drove on, breathing deeply. 'Jock's brought in a bloke who's kinky in a different way. He's going to burn all the hair off your legs with lighted matches. That gives him a thrill. Hard to understand, but it does. He came round to see me the other day,' said Bob, now as in amiable conversation, 'to see whether we could get together. Proper excited he was about these lighted matches.' Edwin knew that this was pure fiction, Bob trying pathetically to scare him. 'But,' said Bob, 'it's whips that appeal to me most, really. And you, you bastard,' he said nastily, 'threw them into the street. All those lovely whips, my collection, worth a fortune, and you chucked them into the street. Sheer wanton wickedness, that was.'

'I take it you must have got them back,' said Edwin, 'or some of them. Otherwise how would you know I'd thrown them into the street?'

'Mister Clever, eh?' said Bob. 'We saw through all your little game. A big pretender, you are, pretending about Perroni's mob and all. Because this is the season when Perroni's mob lays off for a time, Perroni being in the South of France. Didn't come off, that, did it? You trying to push the blame on to poor bloody Perroni. Not that I've got any time for Perroni, mind you. Real bastard, he is. But that's typical of the way your mind works.' He brooded over Edwin's iniquity. 'Had to walk round threatening all the kids of the neighbourhood to get those whips back. And they aren't all in yet. One kid threatened me back, just imagine. Said he'd whip me with one of my own whips, real hard. That put me in a very funny position, that did.'

Bob now had to turn into a wide thoroughfare with shops and lights and people. Edwin could see him grow nervous, his gloved fingers twitching on the wheel. 'Bloody nuisance, this is,' he said. 'Traffic lights there, and wouldn't you just like to nip out of the car when they change. But I'm going to jump them. Untrustworthy you are,' he scolded, 'deceitful.'

'Look,' said Edwin, 'whether you like it nor not, I'm going to put my wig on.' He whipped it from his chest, breaking off a shirt button in the process.

'Oh, all right,' said Bob peevishly. 'Put it on if you want to. Had about enough of you, I have.'

'Good heavens,' said Edwin reverently, looking hard across Bob at a shop window on the right-hand side of the street. He still held the wig in his hand. 'What a wonderful display over there. For Christmas, I suppose. All those whips.' Bob turned his head right, unable to resist, and Edwin clapped the wig on Bob's head. It was somewhat too large and came forward over his eyes. Bob cursed in surprise, took both hands off the wheel to tear the curls away, at the same time slamming both feet hard down. The car stopped, quite correctly, as the amber light came up. Edwin depressed the door catch and tumbled out on to the road. In two seconds he was on the pavement, using a fat walking couple (married, obviously; grown alike in fatness) as a shield. He made various Charlie Chaplin runs and checks, then, seeing a public lavatory ahead, rushed to it with thanks. He pelted down the steps into the echoing vault, saw grave men with both hands occupied at the urinals, the rows of penny-in-the-slot *cabinets d'aisance*. His haste and sudden cry of pain (not a bloody penny in his pocket) were not taken amiss in this place of public relief. If Bob should come skeltering down now –

Edwin saw a man in a lounge suit and homburg,

evening paper under his arm, taking change from his pocket and selecting a penny. As he inserted the coin in its metal bed and pulled at the opening knob, Edwin dashed across, said: 'Will explain,' then pushed the man in the cabinet, followed him, and clicked the bolt. Such places are not roomy. Edwin and the man stood as close as lovers, the man open-mouthed. 'I am surprised, Spindrift, really I am,' said the man, who having cleaned the first daub of shock from his face, stood revealed clearly as Mr Chasper. 'Couldn't it have waited till tomorrow morning at the office? I mean, there are certain places where a man has a right to be alone.'

'I'm being chased,' said Edwin, 'being pursued by a madman.' That sounded ridiculous, but what else could he say?

'It looks as though we're in the same boat,' said Chasper.

'Hardly boat. I've been kidnapped,' said Edwin. 'I just escaped from his car.'

'Yes,' said Chasper. 'Now if you'd be good enough to open that door and let me get out – I'm in rather a hurry, you see.'

'You carry on,' said Edwin. 'I won't look.' Then he heard the thunder of a descent, Bob hurtling in late pursuit, then Bob calling: 'Where are you, you bastard? I know you're there somewhere.' He began banging on the lavatory doors in order. 'Speak,' whispered Edwin to Chasper. 'Say something to him.'

'Whatsh all thish here?' It was the voice, presumably, of the lavatory attendant, annoyed at the noise; it did the place no kind of good. 'Whatsh going on?' Edwin noted the wet palatalization of both the alveolar fricative phonemes.

'It's this man,' panted Bob. 'He got away. I know he's in here somewhere, the bastard.' He hammered at the door next to Chasper and Edwin. 'He's a bloody thief,' said Bob.

'Thish izh a reshpectable plaish, thish izh,' said the attendant.

'Come out of there,' called hammering Bob. 'I know you're in there.'

'You wait your turn,' came the next-door voice, adding the bourdon of a blast of healthy excretion. Bob banged at the cabinet of Dr Spindrift. Mr Chasper called clearly:

'Is it a bald man you're looking for, a man in a hurry?'

'Yes, yes, yes –'

'He came in and went out again. I saw him running.'

'The bastard,' said Bob, and could be heard thundering out and back up the stairs.

'Very bad-mannered,' said Chasper. 'Didn't even say thank you.' He sat, fully trousered, on the lavatory seat and looked up sternly at Edwin. 'You realize, of course, that, though I have no jurisdiction whatsoever over your private life, this sort of thing tends rather to let the side down. Do you spend your leisure time in Moulmein being chased into public lavatories?'

'I'm very grateful,' said Edwin, 'for what you did then. I'm afraid all this adds up to rather a long story.'

'That,' said seated Chasper, 'I can well believe.' Dreamily he said: 'Professor Harcourt, of sainted memory, was arrested in a public lavatory in Nottingham of all places. Showing photographs to people, would you believe it? Well,' he said, throned homburg-crowned, holding his newspaper sceptre, 'I'm glad we've had this little talk. You don't by any chance know what happened to my curly-brimmed bowler, do you?'

'I wish I had it now,' said Edwin. 'It's terribly draughty up here.'

'Well, do drop in again sometime,' said Chasper. 'I'm sorry I have to hurry you out like this, but I've some business to do, tolerably urgent. So glad to have been of use.'

Edwin shot back the bolt, nodded to Chasper, and

205

went cautiously out into the great bare sanitary hall, loud with the fall of waters. Cautiously he surfaced to the street. No Bob. No Bob's car. But here too was the fall of waters. Rain. The first English rain he had seen since the day of embarking for Burma, having come home to hospital in a time of drought. It was heavy rain. The sensation of its needling on to his bare scalp was strange, rather eerie. He hurried to the doorway of a shop, a luminous smart shop full of comptometers. The doorway was already occupied by a pair of lovers, their embraces rustling against the plastic of their rainwear. The plastic lovers, he thought. And then, he thought, he'd forgotten to touch Chasper for a couple of bob. For a cuppa and a wad, guv, and a packet of fags. Fags he had still aplenty. He lighted one. All Chasper had given had been a pennyworth of sanctuary. Brassbold, Harrystonebold, Edwin tapped the male lover on his embracing arm. 'Give us a bob for a cuppa and a wad, guv,' he whined. The male lover impatiently gave poor bald Edwin a couple of sixpences and a threepenny piece. Then he returned, plastically rustling, to his kisses.

Chapter Twenty-eight

A long narrow gallery full of pleasure machines. Edwin stood outside, looking in without pleasure. The brittle needles of rain on his skull were telling him telegraphically that he was near the end. The angels of rain were announcing his tiredness, loneness, hunger for his own kind, sense of self-betrayal, anxiety about the future. He had done for himself proper, he had that. And in the pleasure gallery loud jaunty music distilled, above the rifle-cracks and ball-clicks and cries of hope and frustration, the very essence of clownish sorrow. 'Come on in out of the wet, Dad,' said a man in a white coat, white but not clinically white, not white enough for the goddesses of radiography. Edwin fingered his coins, the gift of a lover. One of the sixpences had the worn bald head of Edward the Seventh – a silver floweret thrown from a heated Pullman in which a hundred-egg omelette had been served; full brandy-flasks in ulster pockets; braces of grouse in the racks; *Rosenkavalier* waiting at Covent Garden. Edwin entered a very different world now. The young and loose-mouthed squandered their pennies at curious games of chance. One, called *H-Bomb*, offered money back for the destruction of the whole world. A trigger sent ball after ball down swift channels, bumping against resistances that doused successively the lights that were Tokyo, Singapore, New Delhi, Athens, Rome, Berlin, London. With the extinction of New York, the whole globe shuddered to silence, the player got his penny back. And, Edwin saw, there was a torture game – a cube of glass with a doll inside on a rack; squeeze the trigger hard enough and strength was rewarded with a most realistic scream. And there was a most compulsive game in which the player battled against lung cancer (diagram of chest and bronchial tubes with flashing lights for zones of infection). And a game for two players reproduced in symbols of prophetic fire the struggle between Red China and the rest of the world. Edwin shuddered and turned to a Rotamint machine. He fed in his Edwardian six-pence, saw wheels whizz and numbers flare; then stillness. He fed in the other, deutero-elizabethan, and, after some seconds of busy mechanic gestation, the tinkling of the birth of the jackpot could be heard. It drew eyes from other machines, even a few spectators for Edwin's gather-ing of the silver harvest. 'Fackin' lacky,' said a youth. Who else had been that? Of course, Nobby of the Kettle Mob, only jailed, not fined nor naffink. Edwin counted six shillingsworth of sixpences. Good. But was it really good? A kip for the night, leaning on a rope that col-lapsed promptly at dawn, a slab of bread and marge, and then what? Living for the day, Christlike. But these im-poverished improvident sects had always sprung to birth in warm climates, where living for the day was possible. Edwin walked out into the cold and wet night, giving courteous thanks to the filial man who had invited him in. He went the way whence he had come, collar turned up and hands in pockets. The lovers were still in the doorway but had reached an embrace of such excruciat-ing intimacy that Edwin hesitated to pay the man back his cold piece of charity. Edwin turned the corner by the buried lavatories and came to a mammoth Edwardian hotel. The bar was announced in lights as open to non-residents. Here would be his last drink. Then let him become finally passive, an ultimate thing, and the agencies of the world take over. His hemlock or viaticum. A double whisky. An olive or so or brittle crisps. Or vinegary gherkins.

Edwin swung in through the swing doors to find handsome or prosperous men buying liqueurs for slim ladies on bar stools with back rests, ladies with ragamuffin hair of cunning cut and elegant stretched legs. The bar was long and lit like a high altar, above it a canopy of intricate carving. The barmen were grave, thin-haired, soft spoken and swift at their priestlike tasks. They inclined to the drink-buyers with smiles of natural deference. Suddenly shy, Edwin turned down his collar, tried to smooth a head already, God knew, smooth enough, and made for the glow of GENTLEMEN. No mere Gents here, no mean apocope. In a fine palace of marble and glass with alabaster steps to the row of urinals, Edwin met an agency of the world – the broad back of a man in a dinner suit, upon his head a coronal of vine leaves, turning with fastening fingers to show to Edwin a fat face with blue chins, the tempering of a nose fitter for lean-headed yelping eagles. 'My God,' he said. 'What have they done to you? Who got hold of you, tell me that? You're so changed, Spindrift.'

Well, there it was. Perhaps the movement of life, which so often meant surprise meetings, was specially helped on by the peculiar atmosphere of mass lavatories. For so many meetings in lavatories could be fateful: that with the lurking corruptor in childhood; the man with addresses and pictures; the anecdotalist who became a friend; the two strangers discussing one's wife; one's boss met when one was being chased by a flagellate kettle-mobster; this man from one's past here, buttoning, crowned with vine leaves. 'Jack Thanatos,' said Edwin. 'Well.' And he grinned at what Jean Cocteau could have made of this encounter.

'Aristotle Thanatos,' said Aristotle Thanatos. 'I don't know where you people ever got the Jack from.'

'I think,' said Edwin, 'it was to protect you from the vulgar and uninstructed. Aristotle, to the British, has always had a ring of the unclean.'

'Yes, yes, and what have you been doing since our college days? I, for my part, went into wine, which you may or may not have heard. That's why I'm here now. A convention of vintners. A conference on the promotion of Greek wines here in England. And upstairs, now, the wines are being drunk.'

'Words,' said Edwin. 'Words, words, words.'

Aristotle Thanatos became instantly irritated. 'It is not words,' he said. 'It is the truth. You come upstairs if you don't believe me. Come upstairs anyway.'

'No, no,' said Edwin. 'I referred to my own studies.'

'All right, don't then. You weren't always so bad-mannered,' said Aristotle Thanatos. 'Is this change of personality something to do with your baldness? And that, I may say, is in very bad taste. It's not at all suitable, not at all.' His accent had absolutely no hint of foreign waters. He smelt Britishly prosperous: Trumper's Eucris, Yardley's after-shave pamperings, mild tobacco, no garlic.

'What I meant,' said patient Edwin, 'was that my studies have been ever-increasingly in the field of words, and that I'd love to come upstairs with you and taste the wines.'

'Why didn't you say so at first?' said Aristotle Thanatos. 'Though, I'm afraid, there's no real tasting going on now. People are drinking. Wine-tasting is, please remember, a serious and daytime pursuit.' He led Edwin from the lavatory, throwing half a crown in the attendant's dish, and walked him up a wide flight of shallow stairs with liquidly yielding carpet and shining rods. Edwin heard vinous noises and song. Aristotle Thanatos pushed in one of the heavy doors and waved Edwin to a heartening sight: drinkers of golden wine from goblets, not glasses, and the wine itself poured from Hellenic jars. In the centre of the huge Edwardian room was what looked like a press, and girls with lifted kirtles crushed grapes with exquisite feet, while men with strong noses stood about, laughing and clapping. Here was drunkenness, but only the holy drunkenness of the wine-bibber. A gross man dressed as Bacchus staggered round with lifted cup, clapping shoulders, kissing girls with straight noses, shouting. But, gloomy, his lips parted to show so many teeth missing, circulated the room none other than 'Ippo, 'Ippo in a sort of ancient Athenian costume, artificial grapes instead of a cap, carrying his sandwich-boards. The backboard said FILL HIGH THE BOWL WITH SAMIAN WINE. As 'Ippo circled towards Edwin and Aristotle Thanatos the fore-board became visible: TAKE A LITTLE WINE FOR THY STOMACH'S SAKE. 'Ippo's secular and religious functions had at last fused. He recognized Edwin with no surprise, saying: 'Had all your hair off,' and then, 'Right bleedin' job this is. Not a drop of wallop to be got nowhere.' He continued to circulate. Aristotle Thanatos beckoned a bare-legged girl with a delightful Cypriot profile. She came smiling with a crown of vine leaves for Edwin. 'Now,' said Aristotle Thanatos, 'you see the names under which some of these wines will be marketed. Heroic names, you see.' There was a display-board with proofs of labels: Odysseus, Agamemnon, Achilles, Ajax.

'Ajax won't do,' said Edwin. 'Ajax was the name of the first water-closet. Hence jakes. But come, let me sample the vintages.'

The wines were bright, some resinous, some smoky, all palatable. 'But tell me,' said Aristotle Thanatos, 'what precisely do you *want* to do with your life? You don't seem to be doing too well in your present position, do you? Bald, for instance. Your trousers cheap and ill-fitting. Your shoes cracking. Your toilet, to say the least, sketchy. Fill the bowl with Samian wine and come and sit over here and tell me about it. Are you married? You are. Are you earning enough money? Don't answer, because I can see that you are not. Are you happy with your words? Presumably you are, else you would not submit so tamely to your present condition of baldness and, to say the least, inelegance. Where are you living? Where is your place of work? Have you any children? A car? Don't attempt to answer all those questions at once.' A charming girl of the Golden Age came up with a tray. 'Try one of these,' said Aristole Thanatos. 'A *dolmas*.' Edwin took a vine leaf parcel of mint-flavoured rice and meat, ate it with zest, and took another before the tray passed on. 'Yes,' said Aristotle Thanatos, 'I can see that you're hungry, too.'

Edwin explained the baldness plausibly. Aristotle Thanatos nodded, sighing with a sort of relief; the baldness had evidently troubled him. Edwin said he was not particularly anxious to return to lecturing on Linguistics in Moulmein. He did not explain why: the scandalous life of the last three days, the rude word spat at innocent televiewers, the chase that ended in a closet with Chasper. He had the feeling that Aristotle Thanatos was going to offer him a job.

'We require, you see,' said Aristotle Thanatos, 'somebody capable of running a sort of public relations office. Somebody much-travelled, a linguist, with broad general culture, in touch with the best people, charming, well-groomed.' He gazed sadly at Edwin. 'It is such a pity.'

'Look,' said Edwin, 'I'm not always like this. You should see me when I'm got up proper.' He gaped with horror at this locution, as did Aristotle Thanatos. In touch with the best people, eh? Edwin smiled it away, a joke, a solecism deliberately used, not unknown among the best people. ''Andsome I look,' smiled Edwin desperately, 'with a big 'ead of curly 'air.' He laughed loudly and gripped Aristotle Thanatos's chubby well-tailored knee. Aristotle Thanatos looked gloomy and said:

'I see, I see, I understand, a joke. Well, I think that you might come to see me sometime when you're feeling a little better. Obviously you're not yourself at the moment. I don't blame you, poor fellow. I don't suppose you've really changed all that much, fundamentally, have you?' He brought his shiny black eyes close to

212

Edwin's, as though conducting an ophthalmic examination. 'I don't know, I don't know,' he said. 'At college you were very different, weren't you? You had, I remember, at least four very good suits. And they've been playing around with your brain, have they? A great pity, to say the least.'

'I still have excellent suits,' said Edwin, 'I have six. But they all happen to be in Moulmein.'

'Moulmein,' said Aristotle Thanatos. 'Rather a disreputable town, as I remember. That was during the war, however. I was in the RAF, you know. Well now, Spindrift, have another drink or something. I'm just going over there to stop Mr Thalassa from falling into the wine press. A charming man, Spindrift, but inclined to gaiety.' And he patted Edwin like an old wet dog and started to go off. Mr Thalassa was making the movements of a sea swimmer, wine dripping from his goat's beard. Edwin said, gulping: 'Jack.'

'Don't call me Jack.'

'All right. Aristotle, Bottle-and-glass, Thanatos, Death, anything you like. Lend me a quid, will you? Two quid. A couple of nicker.' The right word had eluded him. 'For a kip for the night.'

'My dear fellow.' Aristotle Thanatos came back a pace, leaving Mr Thalassa to drown. 'You mean to say you're as badly off as that? I'm terribly sorry. It's my fault, I know, putting you in the embarrassing position of having to *ask*. I should have let you finish your story. I'd just no idea. But I'm an impatient man, you know, and always have been, My biggest fault, my friends tell me. Sit down again. I'll sit down too.' And they sat down.

'Oh,' said Edwin, 'let's not make a big thing of it. I mean, I've got money, or rather my wife's got it, somewhere. Wherever she is. It's only a question of having somewhere to sleep. Just for tonight, that's all.'

'*Women*,' said Aristotle Thanatos, as bitterly as ever Harry Stone could say it. 'I see, I see. She's gone off, eh?

Just like that. Hm. In the old days it used to be the men who left the women stranded. But we've progressed. Well, you'd better spend the night with me. There are two beds in my room. And then tomorrow morning perhaps we can have a talk, work something out. Hm. I'm really terribly sorry.' He gazed round the tipsy room scattered with vine leaves and drenched with wine. His face twitched, for the first time that evening, humorously. 'Now,' he said, 'is hardly the time for a serious talk. But I don't really think you ought to drink any more, either. You don't look at all well. The strain, I suppose.'

'It has been rather a strain,' admitted Edwin. He trailed his left ring finger across his shut eyes in a conventional gesture of weariness. He felt muzzy; the wine probably.

'You go to bed,' said Aristotle Thanatos. 'My room's on this floor. Have a bath and a shave with my electric razor. Then go to bed. We'll have to be up early in the morning if we're going to discuss things, because I have to be at London Airport by ten-thirty. So you go to bed now. I can't leave this party yet, obviously. My room's Number Twelve. The door isn't locked. You go along now and get a decent night's sleep. Poor Spindrift,' he said sentimentally, tweezing Edwin's arm. 'Nobody would have dreamed of calling you that at college,' he added. Edwin searched for some words in Modern Greek, but nothing would come. 'Apothanein thelo,' he said instead, without intending to say it. Aristotle Thanatos laughed. 'You go off now and sleep. You'll feel differently in the morning.'

Outside that healthily drunken room Edwin staggered a little. That wine. He met 'Ippo coming up from the toilet, buttoning behind the shield of his fore-board. 'Bleedin' game,' he said. 'You found your watch yet?' Edwin saw the room numbers dance as he walked the snow-soft corridor. But, without dancing of the eyes or any of the tones of fantasy, he quite definitely passed the two flat-chested daughters of Renate, giggling under their

Eskimo hair-bells, holding hands, off to some assignment in some room. Did everything together, did they? He squinted up at a number, saw twelve, opened the door, found it was the wrong room, very much the wrong room, the two occupants too preoccupied however to notice that he had opened the door of the wrong room. His lips were open, his tongue-point up to the alveolum, ready for 'Sorry,' when his eyes were caught in snake-and-rabbit hypnosis by the sight of the act. The act itself. Complete with sound effects, the train just ready to arrive at the station. 'Sheila,' said Edwin, his tongue-point retracting from alveolum to hard palate and himself, in one compartment of his shocked brain, conscious of the fact. It was Sheila all right, certainly Sheila, for, even in her transport, her head turned. 'Wait,' panted the man, no man that Edwin had ever seen before, an unbearded man. 'Let me finish, blast you.' 'All the time in the world,' said Edwin quite coldly, coldly knowing that he was about to pass out – primrose, Jerusalem artichoke, causeway, penthouse – and then passing out cold.

Chapter Twenty-nine

'Tonight,' said Harry Stone, trouserless announcer, 'to-bleedin'-night, vat is, ve perfesser 'ere follers ap 'is first sensational appearance on ve telly wiv anover demon-bleedin'-stration of bleedin' words. Last time, as ve ole world remembers – and telegrams 'ave been comin' in from China and Peru and over bleedin' foreign spots so vat nobody can't get abaht ve room for bleedin' telegrams – 'e said a word vat can't be repeated no more but now as ve official description of –' He consulted a typed handout. '– Of noun verb expletive wiv bleedin' phonemic structure of unvoiced bleedin' labiodental glidin' onter secondary cardinal vowel number six endin' wiv unvoiced velar bleedin' plosive. Now 'e is goin' to demonstrate ve workin' of an homophone.' That rare aspirate of his blew like a gale through the world. 'Ve perfesser.'

By a singular device Edwin's bald head first filled the monitor screen, inked with the primary cardinal vowel chart. He raised fluttering eyelids and then bled profusely from the nose. 'Pardon, all,' he said. 'A little unwell in the conk.' He winked. 'We have in the studio tonight several homophones. This, for example.' He patted a carpenter's plane, said a secret word, and saw it jet off into the night, BOAC clear on its fuselage. 'Or this,' he said. 'Our little Spanish friend.' He lifted Carmen's skirt to disclose a well-filled stocking. 'You very notty,' she said. 'Oh blimey.' Her teeth champed the screen for two seconds. 'This stocking,' said Edwin, 'has a ladder in it. Now watch.' And there was Charlie climbing the ladder to Valhalla, a spaghetti rope over his shoulder, Charlie complaining: 'Very hard this is. Italian stuff.'

'And here,' said Edwin, 'is a little invention of my own – a ticking kettle, guaranteed to boil any amount of time and stop after only three weeks. Only one nicker. Eight tosheroons. Comes complete with tray on the moor, suitable for picnics.' Money came swirling out of the electricity meter, the jackpot. Edwin picked up a handful of shillings, each of which begged: 'Whip me. Lay it on real hard. If you don't beat me I'll get the mob to beat *you* up.'

'Wonders of philology,' said Edwin proudly. 'Take this here dog, for instance.' He held up struggling Nigger, wearing a fish-head like a false nose. 'This is really a Spade, you see. Give a dog a bad name. Call a spade a spade. All done by kindness.' He put docile Nigger down with a flat metal clank. 'Wooden haft had a bark when it was on a tree. Dogs' affinity for trees. All ties up.' He looked up at the sky-ceiling to see Les walking on the grid. 'World tree withers,' sang Les. 'Gods gormless ghastly. Skylight in the gods, see? For flying Dutchmen.'

'We turn now,' said Edwin, 'from matters of homophones to the whole question of love, love being the hardest collocation of phonemes ever bored by questing squirrel.' Coral appeared, skirtless. 'Bleedin' good pair we make,' said sad Harry Stone, trouserless. 'Phoney homo,' sneered Coral corally. 'Love, eh? Hardest whatever-it-was-he-said, eh? Hard, that's a good un.' 'My wife Sheila will now demonstrate love,' said Edwin, 'complete with seven sacred trances. Do not attempt to brighten your tellies, as much of this must be performed in darkness, being act of darkness. Begin. Commence. There, you see, are words of same meaning but different origin, Anglo-Saxon and French respectively, showing incomparable richness of English. While the demonstration is proceeding, this possibly being somewhat boring for prolonged viewing, I will endeavour to entertain you with priceless philological curiosities. These are normally sold only in public lavatories under VD sign. Special Chasperian dispensation brings them to you, great viewing public, tonight.' Energetic noises of love rose in crescendo. 'Crescendo, Italian loan-word, cognate with crescent as in moon and Mornington. Those noises in the background made by my wife and various persons unknown are, I think hardly susceptible to linguistic analysis. One has to draw the line somewhere.

'Another point,' said Edwin, 'that must be made before my time runs out. Time by courtesy of Kettle Mob, incidentally. It is hardly fair that I should be fastened to a bed, absolutely immobile like Odysseus and other Greeks, wine-dark, lashed to the mast to hear unharmable compulsive music of the Sirens. It is all right, I hear some of you shouting, keep your hair on, mister. Not mister, please. Doctor, if you don't mind. Here is my diploma.' He held out feebly a piece of lipsticked toilet-paper: TWISTER. 'As for keeping my hair on, I should honestly like nothing better.' He smiled up at the camera on the ceiling. He raised a palsied hand to his head. To his profound astonishment hair was already sprouting, the wiry wool of a Negro. In top hat and immaculate tails, twirling a silver-topped stick, Leo Stone danced on stage. He had enlarged his Semitic nose with cunning flesh-coloured wax. 'All together now,' he cried:

> ' 'E's got it on, 'e's got it on,
> 'E's got it on agyne.
> Air in is bed and air on is 'ead
> And air in 'is bleedin' bryne.
> Oh ...'

'A phoney pair of homophones,' said Edwin indignantly. 'Air and air.' Aristotle Thanatos was leaning over him, his head a skull with an eagle's conk. He spoke modern Greek with a slight Turkish accent. His naked skull, by

218

courtesy of the X-ray Department, slowly clothed itself in flesh. 'Carry on,' said Edwin. 'A little more.' But the flesh stopped at a stage of reasonable plumpness only. Edwin blinked at this. All images receded except that of a dressing-gowned man who was not Aristotle Thanatos, burbling his wet Greek over Edwin's bed however, like one whose neural ailment had affected the speech-centres. Edwin blinked a solid white ward into existence, but not the ward he had escaped from. He knew nobody there. Where was R. Dickie, where the sneerer, where the Punch-humped young man? Perhaps this was a different hospital. When one came to think of it, they would hardly be likely to take him back in that first one, not after behaviour they must have considered unpardonable. The Greek-speaker leaning over Edwin seemed mad and happy. He tottered off to the next bed, sociable though monoglot. Men lay in bed all the way along the ward, on both sides, some with dark glasses, most with bandaged heads, one with the dithering limbs of Parkinson's Disease. Edwin tenderly felt his own head. Something had grown there: immovable coils of crepe over a cotton-wool bed. He must have hurt himself hard when he passed out. And then Dr Railton walked in, cheerful, wiping lips that had trumpeted.

'How,' said Edwin fearfully, 'did you get here?'

'I work here,' said Dr Railton. 'How do you feel now, *Doctor*?'

'I know,' said rueful Edwin. 'You were quite right, really. I'm too irresponsible for that high title. But I can't disown it, can I? I can't disown what was conferred upon me, can I?'

'Don't get so excited,' said Dr Railton. 'And stop feeling guilty. Guilt is a big retarder of recovery.'

'So you look at guilt clinically and not morally?' said Edwin. 'But if you had to give a moral judgement on me what would you say?'

'That doesn't enter into it,' said Dr Railton. 'That

doesn't come into the covenant between us. You rest now. Stop thinking.'

'I'm sorry, anyway,' said Edwin.

'If feeling sorry makes you also feel better,' said Dr Railton, 'you go on feeling sorry.' He rose from the bed's edge. 'I'll be in to see you later.'

'Did you enjoy playing the trumpet last night?'

'I always enjoy playing the trumpet,' said Dr Railton. 'The trumpet to me is possibly like the study of words to you. But,' said Dr Railton, 'I have a profession as well.' He smiled quite amiably and then left the ward.

Chapter Thirty

A nurse came in to take his temperature and his pulse. She was a stout Irish body, potato-fed, plum-and-apple-cheeked. When the thermometer had been poked into its warm one-minute nest, Edwin tried a sly question or two. 'Where am I?' he asked. She was of peasant stock that would brook no Saxon nonsense. She said:

'Don't be asking stupid questions. You're in the post-operative ward.'

'You mean they've operated on me? Already?'

'Ask no questions and you'll be told no lies. And I'm taking your pulse, as you can see.'

'What day is it?' asked Edwin. She recorded his pulse-rate in a book, extracted and read the thermometer. 'All days are the same to them who work hard,' she said. She entered a blob on his temperature chart. 'Except Sunday, and even then the work has to go on,' she said, daughter of a poor farmer.

'Was there anything unusual on the television last night?' asked Edwin.

'How should I be knowing? A lot of nonsense, to be sure. I've better things to do than to be watching a lot of nonsense on the television.'

'I'm sure you have,' said gallant Edwin. 'A pretty colleen like yourself.'

'Don't be bold,' she said, and moved on to the next patient. But, standing there at her work, she cast a bold enough look back on Edwin.

Before dinner a Church of England clergyman came visiting. 'I wonder if you'd mind answering a simple question,' said Edwin. 'What day is it?'

'Day? Day?' He was a silvery vague old man. 'Well now.' He fumbled in an inner pocket and drew forth a diary whose entries seemed, to Edwin, remarkably few. 'I don't suppose this would help much. One really wants to know the date, I suppose. From the date one could work out, with the help of this little book, precisely what day of the week it is. I suppose,' he said, 'it's Wednesday or Thursday. I'm not sure. But I'm quite sure,' he smiled, 'that today is a week-day.'

'Thank you,' said Edwin. 'And what time is it?'

'Well,' said the clergyman, 'I'm afraid I'm always leaving my watch at home. But, ah, I see your watch, as I take it to be, is here on the bedside table. And that makes it, ah, nearly six.'

'My watch?' said incredulous Edwin. 'How on earth did that get there?' The clergyman held it close to Edwin's eyes. It ticked away as a naughty cat, on its return from long absence from home, will purr away unperturbed by persons' past perturbations. It was his watch all right.

'Get there?' echoed the clergyman. 'Well, it might be unwise, even blasphemous, to postulate thaumaturgy as an explanation. It would seem more reasonable to suppose that you yourself put it there. Or somebody, not divine, put it there for you.'

'What,' asked Edwin, 'is Spindrift?'

'Spindrift? Dear me, all these questions. Spray, I should have supposed, drifting in from the sea. There's a poem by Kipling, I believe, that uses the word rather finely. "Something something something shall fail not from the face of it, something something spindrift and the fulmar flying free". A poem,' explained the clergyman, 'as you may have divined, about the sea.' He chuckled oldly.

'Is it also a detergent or a washing-machine or anything like that?'

' I have my washing sent to the laundry,' said the

clergyman, rather distantly. 'Why, may I ask, do you ask?'

'Oh, it's nothing,' said Edwin, 'really.'

'Well, I'm glad we've had this little chat,' said the clergyman. Edwin looked sharply at him, to see whether he was sitting on a water-closet. 'Unless, of course, you have any other question to put to me,' he said humorously. 'Forgive me,' he added, 'I don't, of course, mean that if you have such a question I shall cease to be glad. These formulae one uses – quite meaningless. Words are treacherous things.'

'Do you think,' asked Edwin slowly, 'a man is ever justified in leaving his wife?'

'No,' answered the clergyman promptly. 'We are told that we are to forgive unto seventy times seven.' That disposed of that. He got up with arthritic difficulty from the bedside chair. 'If you'd like prayers, you know,' he said, embarrassed, 'or anything of that sort, I should be glad to, that is to say, I should be very happy to –'

'You're very kind,' said Edwin.

'I do believe you've been playing a little joke on me,' said the clergyman, with Christian forbearance. 'I see now from your temperature chart that Spindrift is, actually, your own name. Ah, I see. A sort of riddle, really. Well, good-bye. Spindrift, spindrift,' he muttered genially to himself as he moved on.

Edwin could eat little dinner (shepherd's pie with extra potatoes – mashed, sauté, one baked). He was thinking of what he could say to Sheila if, of course, she came. He could forgive her, naturally, but forgiveness would be to her quite outside the terms of reference, presumptuous as well, for she would believe there was nothing to forgive. Perhaps it was really up to him to ask her for forgiveness, for wives did not usually go around committing fornication and adultery if they were happy at home. All this went back a long way and, he supposed, everything was ultimately his responsibility. What he proposed to do now was already fraught with its potential hangover of guilt. But that should be cancelled out by the guilt she ought to feel and never had felt when committing the sin of hurting him (for she had hurt him, horribly, and it was no good her saying that he had no right to feel hurt). He proposed to leave her because, in failing him when he'd needed her most, she'd given the lie to her own vaunted creed: being together was the important thing, the other thing didn't in the least matter. Leaving her, of course, would merely mean telling her to get out of his life. They were homeless in England, their few chattels were in Moulmein. Edwin was quite convinced that he would not be going back to Moulmein, quite convinced after everything that had happened. The future would have to be replanned when Sheila had been removed from the future.

But, he wondered, had those fantastic things really happened? They must have happened, they still possessed in memory strong reality-tone. The clang of the CAGE chord in that club; Railton's polished trumpet catching the light from the stage-spot; an unsqueezed comedo on the upper lip of Harry Stone. And, above everything, that ghastly snorting busy nakedness, the train coming into the station, Sheila's high demented dying voice. *That* had most certainly happened. And, if that had happened, everything else had happened. But how could anything be proved or disproved? People had such a weak hold on reality, remembering only what they wished to remember. And even with the more cultivated – Railton, Chasper, Aristotle Thanatos – there would be a deliberate withholding, a desire not to add the humiliation of the record to the humiliation of the fact.

Aristotle Thanatos. Edwin began to sweat and pant fearfully. Had he ever really known a man with that name? He racked and sifted his memory for Aristotle Thanatos. It was the sort of name a man might make up, like Mr Eugenides the Smyrna merchant. Would any

Greek be called Thanatos? He tried to relive fragments of his university life, to recall particular scenes, encounters. He seemed to achieve, at the expense of a splitting head, a picture of himself with three or four other men in the pub across the road from the Men's Union – the College Arms – discussing something gravely. Aesthetics, perhaps, or the Fall of France, imminent call-up into the forces or the precise definition of a technical term, the nature of baroque or something. He seemed to see, on the very edge of the group, a plump swart man, maturer than his companions. Edwin looked more closely and found that to be an Egyptian student of technology called Hamid. Aristotle Thanatos. Somebody met in his American post-graduate year? Such a name might well be found in America. He saw the speaker of modern Greek shambling about the ward in dressing-gown and slippers, dribbling, pretending to be a doctor, clumsily nodding over temperature charts. Edwin called him over by shouting: 'Eh!' The man came quickly, blundering into wheelchairs, catching his thigh on bedrails.

'Name,' said Edwin. 'Your name.' He called up gobbets of Greek from the past. 'Kyrie. Onoma.'

'Johnny,' dribbled the man promptly. 'Johnny Dikikoropoulos. Cyprus. Turk man no bloody good.'

'Dunatos,' said Edwin. 'Is it possible onoma Thanatos?' The Cypriot immediately began to cry.

'Damn it,' said Edwin angrily. 'I'm not saying anything about death or you dying. Is the name Thanatos possible? Are there any Greeks of your acquaintance with that name? Mr Thanatos. *Mr Thanatos.* Come back, blast you.' But the Cypriot went off blubbering. There were cries of Shame, insulting the poor bugger like that, just because he's a poor bloody foreigner, oughtn't to be allowed.

'You,' said the ward sister, 'are going to have a sedative. We can't have the whole ward disturbed by one patient. You're too lively, you are.'

'But,' said Edwin, 'I've got a visitor coming. My wife.'

'No visitors for you. You're not ready for visitors yet, carrying on like that. You're going to have the screens round you.' She was a thin fierce woman with very old-fashioned spectacle-frames.

'But I must see my wife,' said Edwin.

'You'll see your wife all in good time. But not tonight.' She wheeled across the squeaking bed-screens, shutting Edwin from the lively sick world. 'Time enough to see your wife when you're better.'

Chapter Thirty-one

'Well,' said Sheila, 'now you seem to be all right. Every-body was worried about you, you know.' She sat, darkly pretty, in a black wide skirt with a lime-coloured sweater, her fur coat sitting on her shoulders. It was the following evening. He felt rested, felt that he seemed to be all right. And various healing forces had conspired to a mood of forgiveness. He forgave himself. He forgave the past few days and all of the past beyond that. He forgave Sheila, but that was a secret, a note passed from himself to him-self.

'Why was everybody worried?' asked Edwin, taking Sheila's hand. It was a cold hand, but the autumn night was cold. It tapped at the window, crying its cold.

'Yes, I don't suppose you'd know much about it, would you?' said Sheila. 'I shouldn't think there's much point in telling you about it, really.'

'After I fell down, you mean?'

'Oh, you remember falling, do you? They decided to postpone the operation. And then, so they say, you had some sort of post-operational shock. You were in a coma, apparently. I tried to get in several times to see you, but they wouldn't let me.'

'And how is Nigel?'

'Nigel? That idiot? He was a phoney, if ever there was one. But why do you ask? Why don't you ask how I am?'

'I assumed you were all right. You look all right. You never looked better.'

'I never felt so cold.' She shivered a little and pulled

her fur coat more warmly round her shoulders, disengaging her lightly held hand to do so. She did not give her hand back to Edwin's hand.

'And how,' asked Edwin shyly, 'is the other man? Nigel's successor?'

'You seem very interested in my boy-friends,' said Sheila. 'As for how Nigel's successor is, I'm afraid I don't know. Or rather I do know. Nigel's successor is suffering from a severe attack of non-existence.'

'Oh, come off it,' said Edwin, suddenly weary, lolling his bound head on the pillow. 'This is unlike you. I know all about Nigel's successor, don't I? Although I want to forget all about him as quickly as possible.'

'Why did you ask about him then? Look, Edwin, I don't have to say this, as you know, but if you think I've been spending this time in London on bouts of promiscuous love-making, you're very much mistaken. I went about with Nigel for a day or two because I thought he was amusing. Then I found he wasn't amusing. He also seemed to have a strong aversion to chlorophyll. He stank. In both senses.'

'Did you get my laundry back from him?'

'No, I didn't, but that doesn't matter.' Edwin looked hard at her. No successor to Nigel, eh? She had never lied before. Edwin said:

'I'm a bit confused in my mind. I don't like to say you're lying, but I think you are. The trouble is that, at the moment, I'm the last person in the world to say that this happened and that happened. I don't know. But I have a powerful impression that certain things happened to me that, quite possibly, may not have happened at all.'

'Oh,' said Sheila, 'anaesthetics, coma. You've been quite ill.' She gave him a hard look back. 'You're the last person in the world, as you quite rightly say, to start talking about anyone lying. I know you don't really mean what you're saying now. Lying's a nasty word.'

'What I meant,' said Edwin, 'was that I didn't want you of all people to join the select group who are keeping silent about what I did, or think I did, during those three days, if it was three days. I know I was ill, but I still want to straighten out fact from fantasy, if there was any fantasy. 'If,' he added, 'there was any fact.' She looked puzzled. 'A question of ontology,' said Edwin. 'We can't go through the world in a state of confusion about reality.'

'Oh, there are worse things than that,' said Sheila. 'Anyway, you're cured now. The operation was successful, so they tell me.' She spoke flatly, without joy or relief.

'Tell me the truth,' said Edwin urgently. 'For God's sake tell me what happened.'

'I can only tell you what I've been told. You passed out and hurt yourself. They decided to postpone the operation.'

'What day was this?'

'Oh, how do I know what day? All days are alike, except Sunday, and Sunday contrives to be even duller than the week-days.'

'So,' said Edwin, 'I didn't see you in bed with another man?'

'No,' said Sheila, 'you certainly didn't. I'd never be such a fool as to put myself in that position, not after that fuss you kicked up in Moulmein. And Jeff and I were not really doing anything on that occasion. It was then I realized that there was something wrong with your brain.'

'And how about the Stone twins and the Kettle Mob and the competition for the best bald head in Greater London?'

'The Stone twins most certainly exist. That competition sounds rather a charming idea. But what is this Kettle Mob? What does it do – mend kettles?'

'They sell dud watches,' said Edwin. 'Which reminds me. How has my own watch – or Jeff Fairlove's, as you tell

229

me it is – suddenly managed to come back again? I could have sworn that the man 'Ippo stole it.'

'So he did,' said Sheila. 'Apparently he sold it to a man called Bob Something-or-other, a man I met in that horrible club of the Stone twins. I saw him wearing it and I got it back. I brought it here while you were still wandering in imaginary worlds.'

'How did you get it back?'

'I got it back.'

'Did this man Bob ask you if you were kinky?'

'As a matter of fact, he did. How did you know?'

'That's what I mean,' said Edwin with energy. 'You see, that's one thing that *must* have happened. I mean, my being kidnapped by this Bob and being made to whip him. I can't have imagined that, I just can't.'

'You seem to have imagined quite a lot,' said Sheila. 'When I came with this watch I came also with Charlie – you remember him, the window-cleaner. It's quite possible that, even though you were dead out, something registered. I told Charlie the story of the watch.'

Implausible, implausible. Why did she lie? Why didn't she help him to get at the truth? What was she trying to hide?

'Now,' said Sheila, 'if you're so keen on getting to grips with reality, I'd better tell you about my meeting with Chasper.'

'I suppose he really knows that I stole his hat,' said Edwin. 'Did he mention it?'

'He had other things to talk about than hats,' said Sheila. 'There was the whole question of your going back to Moulmein.'

'I don't understand this,' said Edwin. 'Why should he talk to you about that? Damn it, he's my boss, not yours. How did you meet him, anyway?'

'He wrote to me,' said Sheila simply. 'Care of the Farnworth Hotel. They had to know where I was staying, remember. Next of kin.'

'But you were thrown out of the Farnworth,' said Edwin.

'I,' said Sheila, 'have never been thrown out of anywhere in my life. Except once from that church in Italy. For not wearing a hat. True, I'm no longer at the Farnworth, but my leaving was quite amicable. I called there occasionally for letters. Dear me, I seem to have played rather a horrid part in your fantasy.' She lit a cigarette, nearly placed it in Edwin's mouth, then thought better of it. Smoking it herself, she presented another to Edwin in the way of acquaintances rather than lovers, striking a match for him.

'Come on then,' said Edwin impatiently. 'What did Chasper tell you?'

'He's sending you a formal letter, but not just yet. He asked me to break it gently to you that you're not going back to Burma, that your contract is being terminated under the provisions of Clause 18. There, I've broken it gently.'

'Very gently,' said Edwin, 'as gently as a whip on a kettle-mobster's back. But I expected this.'

'You did?'

'When Chasper saw me in that public lavatory I knew it was the end.'

'That,' said Sheila, 'suitably edited, might make a nice *News of the World* headline. Clause 18, however, seems to have nothing to do with lavatories. Apparently you've been invalided out.'

'I see,' said Edwin. 'They haven't given me much of a chance to recover, have they? Invalided out, indeed. Are you sure Clause 18 isn't concerned with misconduct?'

'Invalided out,' said Sheila. 'That's what's happened to you. But they're giving you a couple of months' sick pay. Apparently they don't think it safe to send people back to the tropics when they've had the sort of thing you've had. Misconduct, you say? You wouldn't know what misconduct is, my dear Edwin. Bilabial fricatives don't commit misconduct.'

'In a sense they do,' said Edwin eagerly. 'I mean, take the sort of phonemic confusion we get out in Burma. Bilabial fricatives instead of semi-vowels. It was different in certain historical phases of British English, of course. There there was no imposition of alien phonemic habits on –'

'Exactly,' said Sheila. '*Exactly*.'

'Oh,' said Edwin. 'Yes.' And then: 'Two months' sick pay. After that what do we do?'

'I don't know what you're going to do,' said Sheila. 'I personally am returning to Burma.'

Edwin stared at her open-mouthed for a count of five. His cigarette burned slowly towards his fingers. 'I don't understand,' he said. 'What sort of a job? But you've no qualifications.'

'Oh yes,' said Sheila, 'I have qualifications. Jeff Fairlove seems to think so, anyway.' Edwin's open mouth counted seven. He said:

'But you can't marry Fairlove. I won't let you, I won't give you a divorce.'

'There's no particular hurry about a divorce,' said Sheila. 'You'll let me have one sooner or later, I know you will. You don't care enough about hanging on to me. You only really care about bilabial fricatives and semi-vowels and all that rubbish.'

'And how much do you care about Fairlove?' The coal of the cigarette had reached the scarf-skin of his fingers. 'Blast,' he said, and ash scattered all over the sheet.

'I care enough,' said Sheila. 'And I also care about Burma. I like the climate. I like the people. I also like the prospect of not having to be unfaithful any more. Sleeping with a bilabial fricative isn't all that rewarding, you know.'

'Will you,' said Edwin, near tears, 'shut up about bilabial fricatives? You're not being fair to me, you're cruel. I'm still not very well, you know. You just don't care, you never have cared.'

'Oh yes,' said Sheila, 'I did care. Until the bilabial fricatives got in the way. Sorry. The semi-vowels, then. The faucal plosives. The retroflex what-have-yous. Life governed by Verner's Law and Grimm's Law. You see, I know all the jargon. Now I have to learn the jargon of a teak-wallah, I suppose. But I shouldn't imagine he'll bring teak to bed with him.'

'You used to say,' said Edwin slowly, 'that there was only one kind of infidelity. Just not wanting to be with the person you're supposed to love. You said there was nothing worse than that.'

'Oh, all our ideas change,' said Sheila. 'But I'd still say that was substantially what I believe. But when a person ceases to be a person what do you do then? I don't regard myself as having any obligation of love to a bundle of phonemes or whatever you call them. A bundle of bilabial fricatives is just a *thing*, isn't it? You can't love a thing.'

'You may be right,' said Edwin. 'It's queer, but yesterday, *I*'d quite made up my mind to leave *you*. Because it seemed you'd deserted me. Because of that ghastly physical shock which showed me you didn't care a damn about me. I suppose I deserve this, in a way. But I'd made up my mind to change, or try to change. These last few days brought me out of touch with words as words. And it seemed that coming into contact with life made me into a liar, a thief, a whoremaster, a cheat, a man on the run. But you say that these last few days never happened. So that I'm still the same. So there we are. But it was you I was searching for these last few days. I was looking everywhere for you. It doesn't really matter, does it, whether that really happened or not? Even just dreaming about looking for you argues love, doesn't it? And I do love you, I'm quite sure of that. And I could change.'

Sheila sadly shook her dark head. 'I don't think it

would be right for you to change. You're a kind of machine, and the world needs machines. You're like an X-ray machine, or one of those electrocephalo gadgets you were moaning about. You have a use. But I don't need a machine. Not to live with and go to bed with, anyway.'

'We've all got to do something in the world,' said Edwin. 'We've all got to earn a living. My bilabial fricatives and minimal pairs bought you jade ornaments and bottles of gin.' He spoke gently. 'It just happened, unfortunately, that my way of earning a living was one that I enjoyed. Apparently it's sacrilege for a married man to be too happy in his work. I shan't commit that sin again.'

'It's the only sin you've ever committed,' said Sheila, not unkindly. 'But it happened, as far as I was concerned, to be the unforgivable sin.'

'It won't happen again,' said Edwin. There was a pause. 'So now you'll have a chance to be properly faithful. No more casuistry about marriage being divisible into the physical and the spiritual and never the twain need meet. Perhaps this Fairlove wouldn't be so forbearing as I've been, anyway. Perhaps he wouldn't like you to go off occasionally with other men. If,' said Edwin, 'you fornicated with people like Fairlove when married to me, who will you fornicate with when married to Fairlove?'

'You don't know Jeff all that well, do you?' said Sheila. 'He's a jealous sort of man, which is rather refreshing.'

'Oh, woman, woman,' said Edwin. 'How would he like a friendly letter from me, a sad but forgiving husband thinking it only his duty to warn his successor about his wife's promiscuity when he, the husband, lay, or should have been lying, on a bed of sickness?'

'What exactly do you mean?'

'That he caught his wife and a person unknown in the act. That the shock nearly killed him.'

'That,' said Sheila, 'is just plain stupid. That would be just lies and mischief. That would be ridiculous.'

'Oh, I wouldn't dream of doing it,' said Edwin. 'I

couldn't spare the time. I've got to get down to this article on the bilabial fricative in lower-class nineteenth-century London English. But I wonder more and more whether I did really imagine these last few days.'

'I'll come and see you again soon,' said Sheila, rising and smoothing her skirt. 'There are several things to arrange. Your books and clothes and things in Moulmein. That's one of the reasons why I'm able to go back. They're willing to pay a single air fare to Burma to settle matters out there. There's the car, too, and the servants. I'll be back again, oh, why not tomorrow? Yes, tomorrow. And I'm glad you're looking better.'

'Perhaps,' said Edwin, 'you'll have changed your mind by tomorrow night. Because I can, if you think it all that important, become a changed man. Less of a *thing*.'

'I don't think so,' said Sheila. 'I'm pretty sure I don't think so. Anyway, England's so cold, isn't it? I envy you, lying in that nice warm bed. And I have to go out and brave the cold, cold autumn night.' She shuddered comically and left the ward. Edwin heard her heels on the stone staircase, quick and nervous. Then they entered a zone of silence, the carpeting of the vestibule, and that was the end of her. But she had left her handbag on the bedside table. Edwin nearly shouted after her, but it was too late. He tried to beckon a nurse, but the nurse was not willing to be beckoned. Oh well, never mind. She could collect it tomorrow. She could come back and collect it tonight. Edwin wondered whether to open it and examine her private letters, inhaling the faint residua of scent and powder that would give a nostalgic smoky hint of her dying presence. But, unfastening the clip and inserting the tip of his nose into the mouth, he merely satisfied himself that his olfactory sense was back to normal; he did not want to handle anything of hers any longer, he decided. The ward still hummed with the subdued chat of patients and their visitors. He was drowsy. He turned on his side, extinguished all thoughts and feelings — the lights and fires of his lonely house — and sought sleep. It came very quickly. More slowly it ebbed.

'I forgot my bag,' said Sheila. 'I hope I haven't disturbed you. It's early for sleep, isn't it? There are still visitors here. Look, this man gave me a message, a man with vine leaves round his head. He wants you to see him as soon as you can. Can you remember that? I'm sorry the message is so vague, but he said his future plans were a bit vague, that was the trouble. I can't remember his name, but he had vine leaves round his head. All right, sleep if you want to. I've done my duty. Now you can dream about your beloved bilabial fricatives. Brrrr, it's so cold outside.'

Chapter Thirty-two

Edwin awoke with mechanical suddenness, with no hint of a margin between sleeping and waking. He felt well, rested, cured, sickened by the thought of so much sickness snoring around him. The night sister was reading in her improvised tent of bed-screens; a thin beam from a lamp threw a moving golden guinea on her page. The worn silver tosheroon in the sky glowed over a city richer than the sun. The city and the land and all the world were there waiting, full of ripe fruit for the picking. He would not stay here a minute longer. He palpated his chin and cheeks, which were smooth enough. He regretted the turban, but not for long. He would organize things differently this time.

He crept out of bed so softly and slowly – smoothly as the tongue gliding from one phonemic area to another – that the keen-eared sister could not possibly hear. She turned her page, and there was the golden guinea waiting for her, a coin that would never be spent. Edwin stole crouched to the end of the ward, only two beds away from his own bed. Not his own bed any longer, though, a bed he would never see again. He was going to seek again the Great Bed of Ware of the world, a bed lively with wriggling toes and hopping fleas.

He breathed deeply when he reached the bathroom where, for a moment, he rested. The moon illuminated the steel lockers clearly. Where his own clothes were – unless they had been taken away and hidden – he did not know, nor was there time to look. He plucked what was nearest to hand and most suitable. The slight squeak of locker-doors was – and tonight all things would conspire to help him – drowned by a passing lorry, itself followed by a high-powered car, itself followed by a motor-cycle. Edwin chose a good suit that seemed about his size, a pair of socks without holes, underwear that was clean, shirt, tie, a fancy waistcoat, shoes that said clearly on the moonlit sole his own large eight medium fitting, a trilby hat that, to his satisfaction, fitted well. There seemed to be no money to steal. Never mind. That would soon come his way. Finally he remembered that he was now committed for long to the cold of England, so he took a reasonably good Melton overcoat of a subdued blue.

He locked himself in the bathroom and dressed at leisure. When he had finished he looked, he thought, well. Under the hat the bandages barely showed. The shirt was expensive, glossy, with a collar that sat perfectly. These ill-speaking artisans of the ward had both taste and money, thought Edwin. Handkerchiefs; he had forgotten handkerchiefs. He took a random dozen from the lockers – six for show, six for blow – and, last theft of all from his anonymous ward mates, added gentlemanly tone to his outfit with a walking-stick of which, in this place of dodderers, there was a fine selection. Then, fully armed, warm, smart, he walked quietly to the stairhead and openly down the stairs to the vestibule. This new ward was nearer the outside world than that other of R. Dickie and the rest. The night porter dozed at his desk. He was not the one that Edwin remembered from before. He awoke, startled, at the spectacle of a gentleman with upright carriage and twirling stick, checking his wrist-watch by the vestibule clock, finding the vestibule clock five minutes slow, sighing, just come off duty.

'Sorry, sir,' said the porter, 'I'm new on here. What name would it be, sir?'

'Dr Edwin Spindrift,' said Dr Edwin Spindrift.

'Thank you, sir. Sorry, sir. I'll just open up for you, sir. Good night, sir, or good morning as it should rightly be.'

He opened the front massy door and presented Edwin to the freedom of London night, smelling of autumn and oil and distant fires. Or morning, as it should rightly be. Edwin strode off in the direction of the great London thoroughfare which glowed beyond the square and the side-streets. He was off to find Mr Thanatos, who might, of course, be anywhere. There was no hurry, of course. Plenty of time for plenty of piquant adventures. And then Mr Thanatos, vine-leaf-crowned.

On his way to the thoroughfare Edwin met many cats but only one man. This was 'Ippo advertising, front and rear, JOE'S ALL-NIGHT SAUSAGES. 'You got your watch back, then,' said 'Ippo, recognizing Edwin with no surprise. 'Right bleedin' job this is. Workin' nights now, see. The end, that's what it is.

'The end.'